STORMS OF FORTUNE

STORMS OF FORTUNE

A REX RHINEHEART NOVEL

G. D. DUHON

Zavalla, TX

STORMS OF FORTUNE

Front Cover, Spine, and Rear Cover Artwork by Michal Matczak.

Rear Cover Photography by Heidi Steinhagen of Dream of Me Photography.

eBook ISBN: 978-0-9972184-1-1
Soft Cover ISBN: 978-0-9972184-0-4
Soft Cover ISBN 978-0-9972184-6-6

First edition.
First paperback printing.
Second eBook printing.

PRINTED IN THE UNITED STATES OF AMERICA

0 9 8 7 6 5 4 3 2 1

Dedication

This book is dedicated to my father, who was the inspiration for both Johann and Áápi. Sadly, he passed away before this book could be completed. Dad, you may have left this world, but you will never be forgotten—thanks for everything and for always being there.

Sheila, Michael, Amber, Damien, and Erik—this one is also for you. Thanks for inspiring me, pushing me, and for all of the patience which was extended during this labor of love.

Simon W.— I know in another life you might have loved to have been Richard Stratford. Thanks for being you and for sharing that exclusive British humor through the years. I count myself lucky to call you friend.

The VHS class of 1982—I hope that each of you can see a little bit of our childhood within the walls of this book. Thanks for the memories.

Finally, for the friends and fans of Rex Rhineheart on Facebook. Thank you for your patience, though we may have wondered if Storms of Fortune would ever be published, that time is finally here and I hope that you enjoy it!

Prologue

The keel of the frigate sliced through the oily water as the men deliberately went about their work. In the distance, bullfrogs on the edges of the river banks croaked in cadence at a sliver of moon reflected like a platinum mirage on the still water. Over the pulsing sounds of the amphibians, one did not have to strain to hear the whining serenade of the mosquitoes, the bane of anyone within miles of the quagmire surrounding the river.

Though a particularly dark night, enough light was cast to see a moderate distance past the edge of the deck, and the inlet to the river could be seen just ahead. The ship had slowed and was creeping along now on the near-still water. The mainsail and rigging on the deck had to be secured and stowed prior to the ship entering the channel; the captain was a stickler for efficiency and obedience. It had been a formidable, but thankfully short, voyage, even for the well-seasoned crew aboard the *Bienville.*

She had sailed on the high tide out of Galveston, Texas, on a crisp October morning in 1821. The waves crested lightly with foamy peaks, and crying gulls dove for fish in the wake of the ship. At the edge of the horizon ahead, the sun made a grand entrance to the east, tangerine rays stretching their arms toward the stars. She departed, her holds encumbered with massive amounts of cargo—

most on the manifest, but a fair portion cached in a concealed compartment known only to the captain. In fact, she was so heavily laden that she sat an extra foot and a half lower in the water, thus her draft was quite deep.

The *Bienville* was as boisterous as the men who resided within her wooden quarters; she stretched out about one hundred forty feet with a beam of thirty-one feet, and a hold that was almost three times the height of her tall bos'n. Nearly one hundred men were stuffed into every nook and cranny along with her twenty-four guns, powder, and ball, all well-protected within the interior. The crew and galley were housed in the forecastle, with ample storage for foodstuffs, other supplies, and crew possessions embedded within the folds. While she was home to a multitude, they were not overly cramped in the spaces. Ten bunks were allotted to each of the narrow rooms on the perimeter of the ship. Though the life of a sailor was anything but easy, they enjoyed the off-time in their bunks peering out of the portholes at the ocean or hanging their feet over the railing up on deck.

As with most ships of her day, the captain's cabin was at the rear of the aftcastle and had six windows reaching from floor to ceiling. The panes spanned the rear of the ship, thereby allowing the full room to be illuminated with soft rays, be they cast from moon or sun. The cabin was handsomely finished and elaborately furnished with period items that would be the envy of anyone living in a modern home seeking a glance into the past.

The walls were dark oak, hand-polished with pumice until the grain and face of the planks were smooth and uniform. After the wood was polished, it was stained with orange oil and allowed to sit and temper for a few days prior to a final coating of fresh oil. Although the work had been completed nearly a decade ago during a refit, the faint twinkling of citrus still permeated throughout the room, pleasantly overpowering the aroma of salt and ocean.

Although she was designed to sit low in the water, thus giving the ship the natural ability to sail fair and true, this particular voyage seemed to be cursed from the start. Some strange fever had raced through the crew like a flash fire in the powder magazine. Her first mate spent most of the initial days of the voyage leaning over the side, retching until he was quite sure his intestines would twist out of his body. The fever that accompanied his sickness only further served to torment him as the ship powered through the peaks and valleys of watery pinnacles. The illnesses, coupled with the ever-present squalls that threatened to swamp the ship, caused the voyage to drag on much longer than any of the crew wanted or expected.

Upon waking, the first mate sauntered back onto the deck in the hope that a fresh breeze on his face would lessen the waves of nausea that often came and went with the rhythm of the tide. As he passed through the narrow hallway leading to the surface, he soon realized that it was early night and the storm clouds had parted. Sparkling stars and waxing moon, more so than the clean air, raised his spirits and steadied his legs. Yet, for the first time in what seemed like months, he could take more than a step without heaving. *Perhaps,* he pondered as he stepped out onto the smooth and weathered oak planks, *the worst of it was over.* Plus, he knew they were approaching their first unscheduled stop, and the captain was expecting his help.

Antoine Meriwether had served aboard the *Bienville* for some six years. But, as he paused to reflect, he wondered, *had it really been that long?* That timespan was twice as long as most, but only half as long as the captain had called her hollow ramparts home. At twenty-seven years old, he stood a tall six foot-four with a large frame to support his lean but stalwart two hundred thirty-five pounds. His black hair framed a long, lean face, and his emerald green eyes were quick to flash and match the intensity of his ivory smile. His physical and mental strength made him the natural leader that he had proved himself to be.

But, of course, he had not always been the first mate; his initial encounter with the *Bienville* had him boarding as a stowaway on a particularly miserable voyage out of Bordeaux nearly a decade ago. After being discovered by Basile Jandreau, the former first mate, it was Jandreau who threatened to use him for cut bait and throw him overboard a dozen leagues from shore. Had Cookie not intervened,

Meriwether was sure the mate would have done exactly as he stated without hesitation.

The old sea cook was without a doubt the most skilled man with a set of galley knives he had ever met. With a beard made more of gray than black, a belly nearly as wide as he was tall, and an apron that surely displayed a part of every meal he had ever prepared, Cookie was the quintessential image of an under-the-deck chef. More than once, Meriwether had seen him create a delicacy out of something a billy goat would refuse to eat. The crew seemed happy with the meals they were served, and because a satisfied crew normally worked harder, the cook garnered a bit more of the captain's favor than the first mate. To be sure, Meriwether was no one special, but he had struck a gentle chord with Cookie, and the old salt took him under his wing. Openly threatening to serve the man who so much as scowled at the former stowaway as stew to the remainder of the crew, the stout old man protected him as if he were his own son.

Meriwether's early years did not go without incident, for as with all sailors, some must test the boundaries of power, and the second mate soon learned that Cookie meant what he said. On the eve of the fourth voyage, Marseille Vaillancourt, the overly liquored third-in-command, ran screaming from the forward hold grasping the left side of his head where his ear was once affixed. Vaillancourt had cornered Meriwether and was preparing to give him ten lashes for staring him down across the table in the galley. While Meriwether was bigger and carried more mass than Vaillancourt, the older man had years and experiences of brawling over him. After loudly proclaiming his intent, he had advanced to make his threat a reality when the flash of a shiny blade caught Meriwether's eye and then Cookie deftly lopped the mate's ear off with the flick of his wrist. There were no further transgressions after that incident, despite Vaillancourt's promise to even the score.

The sound of the mainsail lowering to the deck jostled Meriwether from his thoughts, and the bos'n turned to greet him. Jules Desmarais had been aboard the *Bienville* nearly as long as he, and was extremely adept at directing the actions of the nondescript remainder of the crew. Watching him instruct the men handling the sails and rigging was akin to watching a conductor finesse a finely tuned orchestra. Whether the men responded to his commands through fear or respect mattered not, for they worked nonetheless. The mainsail was down, stored, and wrapped nearly as quickly as the process started. The men worked in near silence on deck, for they had no wish to be detected by anything or anyone in the vicinity. The mizzen mast was collapsed next, followed along with most of the foresail to complete the opening of the blinds. The wind abruptly kicked up from the south, and the bits of hemp and cotton flapped briskly in the slight gale. In the distance, from the lee bank, the sound of the wagging of the rolled canvas was interrupted by one of the native reptiles—a hefty alligator swashing its massive tail in the dark water as it cornered its prey.

Desmarais turned to the deck crew and muttered something in guttural French too faintly for Meriwether to overhear. When the men instantly padded into action, Meriwether realized he had threatened to slaughter the majority of them if the anchor made as much as a whisper while entering the water. Meriwether moved closer to Desmarais and reminded him that it was also time to lower the captain's launch. Desmarais nodded in agreement, and motioned to the men to lower the skiff. They proceeded to unhitch the fastenings, then guided it into the murky swamp below. As the craft's bottom touched the nearly still water, Desmarais looked over at Meriwether and winked. Meriwether quietly began walking toward the captain's cabin to stir him so the last part of their work could be completed.

The captain of the *Bienville* had been in command almost more years than he could count, and although he was not ready to give it up, there were times when he felt his age. Oh, it was not that he was that old; at forty-one, he was still quite stout and able to spar with the best of them. He kept a razor-sharp cutlass at his side at all times, along with two pistols in his waistband, and a derringer in his tightly fitted boots. Lately, clashes and near battles with the U.S. Navy had left him feeling betrayed—especially after his many years of escort service and assistance in transporting food for them. He had begun to feel pressured and hunted like a wild animal, and he had no patience for their increasingly aggressive tactics.

Some weeks ago, as the crew loaded to leave Galveston, he instructed Meriwether to be certain that nothing was left behind that would indicate they had ever been there. In essence, they were to appear to have vanished into thin air. Their leader had no plans to return to Galveston; he had decided he would drift east toward New Orleans, in the hope of profitable trading and better luck, then later over to Cuba. Meriwether could tell by the captain's demeanor that he did not want to be questioned about the details of his demands. He quietly rounded up Desmarais, Cookie, and a few of the senior men and soberly told them the plan. Along with the remainder of the crew who were not loading supplies, they set to the work at hand.

The reflection of the pyre caused a small section of the city to glow with orange and red hues as the flames licked at the night sky. As the ship headed southeast out of the harbor, a stiff wind and a following sea were silent allies of the craft and its occupants. Meriwether, as usual, smiled to himself as the bow divided the waves and served as a breaker to the leading edge of the water, quite often routing a dolphin or two.

While the crew had labored to ensure their ghost-like exit, the pirate leader had been loading his prized possessions into the hidden holds in the ship. Through his sometimes questionable methods, he had amassed a king's ransom in the last decade of his life, and he was not about to surrender it—U.S. Navy be damned. He had barely managed to load all of it and close the door to the secret cache when Meriwether appeared before him, indicating their work was done.

The captain aroused quickly when Meriwether shook him. He had not intended to sleep on this night, and it took some minutes for him to gather his bearings and realize when and where he was.

Standing at attention and saluting his leader, Meriwether said, "Everything is prepared, Captain. And your skiff is ready, sir."

The captain returned the salute and nodded. He had chosen this location so he could navigate and remember where it was when they returned for the loot. Anticipating heavy resistance to the east of their current location, he wanted to take no chances with their (his) precious cargo. There would be a few unscheduled stops before they came to rest on the docks of New Orleans, so he planned to offload some of the bounty at a few of these locations and bury it until his return to recover it in late spring or early summer.

The *Bienville* sat at a location easily recognizable on today's maps, and he acknowledged that his crew had some difficult rowing ahead of them. The draft of the ship was the problem at the current time and place, as she simply sat too low in the water. He feared they would become stranded until high tide, thereby leaving them exposed to any passing craft—friendlies or no. Though the ship was heavily armed, the captain held no fantasies about defending a floundered vessel in such a narrow waterway, especially with her broadside to the south.

Through the heavy weather and tide, the *Bienville* had made her way into the mouth of the Sabine River that meandered north between the modern U.S. states of Texas and Louisiana. The river's protected boundary would provide a smooth and silent passage to his chosen destination. She now lay anchored about one-half league away from the southern tip of a horseshoe-shaped lake, and was barely able to remain above the numerous sandbars that were just below the surface of the muddy river. She oftentimes dragged bottom, which further worried her captain as he knew the tide would drop yet lower before leveling and then rising again, some hours in the future.

Meriwether nodded at Desmarais, who silently motioned for the men to go below and bring up the boxes and pallets the captain had waiting for them. Despite the absence of the sun, the humidity caused the men to sweat profusely—a meal call to the flying pests surrounding the marsh. The crew moved quickly and quietly. The only sound emanating from the belly of the ship was an occasional curse and hands swatting at the profuse quantity of mosquitoes that were abound.

In short order, the first load was boarded and the men rowed steadily to the rendezvous spot—a humped area on the bank at the back end of the upside-down U-shaped portion of the lake. The destination was nestled between the marshy portions of the river on the southernmost end of a thin slice of land forming a sharp point. Meriwether could not help but notice the long, wispy Spanish moss that hung in abundance as it reached from the cypress trees stretching toward the waiting water, as well as the stench of the sour marsh that quickly filled his nostrils. Knobby knees of cypress trees peeking from the water added extra obstacles to maneuver around as the men stirred the water with their thick oars. The nose of the wooden craft merged with the silty river bottom and one half of the launch's crew stepped off with shovels and torches.

After maneuvering through the tall marsh grass and flushing a reptile or two, the captain indicated a spot, and the torches were placed in a rough square. Wooden shovels went to work on the soft sand between three cypress trees—a large one and two smaller on each side. As part of the crew dug, the remainder of the sailors offloaded the cargo and then started making their way back to the ship for a second, third, and then a fourth and final load. The digging was relatively easy at first, but eventually the mire of the bottom clay slowed the progress by at least half. Despite the delays, the hole was ready to receive the treasure by the time the last load was freeboarded from the skiff.

The captain monitored their progress, pausing to grunt the occasional order in French and force the men to work in an organized manner. As the last of the chests were stacked near the edge of the vault, the wind began to gust, slowly at first, then harder and more deliberately. The gale continued to build until the sound was nearly deafening. Some of the torches had already blown out, and the remainder threatened to follow suit. Without warning, the air suddenly became electrified and an acrid burning smell became so strong it could not be ignored. The last of the torches suddenly went out, yet the entire area was illuminated by a strange blue glow. Some of the crew began stumbling about, holding their ears and faces with their hands. The wind had built to a crescendo the likes of which none of them had ever experienced. Lightning began discharging all around the edge of the hole, striking some of the crew.

Meriwether fought to remain standing as he surveyed the site. Between flashes, he could see most of the men writhing on the ground, holding their ears and squeezing their eyes completely shut. Desmarais reached out to steady himself. A lightning bolt that struck nearby ignited his shirt, so he threw himself backward in an effort to reach the riverbank. Shirt on fire, he rolled until he was submerged in the river, yet his shirt continued to burn.

The captain was down on one knee, struggling to raise his head to steal a glimpse of the scene surrounding him. The pandemonium of the wind, lightning, and screaming threatened to overload his senses. He partially blacked out; when he came to, he saw a blue orb laced with a mesh pattern glowing high above and behind the largest of the chests. The orb, roughly the size of a small melon but rapidly increasing in size, was now hovering slightly below the treetops. Lightning and thunder emanated from the center of the orb and made an evil sizzling and crackling sound as it continued to manifest itself in size and shape. The trio of privateers remained only partially conscious at this point, but they could calculate the orb had grown to some twenty feet in diameter and was beginning a slow descent to the ground.

As swashbucklers, none of the men were cowards or weaklings, but they had never heard of anyone experiencing anything like this. Desmarais, the most religious man of the three, fell to his knees and began praying to a god he was certain had all but deserted them. Meriwether struggled to his feet, only to be up-ended by a near miss from a lightning bolt that left a crater the shape and size of his head near his right foot. The noise was intolerable, and the air was so electrified that hair was erect on every body part of each member of the cursed expedition as the smell of burning continued to encapsulate the group like a heavy fog.

The orb had fully descended near the largest chest and hovered but a few inches above the earth. As they continued to study the ball, a red line, thin at first but slowly widening, ran down the side of the orb from top to bottom. To the captain's ire and terror, it opened and spread apart like the wedges of an over-ripened orange. From the center of the orb, two figures appeared, dressed in white clothing fully covering them but for a small opening on the facial area of the head. A strange light haloed them, the entire area in front of and behind them resonating with the glowing effect. The apparitions held some sort of glowing instruments in each hand. As they moved toward the largest chest, the figures pressed buttons on the devices, and the lights began to flicker in rhythm.

Desmarais and Meriwether could scarcely believe what they were seeing. As they strained to watch, the largest chest began to shake from side to side and then started to rise from the ground. The chest rose to a height of about two feet, and floated with ease between the two figures as they made their way back to the blue sphere. As the figures stepped into the orb, all three men strained to stop them, but rapidly discovered they couldn't move. Helplessly, they watched the figures take another chest, and then one more as they fought to reach the men in white. As the ghostly figures stepped into the orb with the third chest, the orb began rapidly shrinking, imploding upon itself and disappearing into the night as quickly as it formed. As it disappeared, there was a massive explosion, and all of the men were swept from their positions to land flat on their backs staring at the night sky. With that, the heavens went dark, and total silence engulfed the sailors, who promptly slipped into unconsciousness.

Meriwether could not tell how long they had been out, but distant lightning and the roll of thunder jarred them from a state of nether to full alertness in mere seconds. The captain ordered him to return to the ship for the log and writing materials. Though puzzled as to the motive, he knew better than to argue with the captain and made haste to complete his task. The rising tide had allowed the ship to move closer, and Cookie had taken it upon himself to narrow the gap between the ship and land exponentially.

Upon Meriwether's return to the group, the captain made some notes and the crew entombed the cargo as pelting rain and whipping winds enveloped them. Slipping and sliding on the muddy banks, the group scrambled to make it back to the captain's launch. After piling into the small craft, everyone grabbed an oar and rowed without care to rank or position, reaching the ship in one-third the normal time. Wasting little time to store the skiff, the ship was underway within moments. No sooner had they cleared the river's mouth when the first colossal waves began to pound the ship, threatening to capsize her despite the clever navigation of the crew.

Having faced some like it in the Atlantic, the captain realized this was not an ordinary storm, but was indeed the start of the landfall of a hurricane. He knew from experience it was a fool's errand to attempt to ride it out.

"Meriwether! Maneuver the ship as close to the shore as you can without grounding her and have the lookouts watch for the rocks near the shore."

Meriwether saluted and repeated the order back to the captain, then issued his own orders to the crew. The captain remained steadfast in his search for adequate cover. He knew of a few caves to the east of their present location, but they were only useable at the lowest point of the tide, and the weather was surely pushing water to the shore, rendering the caves potentially useless. The rocks and cypress knees protecting the openings could also cause their demise, for he had never attempted to bring a ship this size into these caves.

Meriwether added lookouts to the bow of the ship so the opening could be located with all possible speed, but they made slow progress in the impending storm. The remaining hands were below decks pumping water, but they were rapidly losing the battle. Meriwether knew if the caves were not located within minutes, they would lose the ship and every man on board.

Suddenly, there was a cry from the port side, and the waving lantern signified they had reached the cave. The helm was spun hard over, and the bowsprit targeted the center of the dark opening. The cave was hardly built to hold such a ship, the bottom and sides gouged and likely punctured as they started through. But then the vessel dropped just enough to pass into the waiting maw. Unable to reduce speed in time, rocks at the end of the small lagoon began to dash the bow and were poised to open the hull, had it not been for the captain's scream to drop anchors. The flukes dragged and then caught on the craggy bottom, slamming the ship to a stop. The stern had barely cleared the face of the cave when the brunt of the storm was upon them. Lightning, hail, and heavy squalls lashed at the land; though they were partially sheltered, there was no mercy as the tempest pounded on. The top of the main mast splintered as the rising tide shunted it into the roof. A substantial number of large glass-like crystals fell all around, threatening to impale anyone on deck.

For a brief moment, Meriwether thought they were in a diamond mine, and could not believe their good fortune, but his glee had to be tabled for now. The pause in the midst of the storm did little to place any of them at ease. As the back side of the eye wall began to pound, the sounds of falling rocks and earth boomed all around them. The lanterns, with their feeble light, provided no assistance to identify the source of the failure of the overhead canopy. A blast of wind and storm exceeding one-hundred-eighty miles per hour extinguished every light on the ship. The last sound that anyone onboard heard was the main entrance and ceiling of the cave cracking all around them, followed by the cacophony of total silence.

CHAPTER 1 – A LOST WORLD

THE UNEXPECTED BOUNCE OF THE TRUCK JOLTED REX FROM HIS SLEEPY STATE OF MIND. It was the start of what was soon to be a sweltering Saturday morning, and he had dozed off while riding in the camper shell-covered bed of the truck. His slumber lingered despite the incessant rattle of loose exhaust pipes and the rough ride that could be attributed to shock absorbers in use long past their prime. The bed of the truck was stuffed with his younger brother Sebastien, along with ice chests, food, drinks, snacks, tackle boxes, folding chairs, bait, water jugs, and last but certainly not least, fishing poles. One in particular, a fiberglass 'cane' pole that his dad used in lieu of a regular rod and reel. Rex always thought it curious that his patriarch used such a device when modern fishing tackle would perform the same task with far less effort. At nine years old, it was not something he could comprehend—one of the simple things in life that his father would not allow to be tainted by modern gadgets.

The cab of the blue Ford truck housed his dad, mom, and Stein, his favorite uncle. As seen through the back glass and lighted by the instrument panel, a thick cloud of aromatic smoke was floating about. His father, Johann, was smoking his pipe, and Uncle Stein chewing on a Roi-Tan cigar. He also knew that Gabrielle, his mother, was constantly chiding the two about the impact of tobacco on their health to no effect. The embers on the end of his uncle's fat and leafy roll glowed bright crimson in unison with his respiration.

Stein was a victim of genetics, lifestyle, and the era in which he had lived. Diagnosed as a diabetic somewhat early in his life, Johann had commented more than once that Stein's health had slowly deteriorated through the years. Some of the downward spiral was due to the lack of medical knowledge of the times, but a good portion was due to his behavior. He drank far too much and did not care for himself very well. Despite these unfortunate events, he always remained upbeat. He welcomed Rex and his siblings and had an infectious laugh that could not be resisted.

Stein resided in the same house he, Johann, and their seven siblings had shared many decades erstwhile. Built circa 1920 and situated near the center of a small lot, the old gray house displayed asbestos shake siding, wooden slat floors, and a creaky front door complete with a metal screen door on the outside. Though sparsely decorated, it seemed much larger than it actually was, although it had five rooms including a plain bathroom. Freestanding gas heaters adorned the interior floors, providing heat during short, mild Louisiana winters. Old vegetable cans filled with water placed near the flame-kissed porcelain grates provided humidity. Otherwise, the heaters would quickly dry the air to a discomforting level.

Robbed of his health, Stein was forced to stop working and driving many years before Rex was born. Part of the weekend chores (though he never saw it that way) for Rex and his brother was the delivery of groceries and supplies to him. Johann always picked out the canned goods, meats, fruits, and vegetables, but it was his and his brother's job to acquire two boxes of Roi-Tan cigars from the store shelves. The cigars gave off a pungent plume that frequently burned their eyes, but in the many years to follow, Rex merely needed to close his eyes to recall the smell of them.

Though he had lost his left arm just above the elbow in an accident back when he was in high school, Stein was still quite the fisherman. A machinist he had befriended at a paper mill where he worked as a transportation agent made him a belt assembly that had a mounting point to hold the butt of a fishing rod. When the wearer had a bite, they just pulled straight back to fight and land the fish without worry of the rod slipping. In many ways, it could be seen as a one man trolling rig. Once locked, it functioned similarly to the ones affixed to the stern of charter fishing boats.

Another bump nudged Rex from his thoughts, and he realized they had turned onto old Louisiana Highway 90. Johann and Stein had shared stories about the old highway with him and Sebastien so many times, that Rex felt like he had seen the area in its prime. Prior to the freeways being constructed in the fifties, this road served as the main artery from Texas into Louisiana and handled all of the west-east traffic. Just before the heart of the connection, lay a mile-long bridge of wood, metal, tar, and asphalt. Back then, on any weekend, one could find the bridge lined with hundreds of local residents fishing with poles, bows, nets, and reels. Non-participants would enjoy the scenery while chatting with each other over an alcoholic beverage or a smoke. The lanes were scarcely wide enough to allow two automobiles to pass one another. Crossing the bridge was typically an hour-long affair, especially when stopping every few feet to allow someone to cross to view the latest prize captured from the deep or to dodge the latest malady in the bridge's face. At the time, when they frequented the marshy area, the bridge was beginning to fall into a state of disrepair. With state funding being applied to the interstate system, little remained to support the bridge. As a consequence, there was road base missing and the underlying wood structure had been damaged, leaving gaping openings where feet and tires could easily become entrapped.

Prior to reaching the bridge, there were a number of houses, some used as vacation, hunting, or weekend getaway cabins. There were also families peppered between these buildings, some of them farmers or commercial fishermen that used the bridge area as a launching base for their chosen profession. Affixed just past this familiar plot of domiciles, twin lakes could be found, decidedly parallel in size and shape.

On the northern side of the derelict motorway, Blue Lake was nestled among yellow pine, cypress, and pin oaks along the perimeter of the water. Umber pine needles sprinkled with occasional pinecones carpeted the embankment surrounding the basin. The contents of the earthen bowl were a true representation of its namesake: eerily sapphire but nearly crystal when viewed from beneath the surface, the color of the lake was a rarity in this part of the world.

Mud Lake, situated on the opposite side and unlike its twin, was murky from top to bottom with no hope of visibility. The water was also much more briny than that of its neighbor, thus the habitat that resided within was of a totally different species, though not too far removed. Catfish of different varieties were the main staple that could be harvested from its dark liquid. However, leviathan American alligators could also be found there. When the 'gators were prowling about, any luck that an angler may have had would simply fade away, the fish fleeing to avoid becoming a reptilian meal.

The largest bit of notoriety in the history of the lake was the capture of a twenty-three-foot gator that molested the fish on a regular basis and, on occasion, fishermen who visited the waters. Old Man Patterson, who was not so old but looked fifteen years older than he really was, and his two sons, Tim and Bryan, were considered the foremost 'gator hunters and trappers in the area. They lived in a shack that partially submerged with the tide. The back porch was used as a makeshift boat ramp. Although the Pattersons knew their business in the swamp, they received strange looks and comments whenever they visited the town, and were often treated as outcasts. This was especially true of the eldest Patterson, who had a hook for a left hand.

Rex's dad and Dutch Van Dyke always seemed to go out of their way to speak to the trio. Rex couldn't help but think they were closer than appearances would indicate. The townsfolk were more than happy to allow them to remove the periodic wildlife nuisance that popped up from time to time, or handle a dirty job no one else wanted to do as long as they kept a low profile. Such was the case of Ol' Twisty, as the alligator came to be known. The people in the community didn't care who removed the pest, simply that it *was* eliminated in the shortest time possible.

Though many residents attempted to trap the massive reptile, their efforts were futile as the animal seemed to have extra sensory perception. Evading all order of traps and snares, Ol' Twisty sauntered his way in and out of the lake as if he owned the place. Johnny Chevalier nearly ensnared the old horned back, but gained a right metacarpus to match Eamon Patterson's left. Things moved rather quickly after Johnny lost his right hand to the crushing jaws of the alligator. The Pattersons were called in to deal with the monster, and the trio made short work of the capture, thus making the prior attempts and the architects behind those waylaid plans seem as uneducated and ignorant as the residents of the community viewed the trappers.

One of the local newspapers reported the capture and had accompanying photos which were too grainy to see much detail, but Rex saw the actual photographs of the alligator Johann had in a frame on his desk. The reptile was incredible in size and breadth. He easily hung six feet out of the boat that eventually brought him into the old swamp house. Even after death, it was said a mystery had revolved around Ol' Twisty because, when he was slaughtered, hundreds of multi-colored tubes of differing diameters and lengths were found inside the beast. Puzzling though it was at first, someone later ascertained the tubes were the remains of plastic shotgun shells. The stomach acid of the alligator had dissolved the brass ends, leaving the plastic sleeves behind. A certain level of respect and, to some degree, admiration, was bestowed upon the old man and his sons from that point forward for the slaying of the menace. Though respect should have been automatically granted, Rex was particularly happy to see they no longer received as many disparaging glances when frequenting the town.

On the far end of the highway just beyond the bridge, the land was flat with marsh grass and cypress trees shadowing the edge of the roadbed. There were a number of small roads that led to oil wells situated on land that was leased and operated by a few oil companies. Some locals believed the bridge only existed to allow the oil companies access to these leases; local residents having access to fish was merely a perk. At the far end after the stilted mile-long bridge, the road continued for about another mile, abruptly ending at the edge of the Sabine River where the connecting, center pivot swing bridge had been removed. With the opening of the interstate highway system and to provide more access to the Port of Orange for oceangoing vessels, this "last mile" was dismantled in the sixties. Thus, the old link was severed between the two states and an era ended that had begun on November 11, 1927, with the commissioning of the swinging bridge.

The fate of the mile-long bridge was sealed in the middle of an early summer night in 1973 when an ex-convict who wanted to end it all parked his car in the middle of the bridge and lit both ends simultaneously. The bridge burned for months until it finally extinguished itself at the waterline. Rex wished a thousand times over he had a time machine and could travel back with some of his friends to catch the guy in the act—thus saving the old bridge and the recreational area that people drove from miles around to enjoy.

CHAPTER 2 – A GIFT HORSE?

THE SHARP LURCH OF THE F-150 GRINDING TO A HALT COMBINED WITH THE SOUND OF acorns being crushed under the tires indicated they had reached their destination. As the occupants of the old Ford exited, an early fall could be felt in the morning air as the sun began to peek from the clouds over their shoulders. A slight breeze from the north caused the endless streams of Spanish moss hanging from the trees overhead to sway in unison. When combined with the wind, the gray lichen formed a cyclic motion that resembled enthusiasts at a rock concert swaying with the beat of the music. Although he could not yet see them in the forming light, Rex could hear the leaves that had fallen from the surrounding tallow trees skittering across the lumps of broken road base.

Suddenly, just off the edge of the road, a small animal hissed before dashing into the underbrush in the wake of their arrival.

"Everyone, be on guard for snakes," Johann said, "because they may be where you least expect them."

Stein echoed Johann's sentiments.

"Amen to that! This place has plenty of water moccasins; you can tell they're close by if you smell a rotten stench."

The remaining members of the fishing expedition nodded in agreement.

The road divided the marsh nearly in half, the south marsh containing much higher salinity than the north. The upper side had slightly brackish water, because the river flowed freely through the area. The spot was abundant with sun perch, crappie, and a few bass, but as a benefit from the salt, the occasional goggle eye and sheep's head could also be harvested. The location they frequented was of no scientific or studied choosing. Nay, it was the overhead canopy that beckoned them to sit and pass the time drowning worms for hours on end. The plethora of cypress and pin oak perched at the water's edge had resided there for centuries, growing two to three stories tall. The branches of the differing trees had intertwined to form a rigid, umbrella-like shield of protection against the searing heat of the Louisiana sun.

Standing at the rear of the truck, Rex could hear the red-wing blackbirds starting to exercise their voices in the early morning mist. Crickets, grasshoppers, and the ubiquitous mosquitoes contributed to the pre-dawn serenade that slowly built to a crescendo. Knees of the prolific cypress trees lined the path from the Ford to the sandy bank, and assured firm footing along the muddy walkway. Mounds of stubby knobs continued to the edge of the bank and stretched the full length of the loamy earth, breaking the smooth soil into random plots. As seen from behind on the road edge, the row of chairs must have appeared like pigeons lining the local rooftops, but the fishing positions were separated to allow the sitters to cast their lines without worry of snagging one another.

As the day grew brighter, the party decided flashlights and headlights were no longer needed. His dad doused the lanterns and jaunted back up the path to switch the truck lights off, so as not to exhaust the battery. Hearing a mild expletive, Rex quickly turned, expecting to observe Johann annihilating one of the slithering reptiles that dwelled in the local ecosystem. Instead, he saw him taking in a full survey of the surrounding trees and vegetation. Each of them in turn reciprocated his father's actions and all were amazed at what lay before them.

A few days prior, Hurricane Chantal passed relatively close to the Louisiana coastline, prior to turning toward High Island. Chantal was classified as a category one storm, but most residents of the area would scoff at anything less than a category three, considering it merely a heavy rainstorm with a bit of wind. This latest storm was largely ignored, simply because it did not make landfall in Louisiana and it was thought to be of such low potency. Standing on the river's edge, Rex had difficulty fathoming why adults thought in the manner they did, for to his young eyes, the damage that was sustained by the trees and surrounding foliage was nothing short of spectacular.

Had they traveled only a short distance further, they would have been forced to stop as one of the oldest oak trees in the area had been put to rest across the entire highway. Its massive branches were still shrouded in Spanish moss, and while much of it had remained, naked spots could be seen all along the bark of its limbs. On other parts of the ancient topiary, mistletoe had been pulled from its roots in all directions. Spanish moss had been stripped from the branches of the still-anchored trees. The devastation was nearly complete in spots, but untouched elsewhere. It appeared as though random swatches had been marked to be destroyed.

Never missing an opportunity to educate his young sons, Johann quizzed Rex and Sebastien on the damage around them.

"Rex, do you see the pattern?"

Rex, who considered himself an amateur meteorologist, studied the scene then replied, "Yes, sir! I think we're seeing the circular motion of the storm in action. But, I'm confused by the spots that seem to be untouched."

"Quite right," Johann agreed. "It does seem to be peculiar."

He then prodded the youngest Rhineheart to join into the conversation. "Sebastien, any thoughts on this strange pattern?"

"Well Dad," Sebastien said after a few moments of contemplation, "because the wind spins in a circle, I think the trees will be laid over one side here and on the other side other there. But I agree with Rex. It seems weird that some of this is still standing. It should all be flattened, right?"

"Well boys," Johann said, "I'm not sure why it's laid out in this fashion, but I'm sure it was a heck of a storm. For now, let's see if we can catch some fish."

As Johann led the way with the boys in tow, they made their way back down the rough walkway to the edge of the water. As Johann explained what they saw to Gabrielle and Stein, Rex and Sebastien raced down the bank to see who could cast first. Though Rex was older, his sibling, weightless on his feet, beat him to the mark. His mother and uncle had already been fishing for some time, but the nibbles until now were few and far between. As the hours passed, the sun climbed to its mid-day apex. The heat of a mid-summer day in Louisiana was beginning the simmer before the boil.

Without warning, the growling of Rex's stomach could be heard from a few feet away. Sebastien giggled. "I'm not sure who's hungrier—you or the fish."

Rex rotated the latch and opened the steel Coleman ice chest, tossing Sebastien a cheese and bologna sandwich and a Shasta cream soda. He then grabbed a sandwich and a Fanta for himself. For the next few hours, they bantered back and forth over the loss of bait, missed strikes, and the fact that no one had caught anything. Later, they sat quietly amongst the sound of bait being retrieved and cast occasionally over the water to the song of blackbirds.

"Baby, I don't think they're going to give us much of a contest today," Stein said to Johann, breaking the seemingly endless silence. "This little storm has stirred the water, and they're just not biting."

"Well, we don't have anything else to do, so let's give it a little more time," Johann replied "Rex, have you boys had any luck?"

"It's about the same over here," Rex said. "They're nibbling, but not really biting."

"Babe," Stein laughed, "it may be time for your secret weapon."

"I was just thinking about that," Johann chuckled. He then reached into his tackle box and pulled out a can of WD-40 and a prototype lure one of the guys in the government research department had given him to test in the murky water. Removing the worm hook and split shot followed by the plastic bobber, he replaced them with the tube bait. He gave the tube bait a quick shot of the oil and cast it out into the moving water.

It barely hit the water when the tip of Johann's cane pole bent nearly in half. He jerked back, set the hook, and then proceeded to land a fat two-pounder.

"Wow!" Rex shouted. "Can you set mine up, Dad?"

"Me too! Me too!" squealed Sebastien.

"Now, now, save some for the rest of us!" Stein joked.

For the remainder of the day, they passed the time baiting, hooking, and landing crappie of various sizes. They remained somewhat oblivious to the scenic surroundings and environment that held other wildlife in bounty. Every now and then a splash could be heard in the far distance, indicating an alligator was seeking its prey.

"Well, gang, it's about time for me to prepare our catch," Gabrielle said, "and serve it in a nice meal. I'm sure that Arieanna will enjoy this, too."

Both boys looked at one another and rolled their eyes at the mention of their little sister.

"Stein, will you be joining us?" Gabrielle asked.

"No, my dear, not this time," Stein yawned, "my old bones need to stretch out."

Although Stein and Sebastien were ready to call it a day, Rex protested.

"But I have one that keeps nibbling. I want to see if I can catch him!"

"We've had a full day," Johann said, "don't you think it's time to go?"

Before he could answer, a large splash was followed by an excited Rex shouting, "I've got him! I've got him!"

He worked the reel, but the finny prey wasn't going to give up without a fight. Rex pulled and twisted, but the fish was equal to the task; for every foot of line that he reeled in, the fish pulled back nearly half.

The lunker leapt from the water, and when it splashed back in, turned and made a run for the largest of the river branches. Rex lost purchase, scrambling to remain upright. As he started sliding down the edge of the moist bank toward the water, Stein stepped forward to put his arm around his waist.

"Hold on, boy!" he exclaimed. "You're safe. Now land that fish!"

With regained footing, Rex struggled to reel the fish to the bank, growing tired as the contest endured.

"Rex," Johann called out, "give him some slack and let him swim around a little. He'll tire out, so you can reel him in."

Rex relaxed the drag on the Zebco reel and soon the fish began to wear down, allowing him to make some headway on the landing.

"Can someone grab the net and help me with this?"

By the time that Gabrielle made it back from the truck with the net, he'd nearly landed the fish.

"Wow, that's a fine largemouth!" she cried out as he lifted the immense fish from the water.

Indeed, it was the biggest bass any of them had seen in many a day. Its unique markings and patterns, in addition to its sheer size, made it worthy of some taxidermy skills.

"We'll have to take this to Dutch and have him work his magic on it," Johann said gleefully.

"Really, Dad? That would be awesome! My first trophy, and I only had a little help from Uncle Stein."

"You sure did, kiddo! I'm so glad I was here to see it."

Not wanting to miss all of the excitement but yearning to preserve the moment, Gabrielle climbed the bank again to the truck and grabbed her new Nikon F4 to capture the moment.

"Hold him high and say cheese," she instructed. The flash provided enough lumens to backfill the difference between the sky and the woodsy background.

"There, that was the last one," she noted. "We'll have that one as a keepsake forever. I'll have it developed at Moreau's next week."

Johann and Rex wrapped his prize in old newspapers and packed it in ice inside the Coleman, as Gabrielle, Stein, and Sebastien lugged the remainder of the accoutrements to the truck.

Sebastien poked Rex as the Ford made a U-turn and headed back east, "You lucky dog! I could come here for the rest of my life and never catch one like that!"

Rex smiled. "You're probably right, but you'll have your chance. It's just a roll of the dice."

"Just you wait and see—I'm going for the biggest old Mr. Whiskers there is in the place."

The old truck meandered back towards town and pulled up at Stein's house.

"See you all next time," Stein said as he waved goodbye. "It was a good day. We'll do it again soon!"

Johann had a special place in his heart for his brother, though Stein was more than twenty years his senior. Perhaps it was because he was only able to spend a short time with him growing up. So he made up lost time as best and as often as he could. Some of the best times Rex and Sebastien had as children were those shared with their dad and uncle.

Back home, while Rex and Sebastien stowed the equipment in the basement, Gabrielle started cleaning the fish. Arieanna, like most little sisters, squealed at the sight of them and hid behind her mother's apron.

Rex thought this a little puzzling. His dad usually cleaned the fish while he and Sebastien helped with the scale and gut bucket. There were plenty of times when they would look at the internals of a fish and wonder how all of it worked together. Strange organs in there, yet somehow it magically allowed the creature to live underwater.

"Rex, let's go; you and Sebastien come with me," Johann called.

"Where are we going?" Sebastien asked.

"We have to bring Rex's fish over to Dutch right away, or he won't be able to mount it."

"Cool!" Rex shouted.

Dutch's place was always full of interesting and weird stuff. Rex and Sebastien loved to explore the old taxidermy shop and the projects the old animal preserver had spread around on the workbenches. They climbed into the front of the truck and headed down the long driveway toward town, leaving a ghostly white trail of fine gravel dust in their wake. The trio rolled up to Dutch's shop to find him out back sorting some bags of sawdust that would be used as filler in many of his creations.

"Howdy, Dutch," Johann called as he approached the rear of the house.

Standing outside the shop, Dutch Van Dyke peered over his horn-rimmed glasses, turned, and spit into a brass spittoon. Rex and Sebastien always thought it was neat the way that he did that, because it would ring when the spit hit the brass pot.

"What're you guys up to these days?" Dutch asked.

"Well, Rex here, caught what I think is a nice largemouth this afternoon, and I'd like for you to look at it and tell me what you think."

Dutch peeled back the paper. "Say! Now that's a good'un! What do you want to do with it?"

"What would you charge me to mount it on a board?"

"Let's see . . . Two dollars for the board, five for the paint, some glue, thread, eyes, gills, and sawdust. How about thirty dollars for the whole she-bang?"

"Thirty dollars for the boy's first trophy mount? Let's do it. Of course," he added, "you can pose it so that it looks on the brink of swallowing a lure, right?"

"Why, Johann, you'd think I'd never done this before. Leave it to me; it'll be perfect in every way."

"The only thing I'm wondering," Rex began, "is how much it weighs," Sebastien finished.

Dutch's round belly jiggled with laughter. "Well sure! I've got a scale right here. Let's find out."

A sharp whistle escaped Dutch's lips as he examined the scale's needle. "Sonny boy, you're just a few ounces shy of the state record. It'd be my pleasure to mount this one for you. Let's open him up so you can take the meat home and fry it up."

"You can do that?" Rex asked.

"Certainly! It only takes a few minutes, and since we'll be fillin' this big guy up with sawdust, I won't be needin' the meat or bones."

Dutch worked his filet knife for a few strokes on his leather strop then proceeded to filet the bass. He had barely inserted the blade of his knife and made a long incision, when he let out an exclamation.

"What de heck is dis?!" he said, more than a little of his Dutch ancestry slipping through.

His knife had hit a tough spot in the bones of the fish, or so it seemed to Rex. Instead, he opened the belly of the fish, reached in and pulled out a gold coin.

"What do we have here?" he pondered, stopping to rinse the coin off to more closely examine it. Setting the coin down on a clean, dry cloth, he backed away from the bench for all to see.

"It's a French coin," Johann said, "with a bust of Napoleon on one side and what appears to be a circle of olive branches on the other—both with raised dots on the perimeter."

The inscription surrounding Napoleon's head read:

"NAPOLEON EMPEREUR."

An inscription encircling the olive branches read:

"REPUBLIQUE FRANCAISE."

"40 FRANCS"

"AN 13. .A."

Rex stood in awe and tried to focus on the coin. "Do you think it's worth something, Dad?"

Johann laughed. "Well, it's worth at least forty francs. We'll have to check it out and see; it could be worth a *little* something."

"In all my years, I've never seen a coin like that and in such good condition," Dutch said. "Look how shiny it is and how crisp the lettering stands out."

"Rex, my boy, you may have something here."

"Say," Dutch said, as he rolled the coin between his massive thumb and forefinger, "what is this engraved here? The letters 'JL' are scribed as clear as day in this fancy lettering."

Johann took the coin for a closer look. "You're right. I wonder whose initials these are."

Silence fell over the group.

"Well," Johann continued, "no matter. Let's get going, boys. Dutch, I'll check back in a couple of weeks and see how you're coming along."

"I'll be here," he replied, taking the coin from Johann and examining it one last time before handing it to Rex, along with the meat from the bass.

Rex could hardly believe his luck: *a trophy fish and an old gold coin all in the same day?* Unlike his father, he was certain more coins existed, and he was more than a little confident he could learn the whole story. *Who* was *this mysterious "JL," and why did he engrave initials on the coin? Yes, he was convinced the owner of the coin was male. Were there more? And what did "JL" do for a living?* One thing he was certain of: his search had only just begun.

"Dad," he said, "how do we find out more about this coin? Is there a book or someone that we can ask?"

Johann paused to remove his pipe to allow a puff of smoke to escape his lips. "I'm not sure, Rex. Coins, stamps, and old papers are your mom's department."

Rex thought about his father sitting beside him steering the shiny navy-colored Ford and smoking his large rusticated bent pipe. As long as Rex could remember, Johann had it stuffed with Borkum Riff, Captain Black, or some other tobacco, usually slightly smoldering or in the stages of fading embers. The pipe was dark, with rough, rustic edges on the bowl, and had a curved, black mouthpiece.

His mother had purchased the pipe many years ago in an estate sale somewhere in France, although she could not remember where, other than to describe the mansion as "castlesque". Rex often daydreamed that many years ago a knight had enjoyed the pipe after slaying an ornery dragon.

The smoke would waft aloft from his pipe and float about the room, giving the space a comfortable and kind feeling that was laced with warm spices. Although it would be discovered many years later that tobacco contributed to numerous health issues, Rex would not have had his childhood any other way—Johann's pipe was a quintessential fixture in the Rhineheart home.

The slowing of the truck broke his concentration and he said, "I can't wait to show Mom—she is going to be so surprised!"

"Yeah," Sebastien added, "but when can we go and spend it at the store on some candy?"

"What?! We're not using *my* money for candy."

"Boys, I'm not sure you understand. It may not be worth anything, but if it is, you can't just spend it."

"Huh?" Rex inquired.

"Well, there are a few reasons, namely because it's a foreign coin, and because we don't know how much it's worth."

"But you said it was forty francs," Sebastien said.

"Guys, this is a *French* coin and we're in the United States—the money value isn't the same. Anyway, unless I'm wrong, the coin itself is probably worth far more than its face value."

As the truck rambled down the gravel road, Rex pulled the coin out of his pocket to fawn over its golden luster and crisp details. He couldn't wait to show his mother and ask her if she could look the coin up in one of her many coin books, or if she knew of anyone who could shed some light on the origin of the coin.

"Mom! Mom!" Rex called out as he exited the old truck, "Look what was inside the bass!"

Gabrielle, dredging fish fillets in her secret batter and dropping them into the shortening-filled cast-iron skillet, looked through the kitchen window to see what was causing the excitement. She could see her firstborn running toward her with something golden in his hand.

"What do you have there?"

"It's a gold coin from France, and it was inside the fish, and Mr. Van Dyke found it when he cut it open, and—"

"Whoa, whoa, whoa, slow down and start over. You're so excited I can't make heads or tails of what you're saying."

"Sorry, Mom, I was trying to tell you what we found."

"Well, let's have a look at what you're holding." Rolling the coin between her thumb and forefinger she said, "Man, this really is an old coin."

"But Mom, see how new and clean it looks. How can it be old?"

"Well, although it doesn't seem to be ancient, it is indeed quite old. Do you see these letters and numbers below the olive branches? These are based on the French Revolutionary calendar. It was used for about fourteen years between . . . 1792 and 1806, I believe."

"How do you know that?"

"Simple, my dear, French history was a requirement back when I was in primary school in Marseilles. French maîtresses were unforgiving toward students who couldn't remember their history dates."

"Mom, they're tough here in Louisiana, too!" Sebastien laughed.

"Teachers are mostly the same all over the world," Gabrielle replied with a smile. "Anyway, back to the coin, the French Revolutionary calendar was split into two groups of seven years. The first group had its 'New Year' on September 22nd. The second group celebrated it on September 23rd. So, based upon Rex's date of AN thirteen, we can surmise this coin was made between 23 September 1804 and 23 September 1805."

"Wait. Does that mean it's over one hundred eighty-five years old?" Johann exclaimed.

"Yes, my dear, that is exactly what I'm saying."

"Well now, this coin must be worth much more than forty francs, especially considering its condition."

"I would have to agree with you," Gabrielle said with a laugh. "Let's have a look at a few of my books and see if we can match it with a similar coin."

She walked into her study with the remainder of the clan following and slid a few books from the third shelf of her library and placed them on the desk. She opened a rather thick greenish colored book first, and flipped to a section on French coins.

Within a few minutes she let out an "Aha!" "See here? I believe this is your coin, Rex."

They quickly surrounded her, leaning over to see what she had found. Johann let out a whistle.

"Rex, my boy, looks like you have a *great* example of an early 1800s French franc. According to the grading system, your coin would be set as a fine/fine. That makes it worth quite a lot!"

Rex couldn't stand it any longer. "Well . . . how much?"

"Always counting the pennies, eh Rex?" Gabrielle said. "According to this, it would seem the coin would be worth well over a thousand dollars, depending upon the buyer."

"Over a thousand dollars? I'm rich! I need to find the rest of the coins and we can all celebrate—maybe you and Dad could retire and we could go and search for even more treasure!"

"Well," Johann said, laughing from head to toe, "that would be great, but you have to find it first, and that's a lot of swamp to search—*if* there's any more to be found."

"There must be more! I think the storm uncovered something and the fish thought it was bait and swallowed it."

"Perhaps. Bass are known to strike at shiny objects, which could explain why they like shiners so much," Johann said. "But Rex, I'm not sure how you would begin to search for more coins, the fish could have swallowed the coin anywhere in the marsh. They do swim for miles and miles."

Rex's enthusiasm was quashed as quickly as it had started.

"Yeah . . . You're probably right. I could look forever and find nothing. I do like thinking about finding more coins though!"

"You might want to show it to some of your friends and let them enjoy it too. But then we should put some preservative on it. One of these days you may want to sell it."

"Sure, okay, I won't ever sell it. Not many kids my age have found such a prize. And inside a trophy fish to boot!"

"Mom," Sebastien said, "Is something burning?"

"My fish!" Gabrielle exclaimed, as she ran back to the kitchen to attend to dinner.

Chapter 3 – The Rediscovery

It was hard to believe nearly ten years had passed since the discovery of the old coin and that Rex was preparing to attend Texas A&M at Corpus Christi. He wasn't sure what exactly he wanted to major in. He'd declared marine biology, but mechanical engineering also tugged at his heart strings. "No matter," he said to himself as he packed his bags. "The ocean is where I'm most at peace."

"Rex?" Gabrielle called up to him. "Don't forget to pack all of your clothes, including your jackets."

"I won't," he replied. "I have a few more things to go through and then Sebastien can start moving his things into my room."

While removing the last of his jackets from the rear shelf, he looked up to discover an old wooden box on the shelf at the rear of the closet. He reached up and tried to lift it to set it down to the floor.

"What the heck is in this thing?" he wondered aloud. "Sebastien! Come help me with something, would you?"

Sebastien made his way up the curving staircase into what was soon to be his new room and saw Rex struggling with the old box.

"What? Have you softened in your old age?" he joked. "I thought you'd be able to manage this yourself."

As the chest slid from the shelf and made its way to the floor, he twisted the key and removed the padlock, opened the box and began rummaging through its contents. He found many old toys. The 1974 Cox Dune Blaster was one of his favorites as a boy. There was also a UFO that ran on Cox fuel, a Spider Dragster, a Bell Helicopter and a P51 Mustang along with old fuel cans, tools, and instruction manuals.

Johann had bought all of these at a garage sale back when Rex and Sebastien were young, and they enjoyed many days of playing with them. They had disassembled the engines more times than they could count, and had added numerous stickers and upgrades to the models. Even now, Rex could smell the burning nitro and castor oil simply by closing his eyes. Of course, the old rags that once had fuel on them stuffed around the models also helped prod his memory.

He rummaged around a little deeper and found a handful of marbles, some Star Trek and Lost in Space toy guns, a few trading cards, his battery-powered Robbie the Robot, old video game console and cartridges, and finally, a stack of paper drawings.

He sat for a long time looking at all of his old possessions, reliving the moments he'd shared with them. The Cox models held his interest first. He and Sebastien spent hours in the parking lot of the local horse-racing track setting up ramps and cones to race the two cars. Later, as their ingenuity further developed, they created mounds of dirt to simulate hills and mountains to run the models through their paces. He reckoned they burned through a fifty-five gallon drum of Cox fuel in the prime of their racing circuit. The flying models were fun too, but the cars held a special place in his heart for some reason.

He held Robbie next, and remembered with fondness the times that he would send the robot into the kitchen where Gabrielle was cooking and bump it against her legs. She would normally feign aggravation at him, but he knew she enjoyed his childish interruptions.

The Atari was something of a novelty even in its prime. As brothers, they played for hours—which turned into days in an attempt to beat every villain. Tromping in the jungles of the virtual world, was always an inviting distraction, particularly when they learned all the cheat codes. They eventually bested the game, having assassinated all of the rogues, mercenaries, and monsters with the number of lives given.

He knew that he should hurry along—the trip to the airport was soon impending, but he could not break himself from the old box until he had pored over every item. The stack of drawings was the last thing to examine, so he decided to give himself time to gaze at them one last time.

About halfway through the stack, one drawing prompted a memory. While the majority were of tigers, knights, and superheroes, this one was a map. His eyes widened as he realized this map was a treasure map he had drawn nearly a decade ago to show where he had buried his gold coin for safekeeping. He had all but forgotten about that gold coin. Now that he was headed off to college, he decided on the spot, the coin would be a great reminder of his childhood.

"Mom," he called down, "when do we leave for the airport?"

"About an hour and a half. Why? Aren't you finished packing?"

"Yeah, but I've been looking through my old treasure chest and found a map I drew that shows the way to a real treasure," he replied. "I'll be right back."

"Can't this wait until your first trip home? You know we're pressed for time."

"It'll only take a few minutes, and Sebastien can quit being lazy and carry the bags to the car. It's the least he can do, since he's moving into my room."

With that, he retrieved a shovel from the toolshed and headed for the old pine tree with map in hand. It read:

Place your back to the trunk and take one hundred steps toward the old barn.
Once there, turn spritely for one hundred more toward old McNally's farm.
Aim your toes and step lively for another two hundred toward the old well.
Pivot on your heel and head for one hundred-fifty more toward the ringing of a bell.
Pinch your nose and make two hundred paces toward the smell of a hog.
Finally, go over to the whistle of a train, and dig under the rotted log.

Well, most of these won't be a problem, but the rotted log could be, I don't think it's there anymore, Rex thought as he followed the map as it was detailed. His fears were allayed as he turned toward the train tracks. Though the old tree was long gone, he remembered where it had been, and began digging in the general area.

Within a few minutes, his shovel hit something that sounded like glass, so he widened the area where he was excavating. After several scoops were removed, he could see the outline of an old Mason jar and knelt down to remove it from the hole. The lid had long since rusted away in the wet Louisiana soil, leaving parts of the jar ring and just a small amount of the lid. Taking a gloved hand, he twisted the ring and it came apart in his fist. He tilted the jar into his palm and out came the old gold coin, still covered in Cosmoline grease, just as he had left it nearly ten years prior.

Back in the toolshed, he took a few moments to remove the grease from the coin and was pleased to see the luster had not faded. All its markings were still bright and sharp, including the inscribed "JL." He flipped it a few times in the air before placing it in his pocket, smiling broadly as he walked back to the house.

Sebastien had not moved an inch since he left, so he went back into his room and picked up his bags. He then bumped his brother on the couch to wake him up. Sebastien mumbled as he turned over. Rex laughed.

"Remember this?" he asked as he fished the coin out of his pocket.

"I do!" Sebastien exclaimed, sitting upright. "Where'd you find it?"

"I dug it up, silly. Don't you remember we buried it out back under the old oak?"

"Ah yes, *now* I remember. Wow, it's taken Dad all these years to remove the remainder of that tree, and you still managed to find it."

Rex smiled. "This will be my lucky coin, though I still want to know who 'JL' is, and where the rest of the coins are."

"Let's go boys," Gabrielle called to them. We need to be off. Your dad isn't going to make it, though. He's tied up at the lab on some experiment." She smiled slyly. "You know your father when he gets into something."

"It's alright," Rex said. "I was able to say my good-byes last night. It's not like I'm leaving forever."

"Well, that's too bad, loser . . . it would be great to have the house all to myself," Sebastien chimed in.

"Little brothers are all the same—they think they know it all and want everything the older brothers have."

"You two knock it off! Are we back to being nine years old all over again?"

The two boys looked at each other and laughed. Sebastien extended his hand to his older brother. "All kidding aside, I'm going to miss you. Well, at least until I stretch out on your bed."

"So what time do you land in Corpus?" Gabrielle asked.

"I think about three or so. I'll call you when I land."

"Be sure you do, or I'll do nothing but worry."

"I can't imagine why anyone would go to college to learn about fish," Sebastien teased.

"Marine biology is more than the study of fish, and you know that college is important. You'll be there soon; enjoy high school while you can."

"I plan to party the whole time. Oops, did I say that out loud?"

"Let's go," Gabrielle said, ignoring him. "We have to head to the airport now."

Rex grabbed his bags and climbed into the car for the ride to the airport. He kissed his mother and hugged Sebastien again at the check-in aisle, and waved as they drove away. After walking through check-in, he looked at his watch and realized he had over an hour to go before the flight. Taking the coin from his pocket, he tossed it a few times and thought, Heads—it's a Mountain Dew. Tails—it's a Pepsi. He slapped the coin onto his forearm and laughed out loud as he headed over to the sandwich shop to sample his favorite citrus drink.

CHAPTER 4 – THE OUTING

FROM WITHIN THE FOG OF A DREAM, REX PERCEIVED THE INCESSANT RINGING OF A BELL, but wasn't quite able to locate it. The ringing continued on and off through a few cycles, then he rolled over and realized that his phone was the culprit. He climbed out of the mist, reached out, and picked up his cell.

"Hello?"

"Are you still sleeping? It's nearly ten o'clock in the morning," his father asked.

"Yeah, but Dad, not everyone rises at five in the morning like you do. After the boxing match, I was up late last night studying for an exam."

"They're already hitting you with tests? Didn't your semester just start?"

"I know, but we're really soaking in the data and the professor wants us to be ready for the mid-terms when they come around. They said junior year would be hard, but . . ."

"You still enjoying it?"

"Marine bio's great, Dad. Where else can I work with sea life, modified jet skis, and half-naked girls?"

Johann chuckled. "Well, just don't elaborate too much to your mother. Have you met anyone new?"

"There's this one girl—Christine. She's studying mechanical engineering. I suspect she and Mom will have a few things in common."

"Well, it's not your mother who needs common ground with her—it's you."

"Dad, we're not *that* close; we're just friends. You know me—I'm on a mission to complete my degree, but I'll have a bit of fun along the way."

"I can't wait to hear the details, my boy. Anyway, I'm calling because we thought it might be fun to get together over the Columbus Day weekend and head off to High Island for some fishing and then over to Galveston to let Mom and Arieanna sight-see and shop a little. Why don't you bring Heinmot along?"

"Columbus Day, huh? Well, I'm not sure since we are studying so hard, but I think I can get away for a few days. Although it's only been six weeks, a break from the books would be nice. I'm not sure what Heinmot's doing, but I'll ask and see if he wants to go."

"Sounds good. I know Stein would love to see you again and hear all about your first days in college. Let me know when you know."

"Will do. It was good to hear from you."

"Talk to you soon and take care of yourself—particularly with the half-dressed girls," Johann joked as he hung up the phone.

After setting his phone down, Rex thought about all the times he'd gone saltwater fishing with his Dad, brother, and uncle. The fish were usually slow to bite, but once they started, it was a feeding frenzy. He or Sebastian always caught a sand shark, and cut it up for bait. Their skins were kind of like sandpaper but flexible—slightly smooth in one direction and rough in the other.

Ruminating over the sand shark forced him to make a decision. He knew he should make every effort to make the trip. Stein was getting older and, besides, he had completed all of his studies thus far, he knew what would be forthcoming in the next few weeks, and his job was going well—though he never thought riding a jet ski would be a job requirement.

It was after seeing him maneuver a jet ski in the bay just days in to his freshman year that Professor Brayeburn had asked if he would be interested in working for a consortium involved in the development and modification of jet skis and other personal watercraft. Although Rex didn't quite know what was expected of him, he went for it.

Rex quickly learned that while his driving abilities would be put to good use, it was his mechanical expertise and out-of-the-box thinking they were most interested in. Even though he was just a freshman studying biology, he had spent a considerable amount of time working on small engines, motorcycles, and watercraft at Bluff Small Engines. John, the old man who owned the shop, had taken a vested interest in Rex and taught him all the tricks of the trade.

After meeting with William Jones, head of the R&D department at Personal Watercraft Corporation (PWCC), Rex was quite pleased to learn he could earn a hefty sum for his contributions. But Rex wasn't all about money; his ideas were more important to him. So he'd pushed to ensure that he would retain all rights to any original inventions that he might create along the way. Jones balked at the very idea, but assumed Rex wouldn't develop anything of any great consequence. This would later prove to be an expensive assumption on Jones's part, and a costly one for PWCC. At the time, however, he had been happy to let Rex keep rights to his inventions so long as he worked for half the pay. Rex had thought about it for a few seconds, shrugged his shoulders and accepted the offer. He acknowledged that fifty percent of anything is more money than he had at the time, but he was confident he'd come up with something that would compensate him for the loss of funds. Besides, they were paying him well even at fifty percent. Jones, greedily smiling within, had quickly drafted an agreement, signed it, and pushed it over to Rex.

"I'm looking forward to the project, Mr. Jones," Rex had said with a smile. "I'm sure we'll work well together."

"I'm sure of it, my boy," Jones had smugly replied. "Brayeburn says you're already at the top of his class—best he's seen in years, and the semester has only just started. I'll introduce you to the project team leader early next week."

Sitting on the edge of his bed, Rex grabbed his cell from the nightstand and called his best friend at A&M, Heinmot Iiniwa.

Heinmot was a Native American Indian who hailed from the Little Bighorn area of Montana. His name in English directly translated to Thundering Buffalo, which was a name befitting his heritage. Rex could tell he was quite proud of it, but he had confided in Rex that all of their names had been Anglicized so they could assimilate into the American culture. His father had spoken of it and his grandparents and especially his great-grandparents refused to relent, sticking to their traditions. His mother was Nez Perce, and his father was from the Blackfoot tribe—an improbable union that would have never happened back when the bison freely roamed the prairies.

They almost ran into each other looking for the same book one night at the library. Heinmot was studying for a mechanical engineering test, and Rex was attempting to learn more about pressure and flow of piping when they met over a copy of some mechanical engineering specification. While neither wanted to give up the book, Rex conceded and introduced himself. The customary conversation ensued about who they were, what they were studying, and where they were from.

Rex was surprised to learn his new friend was from the Little Bighorn area, a place he knew quite a bit about himself. "But I thought the Little Bighorn was Crow territory? Were your ancestors invading another tribe?"

"Who's the invader here, white man?" Heinmot mocked in his most serious expression and tone.

After a few tense moments, the duo exploded into laughter and began shaking hands and slapping one another on the back, provoking the librarian, which only served to fuel the hilarity of the moment and resulted in even more of a commotion.

Heinmot answered on the third ring.

"What's up, Rex?"

"Hey man. You up for a fishing trip and some shopping, not necessarily in that order?"

Heinmot laughed. "Shopping, eh? Is your mother involved?"

"Worse. Arieanna! But don't worry. We'll head to High Island over the Columbus Day weekend to do some fishing and then over to Galveston for some sight-seeing and shopping."

"You know me. I'm always up for some fishing."

"Sounds like a plan! I'll have Dad set up the arrangements. Are you going to be at the Quarterdeck tonight? I hear they have a new F355 Challenge game. I'm itching to see how you handle it."

"I'll be there! And you better bring a five-gallon bucket of quarters. You'll need them.

"See you then!"

He and Heinmot had grown very close since that meeting in the library their freshman year, to the point of both inviting the other to meet parents and see their respective home territories. Heinmot had invited Rex on a camping trip near his home in Montana during their sophomore spring break. A chill passed through Rex as he remembered the strong gusts that blasted down from the mountains, pushing the already-cold night air deeper into his bones. Shivering, he had stood and foraged for more logs to rekindle the fire. The sizzling protests of the steam escaping from the green wood echoed in his mind, but within short order, a sizeable blaze had erupted from the heavily bedded coals. As the logs continued their song of whistles and hisses, he had glanced over the flames at Heinmot, who was equally chilled despite his heavy leather outerwear and the steaming mug of coffee affixed in his gloved hands.

"This is your idea of fun?" Rex teased. "It seems like a lot of work for so little fun."

As he chortled in reply, Heinmot had paused to turn his back further against the wind, glanced over at Áápi, his dad, and said, "Dad and I have ventured into these mountains for many years. The hunting and fishing found here have been the source of a lifetime of good times between a father and son."

Examining his desk calendar, Rex realized that Columbus Day was only a few weekends away. Because the drive to High Island and back was some six hundred fifty miles, he thought it best to change the oil in his sports car. He had only a few hundred to go before it was due.

At the auto parts store, he picked up six quarts of Gulf oil in 10W-40, an air and oil filter, and a set of sparkplugs. His afternoon was cut out for him but he didn't mind. Babying his 'Bird was something he had done for a few years now. It was a T-Top model, and the anemic factory 4.9 liter V-8 and corresponding powertrain, which included a 2.41 ratio rear axle, had long since been deep sixed in favor of something that had substantially more power. If Rex loved toying with engines made for the water, he *loved* working with engines made for the road.

As he tightened the oil drain plug, he felt some pain in his shoulder that had to be from yesterday's boxing match. His opponent had been Sammy "Two Tap" Thompson, who was a local favorite. In the middle of the second round, he had laid Sammy out cold with two taps of his own. A jab to the solar plexus followed by a smashing uppercut sealed the win.

Closing the hood, he then headed back inside to shower and call it a day. Upon entering the room, he was surprised to see that it was nearly eight o'clock and thought that it certainly took longer to maintain a car than it once did.

He laughed to himself. That was something his Dad would have said.

He had just started taking a shower when he heard the phone ring. He almost slipped as he stepped out of the shower, but righted himself just in time to grab his phone and growl an irritated, "Hello?"

"Rex? Is that you?"

"Hey, man. Yeah it's me. Sorry. I was in the shower when the phone rang and I nearly fell."

"Oh," he laughed. "I'd been calling most of the afternoon and was about to give up for the night."

"I've been changing the oil and stuff on the T/A for the trip."

"Well, dry off and get dressed—the games are hot, the beer is cold, and it's your turn to buy!"

"Are you sure—I'm *certain* that it's your turn."

"Just get your butt over here and face the whupping that you've got coming!"

Chapter 5 – The Emerald Pier

"Heinmot?" Rex tapped his shoulder to wake him. "Wake up, buddy. Did that morning run wear you out?"

Rex had insisted they head out at 5:30 a.m. on the dot. While Heinmot was an early riser, he wasn't *that* early of a riser.

"I'm up, I'm up," he grumbled, looking out the window for some indication of their whereabouts. "That was a good nap. Where are we?"

"Just outside of Galveston. We'll be going across the Bolivar ferry in about thirty minutes."

"How long's the ride? I've never been on a ferry before."

"Twenty minutes or so. I'll grab a loaf of bread when I fill up so you can feed the dive-bombing sea gulls."

As they drove down Seawall Boulevard headed toward the ferry landing, Rex pointed out and described various landmarks.

"Sea-Arama Marineworld used to be over there. I can't even begin to tell you how many times we visited it during the summer as kids. We stayed at some older motels, but we were happy as clams. Besides, we didn't know any better. Places like the Hilltop or the Driftwood Motel, they were not much to look at, but we had great times there."

"Who cares? You had a good time."

"Yeah, I know; it's just that I always wanted to stay, well . . . over there," he said, pointing at the Flagship Hotel.

"Well, you just had to wait until the time was right. Anyway, I know we'll have a good time this weekend. Prepare to be out-fished!"

"Well, if you get stuck," Rex chuckled, "Uncle Stein will be more than happy to show you the ropes when it comes to fishing—just ask him and he'll tell you everything you always wanted to know."

"Is that the ferry?"

"Yep! Looks like we won't have to wait in line. We'll be riding on the *R. S. Sterling*."

The flagman motioned him into position on the deck of the ferry and then held up his hand to stop.

"Have you been on this one before?"

"Oh yeah. I've been on all of them. In addition to this one, there's the *Cone Johnson*, *E. H. Thornton, Jr.*, and the *Gibb Gilchrist*. They're all named after former Texas Transportation Commission members except Gibb Gilchrist, who was a State Highway Engineer."

"How do you know so much about them?"

"Oh, the information is posted on placards around the decks. We'll see them when we get out and go up on deck."

"We're getting out?"

"Of course! The upper deck will have a fairly good view of Seawolf Park as we pass by it."

"OK. I think I need to stretch my legs and find a restroom anyway."

They stepped out of the Trans-Am onto the concrete deck of the ferry, which looked like most any other ferry, save for its rounded wheelhouses that rose a full two stories above the main deck and contained six large windows. The roof resembled a British driving cap, puffed slightly in front that overhung all its parts, and tapered as it approached the rear of the wheelhouse. The two houses were connected by an oval bridge with restrooms and a seating area. The bottom half of the bridge was I-beam shaped, and contained stairwells on both ends for accessing the upper deck. She was painted light beige with carmine trim.

They made their way to the rear of the ferry. As the engines revved for the trip across the bay, droves of insatiable seagulls encapsulated the deck. Rex opened the bread and began tossing some into the air behind the boat. As Heinmot joined in, the shrieking birds fought each other to gain access to the snippets of bread that rained down, with some diving into the frothy water for morsels. Heinmot scrambled to regain his footing as the deck shifted.

"Whoa, where are you off to?" Rex asked with a laugh.

"Seems I don't have a set of sea legs after all."

Rex pointed out the bow of the *USS Cavalla* peeking out at the edge of the bay.

"I remember the first time Sebastien and I visited that submarine. It was incredibly loud inside because they hadn't yet installed permanent power and were using the engines to generate electricity. I thought I would go deaf before we went from one end to the other."

"Our family visited the *USS Alabama* once on the way to Kissimmee. Those old ships sure have a unique smell."

"Both the ships at Seawolf Park are that way too. If you look over there, you can see the hulk of the *SS Selma*—one of the few concrete hull ships that were made during World War I. These days, there's not much left to it, but you can imagine what it looked like."

"A ship made of concrete?"

"Yeah, concrete ships displace more water than they weigh, so they can float. But this one was damaged, and no one knew how to repair her, so there she sank."

A passing container ship rocked the ferry heavily from side to side. Tossing the last of the bread to the gulls, Heinmot pointed at the approaching coastline, and they returned to the car.

They arrived at the Emerald Pier just as the entire Rhineheart gang began unloading the old truck. Although the Ford was growing long in the tooth, as Johann's primary choice of transportation, it still looked and ran like new due to his impeccable maintenance routines. He had added a few performance items along the way, and had boosted the output of the 390-cubic inch engine by at least forty percent, to nearly four hundred horsepower. This made the task of towing a heavy trailer a simple one.

"Howdy all!" Rex called out. "Everyone ready to catch some fish?"

"You bet! Stein and I have been itching for weeks to wet a line. We drove like madmen getting here."

"Heinmot! How are you?" Gabrielle asked, hugging him. "And how are your parents?"

"I'm good, but I'm a little tired from all the late-night study sessions. Mom and Dad are great."

"Uncle Stein, this is my friend Heinmot Iiniwa from school. I've already warned him he'll have to endure your and Dad's fishing stories. The fish seem to grow every time!"

"Not to worry! *We'll* protect him from all of that," Arieanna chimed in.

"Oh, I'm sure of that, Arieanna," Rex laughed. "You and Mom will fill him in on your shopping ideas in no time!"

"Come on, Rex," Stein said. "Let's make our escape and set things up on the pier while the ladies get settled."

"I'm with you Uncle Stein. Escape."

They toted all of the provisions from the back of the truck to the far end of the dock, pausing along the way to allow Stein to catch his breath. The air had a salty overtone that made their noses itch, and the sky was as blue as Rex remembered from his childhood, complete with streaks of white from the jet wash of high-flying military aircraft crisscrossing the atmosphere. A light breeze came in from the north and, unlike most times, the water was amazingly still and translucent enough to allow light to reflect from the sandy bottom. From the elevated deck affixed about thirty feet above the water, passersby could just make out the silhouettes of several blue crabs foraging the ocean floor for their next meal. A few juvenile sand sharks could also be observed chasing the latest quarry.

Stein chuckled and watched as one determined shark prodded at crustaceans, in hopes of gaining the upper hand. The crab snapped at its snout with a sharp claw, and the sea dog thrashed away in short order.

"Well guys, I think I'm sufficiently recovered; let's haul this stuff the rest of the way," he said.

They positioned the ice chests, chairs, rods, and tackle at the far end of the pier, which was practically void of people, and headed for the bait shop.

Johann chatted with pier-owner Kendall Tremaine inside the bait shop, trying to decide what the lure of the day would be. Rex pointed out a number of old photos hanging on the walls to Heinmot. Rex could remember seeing the "old man of the pier" for nearly as long as he had been alive, and this was in no small part due to the wonderful tales Kendall would spin.

Kendall had been a colorful character for most of his eighty years. He had served in the military in both World War II and Korea. Rex recalled the old man stating in de facto terms that the Korean *Conflict* was, in fact, a war: "It smelled like war, it looked like war, it felt like war, and people died in it like war." Many of the tales he shared with the boys were loosely based on his experiences in the military. Rex could see the wistfulness in the man's eyes when he would reflect on something that happened in those bygone days, as if he were referring to a piece of himself that was lost and could not be recovered.

Tales of the Pacific theater were Rex and Sebastien's favorites. Kendall had served on an aircraft carrier, the *USS Lexington*, and a submarine, the *USS Cavalla*, the latter was now a museum ship anchored in Seawolf Park. The former sat twenty-four hundred fathoms down, at the bottom of the Coral Sea. As long as Rex plied him with coffee, Kendall was content to spin yarns as long as the two brothers were willing to listen.

Thinking back now, Rex finally understood what the old man was feeling when he shared his stories—they weren't just stories; they were a part of himself. Kendall almost seemed to *want* to relive those times, to pass on his memories to a younger generation so they would survive in Rex and Sebastien. He hoped his stories would be passed down by the two brothers in time.

Rex was certain Kendall had been a fireball in his prime. He wouldn't have backed down from anyone or any situation. However, seeing the old octogenarian with most of his crimson hair tinted a silver sheen made Rex a little sad. He could tell that his life had been harder than it needed to be these past few years. The crowds grew smaller with each passing season, Kendall told them. People simply chose other venues to relax, leaving the Emerald Pier with barely enough revenue for Kendall to live on, let alone make much-needed improvements.

The pier was undeniably starting to fall apart, much like Johann and Stein's beloved mile-long bridge had before its demise. Rex wondered how much life the pier had left in it, or if the next tropical storm would sweep it out to sea. He had noted that while the decking was in relatively good shape, there were parts of the handrails that were practically rotted away; only minimum pressure would be required for them to break away and fall into the Gulf. Caution signs along the railing warned about the condition of the rails, with orange cones blocking off other parts.

"Mr. Tremaine, allow me to introduce you to Heinmot Iiniwa."

"Why, any friend of Rex's is like family here. Welcome, laddie."

Heinmot shook the old man's hand. "Nice shop you have here. Lots of nostalgia hanging on the walls. How are the fish biting?"

"Rex?" Johann called out. "Try not to take up too much of Mr. Tremaine's time—he has other customers waiting."

Kendall waved a hand at Johann. "Aye, but it is good to see all of you again." In a lower voice and a smile he covered with part of his hand, he said to Rex, "Stop by a little later, lad, I have something for you."

Rex smiled. "I will. I wanted to say thank you for everything through the years. You've shared your life with us and provided many memories to cherish—not to mention the great fishing we've enjoyed."

"Don't mention, laddie—seeing you and Sebastien grow into fine men is thanks enough. Now go show your friend what fishing on the Emerald Pier is all about."

Rex walked up the slight incline toward the main deck, pausing to take a final look at Kendall before continuing toward the ocean side of the pier. He couldn't help but wonder if Kendall would be around for the next fishing trip. He made a mental note that if he ever struck it rich, he would buy the pier, completely refurbish it, and sell it back to Kendall for a dollar.

The destination at the end of his leisurely walk down the deck found the clan already engaged in fishing, with a few redfish on ice in the Coleman. Stein had baited Rex's pole and propped it against the railing near Heinmot. He opened his lawn chair and sat down, still lost in his thoughts.

"Everything all right there, Rex?" Stein asked.

"Sure, Uncle Stein. I'm just feeling a little sad so few people come out to fish anymore. And the condition of the pier? Man . . . But I guess I'm really thinking about Mr. Tremaine and how different his life should be by now."

"I know what you mean. We've been fortunate," Gabrielle said. "But he seems pretty happy overall. Though I'm sure he misses the large crowds that once frequented this place."

"Yeah, I'm sure you're right. Pass me a cream soda would you?"

As Gabrielle fished around in the cooler for a soda, Stein let out an exclamation.

"Whoa! I hooked a monster! I hope I can land this thing."

Johann set his pole down and walked over to help Stein with his fish. After several minutes and judicious use of the drag, the two of them managed to reel in what appeared to be a bull redfish that was about five feet long. After unhooking the fish, Stein whipped out his tape measure with built-in scale and, sure enough, the monster was over fifty-eight inches long and weighed just under forty pounds.

"Well Stein, it looks like you were right. You *did* catch your record-breaker! He'll need a chest all to himself," Johann said.

Stein snorted. "Well, I'm all in. I think I'll head down, chew the fat with Kendall, and let the rest of you play catch-up."

"Thanks bro!" Johann laughed. "Less competition!"

Rex watched as his uncle sauntered toward the bait shop, bringing his thoughts back to the task at hand as a big red took a run at his bait and swallowed it. In short order, he'd landed a nice twelve-pounder. This was followed by Johann, Gabrielle, and Arieanna all taking turns harvesting their own keepers, rapidly filling the chests with fresh fish. Heinmot was the only one without so much as a nibble.

"Have you checked your bait lately; you should've had a nibble by now," Johann said.

"Let me reel it in."

He worked the Penn 209M diligently until the leader and empty treble hook dangled near the end of his rod.

Rex laughed. "Well, I think I see the problem—your bait's long gone. Didn't you feel anything like a nibble?"

"I'm not sure if I know what a nibble from a saltwater fish is supposed to feel like."

"You should feel the pole vibrate or it'll feel like something bumped it," Johann said. "So when you feel a strong bump or vibration, you should jerk the pole back toward you to set the hook. Then hold on to let the fish run a little and get tired before trying to land it."

Heinmot re-baited his hook with a chunk of squid and cast his line about fifty yards from the pier.

"There you go," Rex said. "Now catch one bigger than Uncle Stein."

"You'll see—" Heinmot said, before letting out a yelp of surprise.

Rex, who had been heading to the other side of the pier to wash his hands, spun back around just in time to see him jerk up out of his chair and land hard against the railing, his rod bent nearly in half. The muscles in Heinmot's arm were straining under the load, but he wasn't giving any ground to the saltwater creature at the end of it.

Rex sprinted to close the distance between the two of them, stepping on a slimy piece of fish entrails and losing his footing. As he regained his posture, he heard an ear-splitting crack, followed by a yell from Heinmot.

The railing, aged and weakened by years under the intense heat of the sun and salt, was giving way. Under normal conditions, the amount of weight Heinmot had placed against the handrail would have been inconsequential, but in its current state, the rails started bending toward the maw of the ocean waiting below.

Before Rex could reach him, Heinmot began to tumble over the edge of the deck. Although Rex was fairly certain that he would not be seriously injured from the thirty-foot fall to water, he couldn't be positive and so he lunged as hard as he could to grab ahold of his friend.

He hit the hard wooden planks with all his weight and heard every cubic centimeter of air escape his lungs. Splinters gouged into his chest and arms as he slid the remaining few feet toward the edge. Although he wasn't sure how, when he stopped sliding, he realized that he had succeeded in grabbing Heinmot's ankle just as he tipped over the edge.

Rex squeezed down on Heinmot's ankle as hard as he could in anticipation of his weight. The jerk came with more force than he expected; despite the fact that he was able to maintain his grip, he heard a muffled snap followed by an excruciating tearing sensation. Heat plumed from within his shoulder and spread across his back so rapidly, it was nearly unbearable.

Through the burning sweat saturating his eyes and between the cracks of the floor timbers, he could see that Heinmot narrowly missed hitting the trusses under the pier with his head. When Heinmot realized he was no longer falling, he stopped yelling, and relaxed his body. It was then that he became even heavier, and Rex began to worry he'd drop him. He strained to see Heinmot's face and saw him flailing around for a handhold, still holding onto the rod and the fighting fish.

"Drop the rod, and I'll pull you up!"

Heinmot released the rod, and Rex started to slowly curl his arm, reaching out with his left hand to grab Heinmot's other ankle. Heinmot arched his back, then managed to grab onto Rex's forearms and began to climb. The pain in Rex's shoulder was past excruciating, but he forced his mind to ignore the pain, tightening his grip as much as he dared. He could no longer feel his hands, and was not sure if he was holding tight enough to prevent Heinmot from twisting free.

"You can let go of my ankles! I can climb over you now."

Rex slowly opened his hands. After ensuring his friend was indeed climbing, he completely released his ankles. Heinmot continued climbing, pausing only to seek better purchase for his hands. After placing a somewhat knobby knee into Rex's shoulders, Heinmot managed to kneel on the pier and lay down beside his rescuer to catch his breath.

Rex lay motionless until he heard thundering footfalls from across the pier, along with Gabrielle's voice.

"Oh my God! Are you two okay?"

"I'm not hurt," Heinmot said. "Just a little shook up. I'll be fine in a few minutes."

Johann knelt beside his oldest son. Through the shroud of pain Rex could hear the concern in his father's voice. "Are you okay, Rex? Are you okay?"

"Yeah, Dad," Rex whispered hoarsely, barely able to breathe. "I think so. But I . . . I . . . think my shoulder is broken."

The nurse within Gabrielle immediately instructed Johann to help her roll him over. Both Arieanna and Heinmot let out a simultaneous gasp. The front of his shirt was partially shredded from the splinters and red with blood.

"Arieanna," Gabrielle ordered, "run down to the truck and get my first-aid kit. Johann, you head down to the bait shop and get Stein. See if Kendall has any blankets and anything that can be used as a stretcher. Rex, I'm going to remove your shirt so that I can see how bad these cuts are. This may hurt a little, but I need to see what's happening here."

She turned to Heinmot as she removed the remnants of the shirt. "Heinmot, are you sure you're okay?"

"I'm a little out of breath and the adrenaline is still hitting me, but I'm good."

Rex, who had been silent the whole time, let out a stifled groan as Gabrielle removed his shirt.

"You have some gouges from the splinters in the deck. There are still a few of them embedded in your chest. I won't even try to remove them here."

"When *will* you remove them? They hurt just a bit," he joked, trying to assure his mother.

"Looks like we're heading to the hospital."

Rex groaned. "The hospital? Mom, are you sure—"

"Yes, son," Gabrielle interrupted, "we need to get these removed. I also haven't checked your shoulder, but from the angle of your arm, at a minimum, it's severely dislocated."

"Is Heinmot hurt?"

"Nah, I'm good man. Thanks for grabbing me."

Arieanna, Johann, and Stein appeared with the first-aid kit, a stretcher, and blankets.

"It was left over from one of the last hurricanes. The Coast Guard never returned to pick it up."

"Gabrielle," Stein asked, "is Rex okay?"

Rex could hear the worry in Stein's voice.

"Guys, I'll be as right as the rain as soon as they pull these splinters out and figure out what this burning in my back is about."

"Rex, I need to disinfect these cuts. It's going to burn. I only have alcohol in this first-aid kit. You ready?"

He nodded, drawing in a sharp, slightly ragged breath as she poured the alcohol over the cuts and quickly dressed them with gauze. She motioned for Arieanna, Johann, and Stein to help her put Rex on the stretcher. Rex cried out as they rolled him onto the stretcher and covered him with the blanket.

A couple of bystanders helped Johann carry him to the end of the pier, but Rex made them stop at the bait shop so that he could bid farewell to Kendall. The old Irishman apologized profusely for the accident, swearing he would repair the railing. Rex waved it off, offering to help the old man when his shoulder was better.

As they lifted Rex to head down to the bottom of the pier, the old man tousled Rex's curly dirty-blond hair and apologized one last time. He then pulled a crumpled envelope out of his pocket and handed it to Johann.

"Rex, that's for later when you feel better. I'm sure you'll have some questions. Come see me and we'll talk about it when you're well."

"Okay, guys, let's get him loaded up so that we can get him to the hospital." Johann commanded. "Stein, will you see if Kendall can keep the fish on ice, until we can come back?"

"I'll do one better than that: you guys take care of Rex, and I'll stay here and clean all of the fish. I'll hang out with Kendall until you come back and get me."

There were no ambulances in the area, so they loaded Rex into the back of the truck and strapped the stretcher down as well as they could to prevent him from sliding around.

"I'll ride in the back with Rex, you all can ride in the front. I'll come back and drive Rex's car when we return for Uncle Stein," Heinmot said.

"Sounds like a plan," Johann said.

Rex was in unbearable pain when they finally made it to the emergency room forty-five minutes later. Gabrielle accompanied him into the John Sealy ER while Johann, Arieanna, and Heinmot remained in the waiting room. Small talk was made about the size of the fish and how good they were going to be when they had a chance to cook them. Of course, that was provided Uncle Stein and Kendall didn't get hungry and devour them before they returned.

Within an hour, Gabrielle returned to the waiting room, much more at ease. She explained that although Rex was bleeding quite a bit, the splinters had all been removed and his wounds dressed. The shoulder injury was quite a bit more serious. It might require surgery to correct, but they would fit him into a sling and immobilize his shoulder for a while to see if it would heal on its own. Rex had been sedated to reset the shoulder, and was resting quietly. Heinmot expressed his apologies and concern, but Johann reminded him that he could have been seriously hurt himself if Rex hadn't caught him.

"I suspect that it'll be a few hours before they allow any visitors." Gabrielle noted. "I'm not sure about the rest of you, but I'm getting hungry."

"I agree, let's go get something to eat; by the time we get back, he should be awake," Johann said.

The four of them squeezed into Rex's small room when they

returned an hour later. As the door closed, Rex opened his eyes, focused, and realized they were staring at him with a questioning look that would not be put off.

"Guys, I'm fine. I can't feel anything just yet, but I'll be okay."

"Your shoulder was dislocated and you had a bunch of huge splinters in your chest. I suspect you're going to feel those wounds in a few hours," Gabrielle said. "You'll also be in that sling for about six to eight weeks, so no crazy stuff until then. The doctor said you could check out of the hospital in the morning. I think I'll stay with you. Dad, Arieanna, and Heinmot will head back to High Island and pick up Uncle Stein and your car."

"Sounds good. Don't let that T/A get away from you," he joked with Heinmot.

Heinmot laughed. "I'll watch it. Get some rest man."

"Before we head out, here is the envelope that Kendall handed me. I think you'll find something fascinating inside it. Since you only have one working hand, I opened it for you." Johann tilted the envelope, and a shiny gold disc fell into Rex's waiting palm.

"Wait . . . what's *this?* It looks like . . ." He trailed off and took a moment to assess the coin. There was no doubt; it was a twin to his own.

"How did Mr. Tremaine even know I had one? Where did he find it? Are there more?"

"Slow down," Johann said. "I'll have him call you when we make it back to the bait shop."

"OK, thanks Dad."

Arieanna, followed by Gabrielle, kissed him on the forehead. As they were walking out, Johann turned and said, "Get some rest son, we still have some good times ahead before the vacation is over—we'll just have to change the venue a bit."

"I'm looking forward to it."

As the door closed, Rex winked at his concerned mother and drifted off to sleep.

CHAPTER 6 – THE MUSEUM

THE PAIN IN REX'S SHOULDER DRAGGED HIM FROM HIS PEACEFUL SLUMBER, AND HE groggily opened his eyes. As his vision cleared, he could see a grinning Heinmot standing over him with a phone in his hand.

"It's Mr. Tremaine, and it's nearly eight in the morning. He said he let you sleep as long as he could. He has something important to tell you."

"Rex, my lad!" Mr. Tremaine's voice boomed the moment the phone hit Rex's ear. "How are you getting along—is the shoulder on the mend?"

"The doc tells me I have some sore days ahead, but overall everything seems to work. It hurts like crazy though if I don't move it just right."

"I'll give you the same advice an old Navy sawbones gave me once."

"I'll bite," Rex said, feeling one of Kendall's jokes coming on. "What'd he tell you?"

"Don't move that way and it won't hurt."

As he laughed, he let out a slight yelp. "Ow! It hurts to laugh."

"I'm sure you're going to be sore for the next week or so until you're well on the way to healing."

"When I check out, I'm supposed to have a prescription for some pain medicine, so hopefully it won't be too bad."

"I wanted to call and tell you about the coin, but I also wanted to share some good news with you."

"Give me the good news first; the coin can wait."

"Believe it or not, after you guys drove away, a random person came into the bait shop and said he saw the whole thing happen. I was expecting a bit of hassle, given he'd witnessed the accident. Instead, he tells me that he wanted to try and find some local help to come out and fix up the dock! Can you believe that?"

"That's great. I'll chip in too, when I can. Why was he so interested?"

"He said that when he was younger he had fished on a bridge that no longer existed, and he saw how the pier was slowly falling apart and he wanted to help. I initially refused, but he insisted and so I accepted with the condition that I post a plaque with the details of his contribution. He refused and said that it was to be an anonymous gift to the cause. I didn't know what to say, so I simply thanked him and shook his hand."

"So you'll have it back in shape soon?"

"And then some! I plan to use four-by-sixes instead of two-by-fours, so that an elephant could bump the railing and not break it. In short order, the Emerald Pier will be back!"

"Well, Mr. Tremaine, I'm so glad to hear it. I was thinking the pier might be standing on its last legs, but it sounds like it'll be fine."

"Aye, I plan to take out a new insurance policy too, so that I'm protected from hurricanes. But enough about that. The coin!"

"Right! Where did you get it? I compared it to mine; it's almost the exact same, including the 'JL' engraved on it. But, I did notice the dates were different, and I'm sure that Mom can decode it and tell me the real differences."

"That's the strange part, laddie. One of my customers caught a nice redfish a few months back; when we gutted it, that coin fell out. I remembered you had a coin like it, and knew it was acquired in a similar way."

"That is really strange—my fish was caught in fresh water over seventy-five miles away and over ten *years* ago. How is it possible?"

"I would agree, *and* I have a theory I wanted to share with you—I think I know who 'JL' is."

"You do? Who—"

Kendall interrupted. "I'll not let on, lad, because I could be wrong and I want you to come to your own conclusions. Since you're already there in Galveston, when you get out of the hospital, you and Heinmot should meander over to the Texas Seaport Museum and do a little research. I think you'll find what you're looking for."

"Alright, sir. If you insist. We'll do that. Better than shopping all day with Arieanna, now that I'm all banged up."

"I don't envy you the latter, laddie. If Arieanna has her way, you'll be on a shopping spree for days."

Laughing, Rex replied, "I'm sure you're right. Thanks again."

"What was all that about?" Heinmot asked, as he hung up the phone and placed it on the desk.

"We have a mission of sorts when I get out of here—which I was thinking should be any minute now?"

As if on cue, the entire Rhineheart clan strolled in, dressed and ready for a day of sightseeing. Arieanna was still fretting over when they would start shopping.

"Well, I see you're as large a pile of lazy bones as you ever were," she teased. "When are you going to get out of bed and get dressed?"

"Yes, and I see you're as easy to fool as ever. I'm already dressed," he sarcastically retorted.

"Well . . . Can we go now?"

"Geez, girl, you're impatient as ever! The stores will still be there in an hour or so. I can't move as fast as I normally would."

"Sorry, I'm just ready to do something since the day was cut short yesterday. Are you really ok?"

"Yeah, but I won't be lifting anything with this arm for quite a while. I'll be fine in a week or so. Let's get out of here. I think Heinmot and I are going to walk down the Seawall and later head over to the maritime museum."

"You? A museum!? Now, I've seen it all," quipped Gabrielle. "You just be careful with that shoulder. Are you able to drive?"

"Nah. Heinmot's been itching to drive the T/A. I'll let him chauffeur me around for a change."

The crew headed out of the hospital and into the parking lot. The wind was blowing stiffly from the south, carrying the smell of the sea deep inland, as it almost always was.

"Be careful with that shoulder," Johann said, "and we'll see you at the hotel later this evening. We'll eat at Gaido's."

"OK, Dad. Give Mr. Tremaine my best."

"Will do."

The groups climbed into their respective vehicles and headed in opposite directions. The Firebird lurched nearly to a stall. Heinmot had to find his manual transmission "legs" again. As they rode, they observed tourists ambling around on the seawall, visiting the various curio shops. Perusing much, but to the chagrin of the shop owners, purchasing little.

"I thought that we could stop by the museum, then head down toward the beach."

"Let's see what this coin is all about."

Rex looked at Heinmot and laughed.

"Indeed! It shouldn't take long to solve. At least according to Kendall."

"Look, there's the museum."

The front of the old museum was as weathered as any ship of yesteryear, with cracks in the face of the wooden planks ever widening from sun and salt. Several rescued houses from the nineteenth century served as the crux of the museum's operations. The largest one housed the lobby and main entrance.

As they entered, an elderly man approached them.

"Welcome to the museum, my name is Ben. Is there anything I can assist you with?"

"This is Heinmot Iiniwa. I'm Rex Rhineheart."

"My pleasure to meet the both of you," Ben said with a broad smile. "Now, how can I help?"

Reaching into his left pocket, Rex continued. "I was wondering if there was anyone who could tell me anything about this coin and specifically the initials 'JL' engraved upon it."

"Let me have a look at that," the old man said. "Looks like a forty-franc coin from the early 1800s. Why yes . . . 1800s . . . Quite interesting. I think I may have something over here that will be of interest to you. Have you ever heard of a pirate named Jean Lafitte?"

"A little. I think I remember learning a little about him in grade school. There's is a festival of sorts in Louisiana based upon his legacy. He was a bit of a pirate and a rogue, right?"

"Indeed he was! If you will follow me, we have a historical section that will provide you with much information as well as several computers with access to historical and nautical databases."

"Wait . . ." Rex stopped. "Are you saying this coin once belonged to Jean Lafitte?"

"I couldn't say that for sure, but it is rumored that he initialed every coin that passed through his hands, and this isn't the first one of these francs we've seen. Truthfully, we've all wondered where the stash of coins is hidden."

"Here we are: *Famous Local Pirates and Folklore.* This section should have some of the answers you're seeking, and the computers are just against the wall. I'll leave you with it. Give me a shout if you need further assistance."

"Thanks, Ben."

The pair of them spent most of the day poring over massive binders and record books. Heinmot handled the larger volumes, thereby sparing Rex the anguish of tormenting his still injured shoulder. As he passed Rex book after book, Heinmot following his passion, researched and carefully made notes on the library PC. When the last page of the final book was read, Rex rubbed his tired eyes and looked up at an equally weary set staring back at him. Heinmot had printed several pages of notes and had resorted to scribbling on the backs and all over the margins.

"Well, what do you think?"

"I found it enlightening—especially about Jean Lafitte," Heinmot said.

"Yeah. Did you know Lafitte lived right here in Galveston from 1817 through 1821 and even formed a pirate colony named *Campeche?*"

"I read that, and also that he had some strange quirks. He was obsessed with the number three and inscribing his initials on nearly everything he owned."

"Well, that proves out our coins, I guess. There must a cache of coins somewhere between here and our fishing spot in Louisiana. It can't be a coincidence that one of Kendall's customers found a coin inside a fish here and I found one inside a fish back home."

"Good point! Now, I—"

"Sorry to interrupt, but the museum will be closing in fifteen minutes," Ben said from behind them.

The pair nearly jumped with surprise.

"Oh!" Rex said. "Right. Thank you again. We lost track of time. We'll put these away."

"Nonsense, young man. Your arm doesn't appear to be in any shape to be lifting these old books. I'm sure your friend and I can handle this."

Heinmot nudged him. "How's that shoulder holding up?"

"Now that you mention it, I think I'm overdue for a pain pill. I'm not sure what throbs more—my shoulder or my chest. We should head over to the Flagship to check in. I'm guessing the clan will be waiting for us."

They headed south down Rosenberg Street towards the seawall. Johann's truck was parked on the side of the hotel as they drove up. As Rex climbed out of the car, he strained his shoulder. Rex stood for a moment and gazed at the monument of a hotel, taking in the view and catching his breath.

"The USS Flagship," Rex read from a plaque on the wall, *"was built in 1965 by Houston banker James E. Lyon. This seven-story hotel contains two hundred twenty-five rooms, and was built on the historic one thousand-foot-long Pleasure Pier structure, which stands entirely over the Gulf of Mexico."*

The structure was rectangular in shape, with three of its sides complete with doors and balconies overlooking the mighty Gulf. Exact dimensions of the pier totaled one hundred twenty feet wide by twelve hundred feet long, and evidence of extensive repairs was apparent all along the rough surfaces. Many of these reinforcements could be attributed to the seasonal hurricanes that permeated the coastal region. The far end of the refurbished wharf boasted some of the best fishing in the area, rivaling even Kendall's Emerald Pier. The seawall side of the building was completely enclosed, with a simple two-story parking lot affixed to the lee side of the street. A wrought-iron banister that extended to a height of about eight feet above the parking surface corralled its upper level.

Gas lamps with large frosted globes were attached to every third post on the railing. At dusk each day they softly flickered on, and began to cast a diffuse light onto the asphalt surface over which they stood eternal watch. Near the street entrance, a two-story-tall sign proclaimed the moniker of the building in bold, red capital letters: THE FLAGSHIP. Three rigid metal flags spread equidistant across the length capped the top of the sign, with the middle flag rising twice the height of its bordering peers. Below the title pane, the other levels of the stand boasted coming attractions and happy hour times, as well as other specials hosted by the hotel.

They entered a lobby ornately furnished in a maritime motif, complete with hurricane lamps on the walls and a ship's wheel and compass at the far end of the reception area. True to form, royal hues of cobalt, ruby, emerald, and amethyst generously adorned the entrance and the halls leading to the banquet and meeting rooms. The marbled captain's desk resembled something taken from the chambers of Henry VIII.

The registration desk was no less lavish, with gold and silver inlays running along the perimeter of the marble top and sides. Alternating patterns of brilliant black and white tiles connected the dull-gray exterior world to the grandiose and brightly lit interior.

Arieanna was the first to spot them, and called out. "Hey, you two, we're over here."

"Are you guys as hungry as we are?" Rex said with a weak smile.

"Indeed," Johann replied. "We've already checked everyone in. Here are your room keys—Rex, unfortunately, you're at the far end overlooking the sea on the seventh floor. There were no rooms closer to us. The rest of us are on the third floor near the seawall on the west side."

"Good! Our reservation grows cold at Gaido's. Shall we go? I'm famished."

"Me too," Heinmot said. "Should we take one vehicle or two, and do they have oysters?"

"Of course they do, and it's only about a mile up the street," Gabrielle chimed in. "But parking is horrific, and it's a nice evening. Shall we walk? That is, if Rex is up to it. How's that shoulder?"

"It's starting to throb, but I think I can manage. I doubt anyone will need to rock me to sleep tonight after I take this medicine."

The group meandered across the lobby and headed west down the seawall. Rex had to agree that it was a nice evening, and with the sun nearly breaching the horizon and the wind carrying the mist of the sea across them, it was a pleasant stroll. As they walked, Heinmot and Rex chatted with Johann, sharing their knowledge gleaned from the long day of research.

"Well Dad, 'JL' looks to be the initials of one Jean Lafitte. He was a pirate and lived here in Galveston. He formed a pirate colony called *Campeche,* and regularly looted and pillaged up and down the coast. He also worked with the US Navy, running supplies for them, and even fought with Andrew Jackson against the British in early 1815."

"You don't say! Anything concrete enough to prove the coins were his?"

"He initialed every coin he ever possessed," Heinmot said. "And the dates are all correct for the time period. And he was almost maniacal about the number 3."

"What if this is just random bits that appear to connect?"

"I think it's a little too random not to be viable," Rex said, "and last but not least, in 1923, some kettles of coins were found under a giant live oak tree on Jefferson Island in Louisiana—every one of the coins had the initials 'JL' inscribed into them. We're not the first."

"Ah, here's the restaurant," Gabrielle said. "We can talk more of this after dinner."

The second they were seated, Johann was back at it.

"I think it's time I share my knowledge about Lafitte with both of you," he said. "We can compare notes later."

"Jean Lafitte was a privateer who heavily scoured the waters from Cuba to Mississippi to Galveston from about 1800 until his death sometime in 1823. He was involved in slave trading, and often frequented the waters between New Orleans and Galveston with an occasional trip to Mexico. While relatively friendly to many of the locals, he was treacherous to those he believed to be carrying valuables at sea, *particularly* actual currency. Rumors of last treasure have been all around him for decades."

"But Lafitte wasn't always a rogue pirate. In the days leading up to the War of 1812, Lafitte ran his pirating operations out of Barataria Bay, on Ile de Barataria, in southeast Louisiana. While out to sea during a looting run, Lafitte and his cronies stumbled across a British fleet poised to attack the mainland. Halting his pirate run, he attempted to warn his henchmen and the people onshore, but the American Navy was also aware of the British. They captured the British *as well* as most of Lafitte's fleet."

"Due to an earlier treaty that declared piracy a hanging offense, Lafitte was forced to fight alongside Andrew Jackson while defending New Orleans against the British in 1815. In return for his actions, Jackson pardoned his crew and family. But much to the chagrin of the Americans, Lafitte soon began working with the Spanish, and moved to Galveston where they built the *Campeche* colony."

"Now more or less, most of what I have just told you is in the history books. You probably read about most of it at the Maritime Museum in Galveston. Am I right?"

Rex and Heinmot nodded in unison "Practically word for word," Rex said, "but there were a few details that weren't covered in the books, and even online, that do help fill in a few blanks. For example, the connection with the Spanish—I wasn't aware of that."

"Earlier, I spoke of the many legends of Jean Lafitte, not the least of which are those that persist about buried treasure and riches. Of all the legends that continue to be repeated, there is one that refuses to fade."

Johann continued to speak and then stopped as the waiter approached the table to take their orders. As the waiter continued around the table, Rex noticed a particularly striking woman with eyes that nearly matched his own. His boyish fantasy was interrupted by the waiter asking for his order.

When the waiter departed, Johann returned to his tale. "The greatest of the legends is that Lafitte sailed to France to retrieve none other than Napoleon Bonaparte. At the end of the One Hundred Days, which marked in history his last period of rule, and shortly after the Battle of Waterloo, Napoleon realized there was no chance he could retake Paris and, therefore, he had lost France. On June 29, 1815, the Prussian Army forced him to retreat to the west toward Bordeaux. Now, of the many things Napoleon was, being unprepared was not one of them. He had made plans months in advance to escape to the United States in the event his campaign was not successful."

"This is where it becomes interesting. Unknown to all but Napoleon, one of his commanders had contacts within the Spanish Army sympathetic to Napoleon and his campaign. Sometime at the beginning of 1815, Napoleon sent a letter via his commander to the Spanish, requesting they relay his communique to Lafitte. The Spanish started the process with all possible speed. The details are somewhat sketchy, but, more or less, the letter requested that Lafitte arrive at the southernmost end of Île d' Oléron, using all possible speed. They should be heavily armed and ready for combat as well as stocked for a voyage back to the United States, carrying Napoleon, his senior staff, and the remains of his family. Along with their possessions was to be Napoleon's amassed fortune, which some estimated to be no less than ten million francs, *all* in gold coins."

"Stolen from a US Naval yard as retribution for the actions taken against him by the US government, Lafitte's ships were the fastest of that time, having been designed to neutralize the threat of slower

British ships. True to their word, the Spanish delivered the message to Lafitte sometime in mid-April. A trio of ships sailed for France a few days later. They arrived as planned in late June 1815, practically setting the ocean on fire in the process."

"Lafitte waited at the appointed meeting site until, sure enough, a few days later a regiment of twenty of Bonaparte's men arrived with heavily laden wagons in tow. Over the course of the next two days, they proceeded to load ten large oaken chests into secret holds within two of Lafitte's clippers, the *Pride* and the *Fleur-de-Lis.* The third ship was a frigate named the *Bienville,* large enough to carry the coins in their entirety. However, since this was so obvious, it served as a decoy to any would-be attackers. The contents of the chests were 1804 and 1805 gold coins in various denominations. The most common coin was an 1804 forty-franc coin. This was Napoleon's first year as emperor, and he wasted no time in remodeling France's money."

"But Dad," Rex said, "doesn't this—" A loud crash halted the conversation as the sound of shattering glass echoed in the room. The tinkling of broken shards was masked by a waiter tripping and falling as he attempted to help a waitress steady herself.

When the commotion faded, Johann said, "Now, where was I? Oh yes . . ."

"After loading the chests and Napoleon's possessions, the troops informed Lafitte that Napoleon was to arrive in two days, and the ships should keep a low profile until then. Lafitte, who had never been known as a patient man, agreed to wait, but told the troops that at dawn on the third day, his armada would sail west with or without Bonaparte. A large formation of Prussians stood between Napoleon and his destination, Île d' Oléron, so he couldn't meet with Lafitte. The pirate and the emperor's gold sailed at sunrise for the US. After a stop in Cuba to resupply and possibly offload some of the gold, Lafitte arrived back in *Campeche* in late fall of 1815."

"Now, I know that you probably have more than a few questions, but let me give you my theory as to what all of this may or may not mean. I believe the legend is true, and that Lafitte and his men did get the gold and made it back to the US with some or all of it. I also believe that one or more of the chests are buried within fifty miles of where we sit. And the reason that two different species of fish in different types of water had one of the coins inside them is due to the wind."

"The wind, Mr. Rhineheart?" Heinmot asked, squinting at Rex. "What do you mean 'the wind'?"

"Simple, my boy, and please call me Johann! I believe Lafitte buried one or more chests around High Island and one or more somewhere in the Sabine River."

"That follows," Rex said. "Since the fish were caught in those areas. But it doesn't explain how they came to swallow the coins."

"Remember the year you caught the bass that had your coin? What did we see on that morning? Do you remember?"

Rex squinted with thought.

"There was a category one hurricane, right? It had just passed through. A fair number of trees were uprooted, and there was some building damage, but it was restricted to a few sections."

"Quite right! I remember that Sebastien was in awe of the damage."

"And the same thing was true at the pier!"

"Therefore," Johann said with a smile, his eyes beaming, "I surmise the *buried* treasure is no longer buried."

"Which means there's more to be found?" Heinmot asked Rex.

"If you stop and think about it, there were no permanent markers back in the 1810s, and trees were usually set as waypoints," Johann said.

"And . . . if I'm following you, you believe the treasure was buried under a tree, the tree was uprooted by the storm, and the gold . . . was exposed?" Heinmot asked with a sweep of his hand over his plate of raw oysters.

"Exactly." Johann said, as he sat back in his seat, "And it's somewhere close."

"But if that's true, why hasn't someone found it already?"

"Who knows? It could be that only some of it's exposed."

The pair of adventurers finally ate some of the meals before them, taking time to let this information sink in.

The night air had chilled from its earlier state. Ocean mist slowly rolled over the seawall, swirling around their feet as they walked. The pattern of spray simulated the waves crashing against the jetties below. The combination of the fog and the sound was lulling and peaceful.

Rex walked quietly, focused on squelching the pain that radiated from the side of his neck and down his upper back and arm. When the walkway to the hotel suddenly appeared out of the fog, he breathed a mental sigh of relief. His pain medicine was only a few more paces away.

"Folks, I'm going to call it a night. I'll see all of you in the morning at breakfast," he said, heading for the elevator.

"Try to get some rest," Heinmot called after him.

The remainder of the group began to say goodnight, the elevator's door closed, and it began its ascent to the seventh floor.

Rex tried watching a little TV, but couldn't seem to get comfortable, despite the ample furnishing of his suite. At around eleven o'clock, he finally dozed off, but he woke again around midnight and couldn't go back to sleep no matter what he tried.

He decided to partake in the magnificent view of the Gulf he was afforded from his balcony. That way, the night wouldn't be a total waste. Leaning against the railing, the cool salt air blew his hair from his face. The moon beamed down onto the ocean, as restless as the waves white capped far from the shore, each crest reflecting the moon.

A rap-rap-rap came from the door.

Remembering the huge bridal party in the hotel, Rex temporarily ignored it, assuming they had the wrong room. But the rapping continued.

He stumbled across the floor, nearly tripping on his own shoes, and opened the door without checking the peephole, to reveal Heinmot holding two frosty mugs of beer.

"I thought you might be awake."

"Man, you're not kidding. Come on in." Glancing at the mugs and raising an eyebrow, Rex continued, "How'd you come by these?"

Heinmot winked and entered, handing Rex one of the mugs as he took a huge sip of his own, and settled into the La-Z-Boy in the corner.

"Thanks for your help yesterday. You saved me, man."

"You'd have done the same."

"I'm not sure I could manage your weight, but—" Heinmot paused and looked at him, and they both broke out in laughter. Rex cut his snickering short, wincing as the pain returned in his shoulder.

"Don't make me laugh. It hurts when I laugh."

"Well, in any case, I would've been seriously hurt."

Donning his best John Wayne imitation, Rex smiled. "Shucks, tweren't nothing pardnah. I'm glad I was there to help out."

The two clanked glasses and drank deeply from their Heinekens.

"Now, about those coins . . ."

As Rex rode the elevator downstairs to join the gang at the breakfast table, his thoughts returned to the coins and his and Heinmot's discoveries. In his heart, he was certain there was at least one cache of the coins. And with Heinmot's help, come hell or high water, he was *going* to find them. A strange peace enveloped him. He was wearing a smile when he exited on the third floor.

"My, aren't you looking a bit more chipper since we saw you last," Arieanna quipped.

"I have to admit, I'm feeling none the worse for the wear."

"How are you, really?" Gabrielle asked.

"I never could fool you, Mom. The truth is, my shoulder is extremely sore in every way possible. But I'm trying not to let it get me down. I'm irritated I'll have to forfeit my next boxing match or two."

"As long as it's just generally sore, I'd attribute it to healing. If the pain gets worse, we can give it a look."

All they could talk about over breakfast was the coin.

"We learned quite a bit," Rex said to his father between forkfuls of eggs. "There's the stuff that I told you about the initials 'JL' we thought might belong to Jean Lafitte, but there was more information. We'll need to do some research to know for sure if all of this is factual or just folklore, of course . . ." he trailed off.

"Well, don't keep us in suspense," Arieanna said, "what else is there?"

"There're a bunch of local Louisiana legends that suggest the treasure we're seeking isn't far from your house," Heinmot said. "There has to be *some* truth to them, or else they wouldn't have stayed alive this long."

"I'm particularly interested in the pistol he always kept by his side. The handle, it's said, contains a map to all his buried treasure. If we can find that . . ."

Johann smiled, winking at Gabrielle.

"Well then, your problems are solved."

"How's that Dad?"

"I know where that pistol is located."

CHAPTER 7 – THE QUEST

FOLLOWING A UNANIMOUS ROAR FROM THE CROWD, THE AZURE SKY WAS SUDDENLY silhouetted with mortarboards, tams, and bonnets being tossed into the sky. The burgundy pieces that comprised the capstone of the regalia contained a common thread; all the tassels were the same color except for a separate color to signify the awarded degree. Goldenrod was Rex's secondary color, the color of science.

From his elevated position on the stage, he slowly absorbed the view of the other graduates congratulating one another, and hugging friends and family. His chest swelled with the pride he afforded himself as he acknowledged his own accomplishments, and came to terms with the fact that he was finally a Doctor of Marine Biology.

Had it really been ten years since he cracked his first book? It seemed like just yesterday he'd enrolled as a freshman with a fondness for dolphins and other marine mammals. Now he possessed one of the most sought-after of achievements: a Ph.D.

In addition to his doctoral work, he'd been heavily involved in the mechanical sector of the PWCC, patenting several improvements to personal watercraft engines. The pinnacle of his work had been the creation of the exhaust muffling system, a multi-funneled design that discharged through a wide, floret-shaped dispersion port. The unique shape of the port, combined with the internal funnels, nearly silenced any engine noise. While not something the general population cared about, the system was immediately embraced by law enforcement and military. They couldn't deploy them fast enough for their Marine Ops units.

Rex found himself in the green almost overnight. Soon after the patents were filed and the project completed, an investment group offered him five figures to acquire the rights to manufacture. After some intense negotiations, he managed to up the deal to six figures along with royalties.

Having entered college at seventeen, he stood as the salutatorian of his doctoral class at a mere twenty-seven, completing all levels of undergraduate, graduate, and post-graduate work in just a decade. Countless hours were spent studying and research alongside his work on his patents. In the end, he was certain all the work was worth it.

Unlike the rivalry that usually existed between the opening and closing speaker at a graduation ceremony, Rex and the valedictorian had been nearly inseparable since they'd met their freshman year. The unlikely pair had battled through all-night cram sessions and project work, were close with each other's families, and had survived their fair share of parties.

Rex had given Heinmot a full fifty percent of the profits from the sale of their inventions, and fifty percent of the royalties. Heinmot had argued that his contributions were minor. He didn't deserve so much credit. But Rex wouldn't hear of it.

Heinmot had taken to using a Hopi word to describe Rex: his long-lost brother. In many ways, they were indeed like long-lost brothers. They had an uncanny knack for completing the other's sentences. When one was in need, the other was always there.

At a meeting about a year prior to graduation, they were in a local pub and had discussed future plans. Both had prospects within the research community, but neither of them knew which way they wanted to go—so many possibilities.

Heinmot said, "Man, as much as I like research, I think I want to continue in more of a practical way, by working for a large engineering firm that has some travel mixed in."

"Yeah, I hear you, but for me, my heart lies with the ocean. Nothing like diving and seeing a reef or pod of dolphins. But there are times when the travel bug bites me."

After a few more drinks, they turned to leave, and Rex looked back at his friend and tossed his forgotten Lafitte coin to Heinmot. "Then again . . . remember this?"

"You know me, brother," Heinmot replied, as he deftly snatched the coin from the air. "I'm always up for a challenge." Tossing the coin in his palm, his face became serious. "I wondered when this was going to come up again. We only have about three hundred fifty miles of coastline to cover." His scowl broke into a smile. "Oh hell, why not? We'll find the treasure in *no* time!"

"That's the spirit! When shall we get started? Of course, we both have to complete these doctoral programs . . ."

As the fog slowly cleared from Rex's addled brain, a ray of sunlight attempted to burn a pencil-sized hole in his eyelid. Although it took a few moments, combined with the smell of maple bacon and flapjacks, he realized he was in his childhood bed. He could hear small chatter in the front part of the house, so he decided to climb into the shower and start the day.

In the dining room, Rex found his mom, dad, and Heinmot setting the table for breakfast. Glancing around, he could see that Gabrielle had outdone herself. There was enough food on the table to feed a platoon. He meandered over to his favorite spot and sat down to collect his thoughts.

At the after-party party, he and Heinmot decided they would entertain his treasure hunting fantasy and would wait six months before further pursuing a career. It wasn't like they were strapped for cash. The PMCC income was steady enough, and both could afford the break.

Looking around, he smiled because the old home held so many memories for him. The sturdiness of the log cabin and its sound-deadening properties were far superior to the brick or stucco siding frequently found on homes in the area. Sebastien used to say a tank could drive right up to the front door and no one would know it.

"Coffee, Pahana?" Heinmot asked. "You sure look like you could use some. Didn't you sleep well?"

"Thanks, mon ami, but I'll think I'll stick with my Mountain Dew. I slept well, but geez what a party. And what a drive afterward! And, by the way, congratulations, Dr. Iiniwa. Can't remember if I said so yesterday."

"It's a little foggy to me too! Seems like it has been one continuous party these past few days, and thanks for the congratulations. You too, Doc."

"All right, Doctors!" Gabrielle said. "Help me get the food on the table before it gets cold."

"Guys," Johann said as they sat down to eat. "Gabrielle and I want both of you to know how proud we are. A Ph.D. is no joke, and the two of you make a great team."

"We're both just over the moon about it, and we're sure your parents are as well," Gabrielle said to Heinmot.

"Any immediate plans? What will the two of you find yourselves into now?" Johann asked.

"Funny that you should say that, Dad. I have had an itch that's needed scratching for about fifteen years now. I've coerced . . . *convinced* Heinmot to help me solve the riddle of the golden tide."

"The *what?*"

Rex slapped the gold forty-franc coin on the table and said, "The golden tide, Mom. At least that's what we're calling it."

Turning to Johann, Rex continued.

"Dad, if we can find that pistol, the one with the map in the grip you claim to know the location of, we might find Lafitte's treasure. As crazy as it sounds, and although I know that it's a long shot, it's just something that Heinmot and I need to do before things fire up at our new jobs—me at the Marine Center in Corpus, and Heinmot at Garner Engineering in Dallas. Before, the timing was just never right, too much school and research—now, with a few months to kill before starting those lifelong endeavors, we thought that it would be a good time to put this legend to rest."

"I'd hoped that when you grew into adulthood and matured as you went through college that you would forget about the legend. But when you get an idea in your head . . ."

"Dad, I don't think I could live with myself if I didn't at least try. What's the harm?"

Johann looked around and settled his eyes on Gabrielle's. After a moment, they both sighed deeply.

"Alright, Rex. Heinmot. You know what's best. Let's talk details after we eat."

Johann sat at his desk and pulled out the makings to stoke his pipe. Rex and Heinmot sat on the large, padded leather sofa and gazed at the office walls. The wall behind Johann was filled, floor to ceiling, with books of all types: fiction, non-fiction, reference manuals, specifications . . . you name it, and this bookshelf had it. Johann's work in research and development for the government required that he maintain such a library along with multiple computers sporting the latest encryption technologies—something that piqued Heinmot's interest. The other walls displayed artwork from various periods that, taken together, comprised a nautical theme.

A French eighteenth-century desk acquired from the same estate sale as his pipe made a handsome fixture against the rough logs walls of the cabin. Electric floor lamps from England sat at each side of the desk and in a corner of the large room. A massive chair with huge animal-shaped legs and arms stood behind it, completing the look of an ancient tax collector's work space. A small lamp illuminated the surface of the desk that held various pens, pencils, and papers scattered across the desktop. The gray of Johann's hair and beard and the half-glasses he wore only served to complete the picture.

As a ring of smoke curled about his head, Johann set his glasses on the desk, and leaned back in his chair.

"Would it change your mind about searching for those coins if I told you there were no less than ten men I've known who spent the majority of their lives looking for them? They've spent fortunes and wasted away their lives, never finding as much as a clue about the coins. Does that make a difference?" He paused to puff on his pipe, waiting for a response to his rhetorical question he knew wouldn't come. "No? Well, you know two of them yourself, Rex."

"I do? Who?"

"Eamon Patterson and Kendall Tremaine."

Johann let that sink in for a moment.

"Both have spent years and fortunes launching expeditions into both of the areas we've been discussing. This is why, in some ways, I think you and Heinmot would be wasting your time looking for the gold, even though we all know it's out there. Does any of this change your minds?"

"I wasn't aware of the men searching for the gold. I think knowing me as you do, you know I have to look. That gold's out there *somewhere*."

"I'll agree with you there—it's *somewhere.* But finding that somewhere will be a whole different story."

"But Dad, in Galveston, you said you knew where Lafitte's pistol was located. If you know that, why haven't you gone after the gold?"

"Ah, yes, about that. There are many rumors about where it may be. When I said I knew where it was, what I actually meant was I know someone who might know where it is."

"And that would be?"

"As I said, you already know him. Eamon Patterson. If you're truly serious about searching for the gold, you won't be able to do it without his help."

"Why would *he* tell me where the pistol is located? He's been searching for years for the gold. Why doesn't he go get it himself?"

"It has to do with time or, rather, lack of it. Patterson was getting old when you were a kid. He's ancient now, and I've heard rumors that he has cancer."

"What about his sons—Tim and . . . Bryan?"

"Rex, Bryan died in a boating accident a few years ago, and Tim got married and moved out to California. I'm not even sure he checks in on Eamon, and he didn't know anything about the pistol until well after he gave up his search. Mrs. Aldridge, who lives down the road from him, stops by a few times a week to bring him food and pick up the place. The legend of the gold is slowly fading away, and no one wants to look for it after so many years of failure."

"How can I convince Mr. Patterson to share what he knows with us?"

"I think that's how I can help you. Through the years, most of the townsfolk tended to shun the Pattersons, but you'll remember I always went out of my way to help him out or just say hello when I saw him out fishing or in town. Not many others except for Dutch ever did that; I think he'll remember my kindness, and I think he'll remember you." Something twinkled in Johann's eye. "But before you go to him, head over to Boudreaux's and pick up a few pounds of boudain, some cracklins, and maybe some beer. That'll help stir his memory."

"You know the way, Rex. Just follow the road toward the burned-out bridge, and you'll find the road to Eamon's shack at the edge of the woods."

"Does his shack still rise and fall with the tide?"

"It does. Although some things change, there are plenty more that never do. If his health allowed for it, I think he'd still be in his pirogue chasing alligators through the swamp."

Armed with a few bags of boudain and cracklins, Rex and Heinmot headed down Highway 90 toward the Sabine River in Rex's graduation gift to himself, a brand-new Corvette. It probably would have made more sense to take Johann's truck than to try and dodge the pot holes in the ancient highway, but it wasn't much of a challenge, especially given the upgrades he'd made to the suspension.

"You know," Rex said, turning to Heinmot, "I know this is a bit extreme. It's not too late to back out if you want."

"Rex . . ." he started. Heinmot rarely used his first name anymore, so something was clearly bothering him. "It's not that; you know I'll be with you until the bitter end and that's just how it is. I'm not superstitious, but in the words of my grandfather and based upon what I recall you saying about him, this Patterson fellow seems to be 'bad medicine,' if you know what I mean. Are you sure you want to do this?"

"Hein, I don't think we have a choice in the matter. It'll be a dead end otherwise. My only concern is that I'm not my dad, and this old guy doesn't really know or owe *me* anything."

"Well, based on all of the information your dad shared, combined with the two coins that you have, there's definitely something to this legend, but if we have to start with this Patterson, I guess we just have to."

The road down to the Patterson shack appeared as they made the turn in the highway. Rex cringed at the sound of his new 'Vette scraping bottom as they dropped from broken asphalt to a scantily clad shale road that had some huge craters in it. Although, he had never driven to the house, he believed it was even more overgrown now than in the past. Pampas grass and briar patches threatened to reclaim the land. Seeing the moss hanging long, web-like beards from the overhanging canopy of jungle, and smelling the sour, decaying stench of the festering marsh permeating the air, Rex now lamented removing the targa top. With all the low-hanging branches, it would be a miracle if a cottonmouth or copperhead snake didn't drop down in their laps. As they zigzagged down the road, he and Heinmot heard the rustle of scrambling critters; the brush around them moved so much with wildlife, it seemed alive itself. There was no doubt a box office slasher movie could be shot along this road. Despite his familiarity with the overall landscape, Rex was surprised at how far off the main road the house sat. The odometer indicated they had traveled more than three miles, and there was no house in sight.

A deep ravine in the road suddenly popped up before them as they rounded a shallow curve. Rex had to slam on the brakes to prevent the car from going down into it. As the 'Vette slid to a stop at the edge, he set the emergency brake and they stepped out to inspect the roadway.

"Are you *sure* this is the way?" Heinmot asked. "I don't think even your dad's truck could have navigated this part of the road."

Rex sighed.

"Well, I guess it's Pete and Joe from this point forward. Let me grab the food; we'll hoof it the rest of the way."

"Wait," Heinmot said, looking around with squinted eyes. "Have a look here; the road continues around the ravine to a makeshift bridge to the right. You couldn't see it from the car."

"I think that was the general idea."

"But why would someone want to hide . . ." He trailed off as he answered his own question. "You know," he said, "this just went to the next level, right?"

"Agreed," Rex said, then smiled. "Shall we?"

After a mile down the slipshod road, a field of pumpjacks, slowly nodding up and down as they sucked black gold from the marshy ground, appeared along the edge of the swamp. Around the next turn, they finally found the house on the swamp's opposite edge. It stood against the wood's edge, partially engulfed by the moss hanging from the cypress trees. The gray of the slate siding had long since been erased by the green tint of algae, and the windows were likely cleaned last when they were installed. Rex stopped at the back edge of the clearing, and the pair slowly exited the car, doing their best to look friendly.

The surrounding cypress trees and their knees threatened to trip them as they approached the porch. The Spanish moss swished in the wind, and the stink of rotting carcasses enveloped the space surrounding the property. A moderate-sized garden was in full bloom on the left side of the house with corn, okra, green beans, potatoes, and tomatoes. Rex was shocked to see a rose garden bordering the outer edge with wisteria. The flowers released a powerful fragrance that overwhelmed the muddy stench that wafted along on the breeze.

"He must have a generator," Heinmot said. "No power lines coming in, but he's got spotlights on the corners of his house? Either the old man is paranoid, or he often receives unwanted guests."

"Yeah. Like us . . . And those elongated crosses at random places on the outside walls of the house? Those are embrasures someone can fire a gun from without being seen."

Abruptly, a gruff raspy voice called out from the house, "Stop right there! Who're ya and what do ya want? What's in those sacks?"

Rex and Heinmot froze. "Mr. Patterson? It's Rex Rhineheart."

"Rhineheart, huh? Rhineheart . . . are ya any kin to *Johann* Rhineheart?"

"I'm his oldest son. You might remember we met many years ago near the supermarket? I was a boy scout and stopped the traffic so that you and your wife could cross the street? She twisted her ankle and fell. She hurt her leg and I helped her up and walked with her back to the curb while you went to get the truck."

"Ah, yes—I do recollect that. And the other one. He looks Indian."

"I'm Heinmot . . . sir," Heinmot replied, waving his hand awkwardly, not sure how to take the old man's comment.

"My father sent me. We've brought you some boudain, cracklins, and some cold beer and sodas," Rex said, holding up the bags.

"I reckon you can come on up, but yer friend will have to wait there. I don't like strangers around here."

Rex looked at Heinmot, then back at Patterson.

"Not to be a bother, but it's both of us or neither. This food is growing cold and the beer hot. If you want this stuff, you'll have to talk to both of us."

The door to the old hovel creaked slightly open and a double-barreled shotgun pushed it open the remainder of the way. Aged much more than Rex remembered him, Eamon Patterson was barely recognizable. The old hermit's thin hair was a ghostly gloss of white, and as he walked his right leg dragged slightly behind him. He had the shotgun cradled in his left arm and a walking cane in his right hand.

Patterson laughed heartily as he emerged into the sunlight and lowered the gun.

"Just like your dad. You drive a hard bargain, son. Come on up but both of you keep yer hands where I can see 'em."

As they slowly approached the front porch of the house, Patterson's facial features came into focus. Rex couldn't help but feel sorry for the old man. Life had not been overly kind to him. Deep lines and crevices covered his face. The skin of his arms was dark as tanned leather. While Rex guessed he was somewhere around seventy-five, he looked to be in his mid-nineties. Coffee-colored eyes stared out from under gray eyebrows; though old, they were as sharp as any predator's. Beneath the ashen beard that hung to the middle of his broad chest, his granite jaw chewed hard on a toothpick. Once a brawler who could likely stand toe-to-toe with Rocky Marciano, the old man's physique had dwindled, but Rex figured he was still no one to be trifled with. As he stood there, bare-chested in overalls, Patterson was a dinosaur of the modern age.

"Anytime somebody comes up here carrying sacks like you two fellers are, they usually want somethin' . . ."

"Well I suppose that's true, Mr. Patterson. My friend and I would like to talk about Jean Lafitte."

"Ha! What you mean is you want me to tell you where to find his gold."

"Well . . ."

The old man held his up hand and propped the shotgun up in the corner of the porch. "Sonny, you don't get to be my age without learning a few things about folks." Looking at both of them, he chuckled. "Besides, I didn't think you were here to ask me to the square dance."

Astonished by the fact the old man had a sense of humor, Rex looked at Heinmot and back at Patterson before they broke into laughter and proceeded to soundlessly enjoy the beer and food. When they'd presented the boudain and cracklins, his eyes lit up, but the two six-packs of Lone Star sent a smile ear-to-ear, revealing a relatively full set of slightly yellow teeth.

Rex started his story immediately, from the first fish he'd caught to Johann's theories.

When he finished telling his tale, Patterson looked first at Rex and then at Heinmot. "That's a good story . . . but what do you need from me?"

"Well sir, Dad tells me that you may know the whereabouts of Lafitte's flintlock. That pistol would seem to hold the key to the whereabouts of the treasure."

"Son," he replied sadly, "that rumor's been around nearly longer than Lafitte was around. If I knew where that pistol was, I'd already have the treasure. I've torn up this marsh for nigh upon forty years and all it got me was the loss of my left hand to a gator when I reached into a hole where the gold was supposed to be."

"So you don't have any clues or ideas about the treasure?" Heinmot asked.

"So you're Johann's boy, huh?" he said to Rex, before turning back to Heinmot. "I'll tell you something about this boy's daddy. There was a spell when the people in this town wouldn't give me the time of day, or worse yet, would cross the street when they saw me or my boys comin'. His dad and that old taxidermist in town were the only ones that didn't treat me like I had the damn plague, just because of the way I look and dress and the like. Now, that may not mean much to most folks, but it means a helluva lot to me. I never forgot the kindness those two showed me and my kin." He turned back to Rex. "I also suspect your Dad had a hand in having that Aldridge woman come by and check on me. So I'm going to tell you something that I haven't talked about since I lost my oldest . . ."

"Your dad's a smart man. He almost figured out the biggest part of the legend. He just needs some details to fill in the gaps. As you already know, Lafitte would hang out on Jefferson Island with his relatives when the heat was on and he needed a hiding place. He buried treasure there that was discovered under a giant live oak back in the 1920s. I suppose ya already know that?"

"Yes sir. We found that in a Google search on the computers at the museum in Galveston."

"Now for the part you may not know. Did you read how many pots were found there?"

"No . . . I don't think there was any mention of that, just that gold coins were discovered in some kettles."

"Well, sonny, I happened upon this information just about a year or so back from a feller who was on his deathbed—and now I'm more or less on mine. I'd given his family a steady supply of wild game back years ago when they were nearly starving to death, and just like the kindness your Dad showed me, he never forgot it. So here you are. Apparently, Lafitte was highly superstitious, and did everything in groups of three. He also told me other locations Lafitte frequented. I see the doubt in your faces, but I'll prove it to you. Answer a few questions for me. How many ships did Lafitte sail to France with?"

"Three."

"How many pots of gold were discovered on Jefferson Island? You don't know that one, so I'll answer it for you. Three."

"On most ships of the day, there were only two lookouts on duty. Any idea how many Lafitte used?"

"Three?" the pair of adventurers asked at once.

"Three," Patterson said with a rap of his cane on the porch. *"Everything* he did revolved around the number three. Your dad was right: Lafitte made it back from France with Napoleon's loot and he buried it right here in Louisiana—all nine *million* francs of it."

"Nine million? Dad told us it was ten million."

"Is ten divisible by three? No, it's not. Old Lafitte left one million of that loot back in Cuba or in Mexico. He was so superstitious he believed it would bring him bad luck. There are persistent rumors that he also left it because he planned to retire there. For two other tidbits, that will bring the grand total to, yep, three."

"Lafitte used several of the islands in the eastern part of the state. They were in groups of three as well. I checked the maps not too long ago and learned that Weeks Island was the third island in a straight line away from Jefferson Island."

"You also need to need to know that he always buried his treasure in clusters of large live oak trees—just like the ones on Jefferson Island. But like everything else, they had to total three. So what you need to do is head over to Weeks Island and, in the center, find a great grove of live oaks—I hear tell it's one of the biggest groves in the area. Look for some massive live oaks in clusters of three. *That's* where his treasure'll be. At least some of it."

Rex and Heinmot looked bewildered. *How would they ever pull off something like that? First they had to get to the island, then find its true center—a feat of geometry that would take quite a bit of reckoning—then they had to find the exact trio of live oaks to dig under?*

Seeing the look of helplessness on the would-be adventurers' faces, the old man continued. "I have some connections who might be able to help you. You have to approach by water, and you'll have to be fairly quiet—the entire area is posted, and there is a military base, so it will require some light footwork to slip in and out undetected. Head down to the Pelican's Perch in Cameron and ask for a guy named Fats Melancon. You can't miss him; he'll be the biggest Cajun in the bar. But don't be too surprised if he's skittish; he doesn't like the law, and may think you're a cop. When you find him, tell him PawPaw Patterson sent you and it'll save you a bruise or two. Fats will take care of you, he knows when to keep his mouth shut, and he's one of the best boat captains I've ever known. You're going to need a few greenbacks to grease his palms, but it'll be money well spent."

"We really appreciate it, but I don't understand why you don't go after it yourself."

The old man's face suddenly lost all of its expression, and his voice took on an edge.

"Boys, look at me. I'm just too damn old to start on an adventure like that. Hell, as much as I don't want to admit it, I've been too old for decades, and now I've got cancer. As for why—well, I've already told you that. I owe your dad something, and I figure this will help clear the books. I can see the mystery burning a hole right through you. It has inside of me for decades. Now, go find your treasure."

Chapter 8 – The Trek

The sky was beginning to darken as the Corvette rambled back up the pockmarked highway to Rex's house. They were both excited at the prospect of finding Lafitte's loot, but neither knew what to say.

"Okay," Heinmot said, "so what *is* the plan? I can hear the gears whirring in your head from here."

Rex quickly laid out his plan.

They would need to rent a truck and trailer, then pick up two of their silent jet skis and bring them to Johann's. They would use the log cabin as a base from which to launch their operations.

Heinmot would also need to gather some metal detectors as well as the small ground-penetrating radar units. Headlights, backpacks, folding shovels, hatchets, machetes, and other miscellaneous equipment, including a small tripod gantry crane and a winch would also be needed.

While Heinmot gathered supplies, Rex would meet with Melancon to procure transport to Weeks Island, as well as the necessary logistics needed to support an at-sea launch on the jet skis. He also needed to fill Johann in on all of the details, and borrow a few devices he'd seen him working on as part of a government project.

The two agreed to meet back at the log cabin in three days. Upon reaching the house, Heinmot wasted no time and prepared to head west to Corpus Christi to retrieve the jet skis and the necessary equipment. Shortly after, both smiling, with their eyes dancing in excitement, they shook hands and then headed to their respective destinations.

Salt from the frothy seawater burned Rex's eyes, yet his heart pounded in his chest as he and Heinmot neared their objective. Although the *Gittaloadodis* and its crew didn't come highly recommended at some of the local watering holes, the old trapper had already informed him that Fats and company were top notch and knew when to exhibit total memory loss. Nine times out of ten, any other captain would have been more than a little suspicious of Rex's request to haul unmentioned cargo to an undisclosed location in the heart of the night deep in the swamp. But Al 'Fats' Melancon just waved a thick hand in the air when Rex presented him five crisp hundred-dollar bills. "Coun' me in," he said. "Da Franklins talk and bulls—err . . . cow patties walk. "We'uns has no cares about yo' intents—kosher or udderwise."

Rex then informed him that Heinmot would travel to the jetties southeast of Cameron to meet with him to drop off the equipment where it could be loaded onto the boat the night before the voyage. In return, Fats told him they were to travel along the coast and enter into Vermilion Bay, where they could slip away unnoticed. He practically guaranteed Rex no one would pay much attention to the old trawler. It was regularly seen up and down the coast trolling for shrimp late at night.

Darkness shielded their departure in a total blackout. The aging boat wasn't much to look at, but it operated perfectly. Fats pushed the starter button and the diesels fired immediately. Though Rex was a little surprised, the initial shock wore off quickly when he realized the engines appeared to be only a few years old. The old captain wasn't messing around.

Light surf and a warm wind met the barnacled bow as they headed silently eastward, communicating via hand signals and body language. After casting off, the crew headed down below for a quick nap, passing Heinmot on his way up with three steaming mugs of chicory-laced coffee. Rex glanced at the wake of the boat once more and the tarpaulin-covered cargo, and then turned to follow his friend into the windowed cabin.

Handing one of the cups to Fats, he slightly smiled and said, "Well, Cap'n, at least there is a slight wind to help keep the mosquitoes at bay."

Sloshing a goodly amount of the piping hot liquid into his mouth, Fats nodded and replied, "Aye, but those lil' bloodsuckers don't like to give up none too easy. They'll be back if'n the wind switches directions."

Rex took his cup and said, "Thanks, mon ami. I would've made a pot had I known we had any down below."

Upon hearing Rex use some French, the shrimper let out a soft laugh and said, "Boy, it's good to hear some of the old words continuing into the younger generation. Most young folks have no use for it, and think it's too backwards for modern use."

Rex choked on his coffee and said, "Now, don't let my mother know about that. She would ring my neck if she thought that I was afraid to speak French or that I thought it had no use in present-day vocabulary. She was born in Marseille, and insisted that my sister, brother, and I learn every word of it before we were ten years old."

He continued, "Heck, I'm fluent in three languages—English, French, and German. It was a little hard growing up having a German dad and a French mom, because both of them wanted us to learn their native languages first. Sebastien and I did okay, I guess, but Arieanna only wanted to learn French. She always thought that German sounded so harsh, but French was flowery and nice."

The wheelhouse roared with laughter at his last statement and Fats said, "That's okay son, you ain't lived 'less'n you have a Cajun granny. I s'pect your ma had a proper French schoolin', but my gran' taught us the bad words before the good 'uns and my mammy would rap us with a willow switch every time we used one of 'em."

Heinmot shook his head and said, "Nope, I've beaten both of you. Try having one Blackfoot and one Nez Perce grandmother to know what trouble is all about. Why, my brothers and I could do nothing right!"

"Pahana, I know you know, but Fats may not, that those two tribes were mortal enemies and neither respected the opposite's traditions. We quickly learned the differences and would help each other remember so that we didn't get into trouble. Try learning two different Indian languages and remembering which was which in front of the two grandmothers. Why we couldn't sit down until we were nearly seven from having sore hind parts."

The conversation continued for some time, with the three acting like long-lost friends reminiscing about their childhoods and the old ways of the grandparents. The old trawler made good speed in the smooth waters along the coast, and was less than thirty miles from the turn at the bay before they knew it. Fats stomped his foot twice on the floor of the salty cabin and a rustling sound down below signaled the crew to get back to work.

Rex followed the crew out onto the main deck and allowed his eyes to focus in the dark. He had taken a bearing at the last turn. He knew the island couldn't be too much farther, but wanted confirmation. Setting his cup of coffee on the railing, he called up to the captain, "How much longer?"

Fats scratched his grizzled jowl and pondered for a moment before answering in his Cajun drawl. "Sha, canna be mo' dan some few minutes from dis point."

Though he wanted a more precise number, it roughly matched Rex's calculations, so he nodded in affirmation. Turning and bracing himself against the slowly rolling deck, Rex floundered toward the stern of the boat to check on the personal watercraft and tow skiff affixed to the transom. Matt "PeeWee" Bergeron and his brother Mitch were going over the rigging. They didn't want to lose time figuring it out when it was time to release the vehicles. Heinmot fought the rolling of the deck as he made a few last-minute adjustments to the equipment.

PeeWee readied the winch and davit that was attached to one of the watercraft, while Matt connected the second Kawasaki to the opposite davit. Heinmot stood admiring their handiwork, performed so quickly and silently on the rocking deck.

Rex made a few modifications on both the Kawasaki machines. A turbocharger pushed the horsepower to well over two hundred—thus making a quick escape almost guaranteed. Shielded lights with red filters would save their night vision, and non-reflective paint would reduce the chance of being spotted with any of the multi-million candlepower spotlights used to light game, an illegal yet common practice. The pièce de résistance was the triple-funneled, submerged exhaust system the pair had invented that all but ensured the jet skis would skate silently along the bayou.

Fats cut the engine, and the boat drifted to a silent stop in the murky water. All hands on deck paused to listen for any activity within earshot. Nothing human was to be heard, but the whine of Louisiana's unnamed bird, the croaking of frogs, and the occasional splash filled the air with a racket that would cover any moderate noises they might make. The jet skis were silently cranked down until the hulls bobbed in free-flowing water. Rex and Heinmot slipped over the side like ninjas and mounted the jet skis.

Rex tossed a small roll to Fats, who deftly snatched it out of the air with one of his fists the size of a small ham.

"Mon ami," Fats said, inspecting the roll of bills, "dis is much mo' dan what we agreed on."

"Keep those engines warm, my friend, we may be coming back to you with a swarm of bees on our butts."

"If we're not back by six o'clock," Heinmot said, "you guys get out of here and don't look back."

"Don't worry. We'll be rit here."

With that, they both fired up the Kawasakis and turned north, heading deep into the marsh. They were making nearly fifty knots, and the engines were barely making a sound. When Rex saw the rotating beacon of the lighthouse, he knew they were on the right track. Weeks Island awaited just minutes ahead in the enveloping darkness.

He smiled, nodded at his friend and hunkered down to enjoy the ride.

CHAPTER 9 – LAFITTE'S LOOT

THEY SHUT DOWN THE JET SKIS ABOUT A QUARTER MILE FROM SHORE AND COASTED IN absolute silence. The pair made a quick assessment of the surrounding marsh to detect any unnatural movement and to locate a suitable landing spot. The military complex not far from the purported location of the treasure gave the pair pause.

"Pahana, over here," Heinmot whispered, pointing at a thick patch of growth along the bank. "This is perfect."

They'd skirted around the populated area on the west side and circled northeastward through the marshy waterway from the southwestern edge of the island until reaching Plantation Lake. There, the swamp made a double switchback. They'd been lucky to find a small tributary that peeled away from the main branch and led straight to the small lake. They easily hopped the berm and scooted across the water until they found an overgrown area of the bank. The cypress trees and blackjack vines formed a natural gate to the small inlet. The selected spot would not be seen even at mid-day, but they planned to be long gone by then.

According to the directions Eamon Patterson had disclosed, from their current location the large live oaks should be less than two miles in a northwesterly direction. Rex nodded at Heinmot, and the duo strapped on their backpacks, switching on the AN/PVS-7 night-vision goggles Johann had 'acquired' for them. Rex carried the ground-penetrating radar unit with Heinmot packing the metal detector. Both had folding shovels, canteens, and red-filtered flashlights, and were covered head-to-toe with military-grade DEET mosquito repellant. Heinmot led the way, but he did so from experience leading hunting parties in Montana, as opposed to any natural ability supposedly granted to all Native Americans. When Rex commented on how suave he looked leading their expedition, he couldn't help but laugh. Rex was usually the one in the lead.

The night air was clammy. A wet fog crept around the bases of the trees and through the marsh grass. The extra humidity would help mask the sounds of their footfalls, which, on a normal night, wouldn't carry more than a few yards anyway.

A sudden splash to the left caused Heinmot to hold his left fist in the air: a signal to freeze in place. After a few moments, another splash further out indicated whatever they disturbed was moving away from them. They continued, carefully high stepping through the marsh grass and brackish water. A thin sliver of a moon provided little light. Luckily, the green light of the googles enhanced the ground and undergrowth surrounding their path.

After a while, Heinmot held up a finger to indicate they had navigated about a thousand yards, a bit more than half a mile. Rex snuck a peek at his new Luminox diving watch. The glowing green tritium on the hands and dial made it a simple task to calculate they had traversed the distance in about twenty minutes, which, at the present rate, left them about an hour and half to go. He smiled as he thought about the mate to his watch resting on Heinmot's left wrist. Johann had given one to each of them after the graduation. Rex did not ask how he got them, but he guessed one of his many military contacts had assisted. The watches both bore the same inscription: "Follow your heart and your feet will never stray from the path. Love Mom and Dad."

He and Heinmot really were like brothers. Both sets of parents including all of their siblings shared that same relationship. Rex had met Heinmot's parents some years ago. They had taken him into the family as if he had always been there.

Heinmot snapped his fingers right in front of Rex's face.

"Hello? You still with me?"

"Sorry," Rex said, shaking his head back to the present. "Where are we?"

"Another two thousand yards should have us close to the mark. We don't have too much farther to go."

Hearing muffled chatter in the background, they crouched down and waited. A patrol could be heard moving through the marsh toward the south. The throbbing sound of rotors off to the southeast reminded both to maintain their stealthy approach—a chopper in the air would make short work of detecting an intruder. They continued northwest toward the live oak grove, managing to remain unnoticed despite the regular military patrols. After passing a small power transfer station, they held still for a few minutes, to be certain no one heard them. The weight of the backpacks was slowly becoming a burden. All four arms ached from the balancing act they were doing with the detectors. Varmints of unknown size and origin scampered through the salt grass as they walked past their nests. Finally, after another hour had passed, they broke through a high mound of blackjack and thorns, stepping into a ring of trees that had short patches of thick razor grass growing all around.

Heinmot reached up to switch off his night vision, but suddenly stopped and held up his left fist. Not hearing or seeing anything out of the ordinary, but fully trusting him, Rex froze in his tracks not certain what was spooking his friend. Slowly setting the radar unit down into soft pampas grass, Heinmot crouched and motioned for Rex to do the same.

"What's—" Rex started, but was cut off by a horizontal motion from Heinmot to remain quiet. He then pointed up into the trees with one hand and made a gesture to look at where he indicated. Rex studied the trees and caught a glimpse of motion, but couldn't quite make out what it was moving there.

In a one swift movement, Heinmot grabbed a large piece of oak, slung it into the tree above them, and slid to the side. The sound of solid wood meeting soft flesh was heard followed by the sound of a woman screaming and something crashing down through the trees. A split second later, they heard a thud along with snarling, and then the sounds of something running through the swamp.

"Pahana, we nearly had a tiger by the tail or, more fitting, *he* nearly had *us* by the tail. I could see two glowing rings through my goggles, but I wasn't exactly sure what it was until the panther flicked his tail and I saw the motion silhouetted against the tree limbs."

"I guess we should wait before we start digging up the rest of the swamp."

"We can't dig up the entire swamp. Where are you thinking? I have no idea *where* to look."

"You remember Lafitte did everything in groups of three, right?"

"Yeah, but I haven't seen any trees in groups of three."

"Gold is heavy, right? So it would stand to reason that even in the best condition, a small group of pirates with no machinery wouldn't be able to carry three heavy chests into the outlying area of the swamp. Agree?"

"Shoot, we're in pretty damned good shape and lugging these backpacks and the detectors has us sweating like a fox in a forest fire. A band of rogues couldn't possibly make multiple trips this far in. If Lafitte was as superstitious as we've been told, he would've wanted to get in and out as quickly as possible."

"So do you think they would've trod in this far?"

"If they had three chests, this would've been a killer for them. So what are you thinking? It'll be light soon."

"While you were tracking the panther, we passed through groups of large live oaks loosely arranged in rings that have a decreasing radius. I believe that we need to look between the third and fourth ring and we may have some luck."

"The innermost ring is only about another hundred yards or so, why not bury it there and make it easy to find?"

"Too obvious and I believe his superstitions preyed heavily on his convictions."

"Rex, the third ring has to be more than six hundred yards in circumference and more than fifty yards wide. I can't even see the other side from here. Surely, you don't mean to dig up the whole thing?"

"Nope, but I have a theory. You have to remember that Lafitte was a pirate, but he was also a really good sailor. He could probably read the stars better without a sextant than half his crew could *with* one."

"Okay, but how does that keep us from digging up half the marsh in less than six hours?"

"Simple, my dear Dr. Iiniwa. First, we take a bearing and find the northernmost tree in the ring. Then we divide the circle into three, which would make three 120-degree wedges. Then we take the third section, which would be the 240-to-360 degree wedge, and start scanning. If that doesn't work, we'll scan the whole area and come back tomorrow when it's dark again."

Heinmot let out a slow whistle.

"Not too shabby, Pahana. I'm not sure how you deduced that, but let's test your theory."

The duo quickly found the northernmost tree in the ring and started dividing the ring as Rex suggested. Within twenty minutes they had located the potential area. Heinmot connected the battery pack to the radar and got ready to scan. "You know ground-penetrating radar doesn't operate effectively in wet ground, right?"

"Yeah . . . but have a look here. In this wide span of grass the dirt is dry and sandy. Go ahead and fire her up."

Heinmot switched on the unit and began to pace back and forth in a systematic pattern. Rex activated the metal detector and followed in his exact footsteps to ensure no square inch was left un-scanned across the five thousand-square foot area. As much as he *wanted* the gold to be there, after making multiple passes, they found nothing, not even a rusty Coke can.

"Well," Heinmot said, "so much for your theory about the rings of trees. We have about four hours until daylight, why don't we go a little farther in and see what is there?"

"Agreed. Nothing here. Lead on, mon ami."

After wandering around the area for half an hour with the metal detector, they found nothing of interest. Rex passed Heinmot a canteen and an energy bar while surveying the area. They'd passed through the center of the tree rings and had cleared the second-most ring on the other side. Both decided they would go as far as the outermost ring before giving up.

Heinmot was relieving himself when a flash of lightning illuminated the area. He noticed a group of trees that formed a slightly curved double H as the light flickered and faded.

"Take a look at this group of trees. Notice anything peculiar about them?"

"Not really. They look more or less like all the other trees."

"Yeah, but what would you have if you removed the cross-connecting parts of the trunks?"

"A group of three trees! In fact, it would be the only group of three we've seen all night."

"Hand me that radar unit, bro."

Walking in a diagonal pattern, Heinmot began scanning the area from the base of the trees outward. On the fifteenth pass, the radar unit indicated something was about three feet below the surface.

Heinmot fine-tuned the radar unit. As he adjusted the knobs, the picture came into focus. Arranged in a triangular pattern beneath them were three, small rectangular blobs. Another sudden flash of lightning hit to the south, followed by a heavy rumble.

"One, two, three, four, five," Rex counted before thunder echoed through the swamp. "Sounds like it's moving our way. Wouldn't be Louisiana if we weren't caught in the middle of a downpour. We better start digging."

They shut down the scanner and broke out the GI-surplus folding shovels. The digging was slow at first, but once the top layer of dirt was removed, moisture began to pool in the base of the hole and the digging became much easier. They decided to make the hole about four feet in diameter so they wouldn't have to move away too much soil the deeper they dug. After about three feet, the shovels struck something decidedly hard. Heinmot reached down and brushed the mud to the sides of the opening and twisted on his small aluminum flashlight to examine the source of the blockage.

The narrow white beam illuminated a section of rough-cut wood, possibly a plank, in fantastic condition considering its theoretical age. He motioned to Rex to continue digging from the center outward so they could find the edge of the wood. The pair continued to hack away at the soft ground, and the edges of the boards were soon exposed. They paused for a moment to drink water from the canteens; they were soaked in sweat from head to toe.

As Rex mopped his face with a rag, he thought he saw motion out of the corner of his eye. Another bolt of lightning illuminated the space surrounding them, but he couldn't discern the source of the perceived motion. He'd all but shrugged it off as lightning playing tricks on him when it caught his peripheral vision once again. He wiped his face again and kept his eyes shut for a moment to allow them to focus. When he opened his eyes again, he was sure there was something lurking behind Heinmot.

He grabbed his shovel and flashlight and slowly circled their small excavation. Heinmot stood still as a statue, wondering what was happening just behind him. Rex let out a grunt, and Heinmot heard a heavy crunch as the shovel made contact with something.

After a moment, Rex touched him on the shoulder. "You can turn around—that, my friend, was close."

Heinmot spun around to see one of the less-than-friendly denizens of the swamp sans its business end on the ground behind him: a four-foot cottonmouth. The dark, fat, serpentine body twitched as if in an attempt to locate its missing head a foot or more away. Using his thick-soled military boots, Rex kicked the snake head deeper into the swamp and heard a satisfying splash as it made contact with the marsh water and sank into the murky deep.

"Damn, that was close!"

"No kidding. Let's uproot these boards, shall we?"

Nodding, Heinmot placed the pointed end of his shovel between the edge of the pit and the board and began to pry upward and out. Rex joined him on the opposite end of the board, and, in moments, the plank gave way, and they removed it from the hole. The process was continued on the second and third board until only a five-by-four foot opening remained in the ground.

"Well, that's not what we're looking for. I wonder what's down there next?"

Heinmot shined his flashlight down into the small pit only to have the light reflected back into his face. Just below the boards, the pit had completely filled with water. When they tried to bail the water out, it simply ran right back into the hole.

Rex sighed. "I think we're going to have to dig a side hole to force the water to a lower level."

"The tide's now working against us too. It's three-thirty. We need to hurry or daybreak will catch us in the act."

Another bolt of lightning hit and thunder rolled across the swamp.

"Not to mention if this downpour happens. I think we'll just have to grin and bear it."

"I'll flip you for it. Heads, and I dig and dive. Tails: you do."

"No need for both of us to end up smelling like marsh rats. I'll do it. There can't be much digging left."

Rex stepped down into the hole, water up to his knees, and started digging. Though it was hard to tell, he knew that headway was being made because the waterline continued to rise up to his chest. Although he was a tall six-foot-two, he had no qualms about the fact that it would be over his head before the task was done.

Suddenly, the ground beneath him gave way and he had to tread water to avoid going under as pieces of broken boards floated to the surface. He searched with his feet and felt three distinct mounds beneath him, probably the objects he and Heinmot had detected with the scanner.

"How much water do you calculate to be in this hole?" Rex asked, looking up at Heinmot.

"Let's see—pi multiplied by radius squared . . . multiplied by height. Roughly ninety-eight cubic feet in the pit and a cubic foot contains about seven and a half gallons. So about seven hundred and thirty-five gallons."

"Ok. We need to be able to see what's down there before it fills back up. There's somewhat of a berm behind me we can bail the water over. That way the water won't be able to drain back into the hole. If we don't start soon, the rain is going to drown us. That last flash was so close it can't be more than thirty minutes off, now."

"How are we going to bail out seven hundred gallons of water in less than thirty minutes?"

"Only one way that I know of, we have to use the covers for the scanner. I figure each of them hold about ten gallons so we have to work like mad. Ready?"

"Let's do it!"

They quickly removed the thick fiberglass covers from the scanners and set to bailing the water from the hole as fast as they could. Within minutes, the water level had dropped by more than half, but as they neared the bottom the bailing became harder. When there were mere inches of water covering the bottom, Rex grabbed his shovel and created a runoff hole off to the side of the main dig. The water receded into the smaller pit, revealing broken pieces of wood and more Louisiana mud.

"We need to dig a little more and see if we can uncover whatever's down here. We have to be close—the scanner had a reading at five feet, give or take a little and we're just on top of that now."

Sweat running from every pore, mosquito repellent long since washed away, and drops of rain beginning to fall, they dug as though it were the last march in a long campaign. After about four additional inches of slop had been excavated, Heinmot's shovel struck something hard. He dug around the area to reveal the dome-shaped top of a chest a foot-and-a-half wide and two feet long.

At nearly the same moment, Rex encountered a second, similar object, and they both started digging to the side, quickly finding he third chest slightly deeper than the other two. The last one was markedly larger than the other two.

"Heinmot, this is getting dangerous. We're nearly seven feet deep in a hole in the marsh. With this rain, it wouldn't take much for this whole thing to cave in and bury us along with these three boxes. Why don't you hop out and set up the tripod while I dig a little more."

"No joke. This *is* dangerous. We'll have to be better prepared next time."

The tripod was assembled between flashes of lightning and the winch skillfully attached to it. A long, wide strap was attached to the hook and lowered into the pit where Rex threaded the strap over and around the chest and signaled for Heinmot to start cranking. As the strap tightened, Rex put his weight against the box and attempted to rock it. The tripod began to creak with the pressure being applied to it, but Heinmot kept cranking on the winch to lift it as quickly as possible.

Jagged blue flames arched across the sky as the strap creaked with the weight. Soon, the chest would either come loose from the mud or the strap would snap.

"Heinmot, toss me something to use as a pry bar. There's too much suction on the chest."

Heinmot found a thick, long, branch and handed it down to him. Rex jammed the branch under the edge and as he pried up on the chest and Heinmot rocked the strap and kept cranking the winch.

A wet, sucking sound escaped from the hole as the vacuum was broken and the chest swung free. Heinmot cranked it the rest of the way out of the hole, surprised it was so light. He quickly cranked on the winch as Rex climbed out of the hole. Together, they grabbed the old coffer, lifted, and set it carefully on the ground. Both were astonished at the overall condition of the wood in the beams of their halogen headlights.

"It seems as though it were buried yesterday. Hell, even the hardware has no patina on it."

"Look here," Heinmot said, "even the outer layer's only *slightly* rotted. But we can study this back at base. We need to hurry."

The rising mosquitoes providing ample additional incentive, they repeated the process to excavate the second trunk. Just like the first, it was far too light to hold much gold. The third chest, however, was much more promising. Rex began rocking it as he had on the others, but he noticed something was amiss.

"This one feels like it weighs a *ton!* I'm not sure we can handle this one, but keep reeling, and I'll do what I can from down here."

He jammed the branch under it and pushed with all of his force. The chest barely moved, the strap groaning and stretching much more than before. Heinmot cranked on the winch as though his life depended on it, but his arms and shoulders burned to the point of a white light blinding him from within. He dared not twist the winch another click for fear it would explode and fall into the pit on top of Rex. A quick check of the tripod confirmed his thoughts. Its legs were nearly buckled and the winch bulged awkwardly. Any further pressure would result in complete failure.

"Rex, if I keep cranking, the whole thing may fall into the pit on top of you."

"If we both try down here, we can break the suction, and it'll come right out."

"Let me find another log and limb to help pry on it."

Heinmot reluctantly dropped into the pit as Rex removed more slop on each side to reduce the surface area on which the water could form a vacuum. Rex tossed the shovel to the side, then they pushed their branches further under the chest and leaned against them with all the force they had left. The suction on the bottom of the chest broke, then grabbed again.

As they applied more force, the chest rocked, but refused to break free. Rex slacked off and hit his branch with every ounce of strength he had. The veins in his neck popped. His triceps bulged. He braced against the wall of the pit and used his thick thigh muscles to increase leverage. Heinmot reciprocated and the chest lurched. Rex's branch snapped in two, and he landed face down in the mud, his shoulder slamming against the side of the chest just as it broke free and swung back, striking the side of his head. He lay still for a moment, then shook the haziness from his brain and pulled his legs under him to stand.

The rain was now pouring, lightning crackling all around them.

They had to use hand signals to communicate, it was so loud. Rex motioned for each to grab a side of the chest; together, they lifted to test the weight. Even with the help of the winch, lifting the chest from the pit was going to be nearly impossible. Even if they could, they wouldn't be able to get it back to the jet skis before daylight. Still, they had to try.

Heinmot steadied the chest so that he could grab the strap and climb out. Just as he was about to climb out, lightning flashed, and they saw a thoroughly drenched Fats Melancon, with Matt behind him, standing at the edge of the pit. Rex couldn't help but notice the shiny .45 Colt Fats had pointed right at them.

CHAPTER 10 – THE VOYAGES

STARING AT THE BARREL OF THE GUN, THE PAIR SLOWLY RAISED THEIR HANDS IN surrender. Inner rage began to build within Rex. He silently cursed, and quickly began to calculate how they could free themselves of this mess without being shot in the process. He looked at his friend with fury-induced desperation. Heinmot's eyes echoed his.

Suddenly, Fats broke out in laughter, his large belly jiggling under his soaked clothes.

"Sha," he said to Matt as he stuffed the Colt in his belt, "we got two drowned rats here."

"Mah, two rats that might need some help, I think."

"Put yo' hands down! This ain't no stick up. Me and the boys figured since you hadn't come back, something must be wrong. Dis pea shooter in my pants is for the moccasins that slither around here. And since ya'll left a trail a blind man could follow, 'twas preety easy to find you."

Rex and Heinmot laughed as they lowered their hands.

"Well in that case, it's good to see you boys! You're quite right, we are two drowned rats in need of some help. We need to haul these chests back to the jet skis before the sun comes up."

"I don't think ya'll have to worry about the sun just yet. This storm will keep it hidden for another hour past sunrise." He paused and looked around at the sky. "But we should get this show on the road, just in case."

Fats grabbed one side of the chest and Heinmot the other. With Rex pushing from below, the large chest was finally lifted and set to the side of the pit. Heinmot quickly created harnesses from the straps so the two smaller chests could be dragged by two of them and the larger chest pulled by the other two. Matt stepped into his makeshift harness and placed a strain against the load to take up the slack. Fats wrestled the straps over his bulky shoulders and around his chest. Rex and Heinmot grabbed their straps and the unlikely foursome trudged away through the mud.

As they made slow but steady headway through the blinding rain, Rex's mind was racing with dreams of what they might find in the chests. Gold? Jewels? Maybe both. Or nothing at all . . . . No matter the prize or lack thereof, he was glad he'd listened to Old Man Patterson. The adventure itself was worth the effort. A quick glance at Heinmot told him his friend was equally satisfied with their discovery. Pulling as fast and hard as possible, the group arrived at the jet skis still under the cover of the storm.

Fighting the slippery bank and the torrent of water that was draining out of the marsh back into the bay, Rex strained to hold the jet ski steady as Matt and Heinmot loaded the chests. The duo along with Fats made the loading of the large chest simple by comparison; though his silhouette hinted that he was mostly comprised of blubber, only a fool would believe that. Matt ran down the bank to grab the small boat making it ready for the trek across the bay. The pair departed and headed back to the trawler to be ready to receive Rex and Heinmot.

On the return trip, courtesy of the squall, the bay was much rougher than their entrance. Though each Kawasaki had plenty of power, their progress was slow-going as the waves threatened to capsize them and the precious cargo. Twice, despite their efforts to navigate around and through the soup, they each saved the other by gunning the jet skis in a diagonal motion to offset the physics of the agitated water. Holding the machines steady against the side of the *Gittaloadodis* proved to be an insurmountable task as the boat continuously slammed against the jet skis, threatening to smash the riders. After thirty minutes, Rex gave up and motioned to Fats to lower the winch line so they could haul the chests aboard. Within an hour, they were aboard with the chests stashed in the hold, the remaining hardware lashed down for the stormy ride back to Cameron.

Much like the vessel in another ill-fated voyage, the ship was tossed about in the sea as if some invisible hand stirred the currents deep beneath the surface. At more than one point, Rex was sure he would empty the contents of his hollow innards as waves of nausea struck him in rhythm with the churning ocean. He moved from the hold to the wheelhouse to breathe some fresh air and to add some point of reference to all of the motion. He found Heinmot and Fats gulping steaming mugs of coffee strong enough to curdle the cream.

"Sha," Fats said, "you should have a bite to eat."

Smiling, Rex waved him off.

"I'll be fine once the waves settle."

As if on cue, the sun began to break through the clouds from the west, and the rain slackened to a drizzle. Within a few minutes, the rain stopped completely. To give Rex a break, Fats moved the old trawler a little further out to sea into a patch of smoother water. Clearing from west to east, the sky above and westward was free of clouds save for a few wisps, which served as a further calming effect on man and ocean.

The full effect of the sun was evident around them as the humidity increased, reminding Rex of the old saying "If you don't like the weather in Louisiana, just wait twenty minutes, and it'll change." Ahead and to the right, he could see jetties extending from the shore where groups of fisherman tested their luck against the recently agitated water. Farther ahead, the last jetty protruded; the landing at the Pelican appeared in the distance.

Fats went about his work like the seasoned professional he was and, as expected, he dialed in on the landing in one try. Matt and Mitch were on the dock before the old scow slowed and had her fully cleated when she came to a groaning stop.

His legs firmly beneath him again, Rex let out a slow breath. "I suppose you and the boys know what we're after now."

"I wonder what's in those chests," Heinmot said, eyeing them excitedly.

"Sha, as they say, 'curiosity killed the cat,' but we've no intentions puttin' our noses where they don't belong. If and when you're ready, I expect you'll tell us what we need to know. We weren't paid to learn anything; we were paid to *forget* everything."

Smiling, Rex took a sip of a Mountain Dew. "And that, my dear captain, is exactly what you've done so far." He extended his hand to the old salt. "It's also the reason we'll be using your services exclusively from here on out—assuming you want in."

Fats slapped Heinmot hard enough on the back to make him choke on his coffee, and crushed Rex's right hand in his ham-sized fist. "It'll be our pleasure. I've grown to like the two of you boys . . . and we can't complain about the pay either."

Reaching into his pocket, he pulled out a nub of a pencil and scratched something on a tattered piece of paper. "Here's my direct phone number. Call and you'll either get me or one of the boys instead of the bar at the Pelican. Just let us know when you're ready, and we'll be there. Everything's loaded up for you."

"Thanks, Fats. We'll be back in the next few days to pick up the jet skis."

"Unless you need them right away, I can store them in the warehouse. No one'll go in there snooping around. The boys'll hose them down to remove all of the salt."

Rex reached into his pocket and handed Fats another small roll of bills and shook his hand again. "Thanks again for everything. We'll be in touch."

Rex and Heinmot climbed into the Ford and headed north toward the log cabin. As they drove, all they could talk about were the chests. Neither was sure what was inside, but they agreed the smaller chests were too light for any gold coins.

"Jewels and precious stones then?" Heinmot joked. "Hopefully, there's enough to at least finance this adventure. We've spent a fair amount already."

"Yeah, but you have to admit it's exciting either way. I'm thinking that large chest has something in it—rocks, cannon balls, or lead, *hopefully* gold . . . there's definitely something heavy."

"I'm thinking we should have your dad in on the cracking of the seals."

"I was thinking of adding another person to the mix—Old Man Patterson. If not for his 'confession' we wouldn't have these three chests in the first place."

"Let's swing by and pick him up on the way."

"I've got a better idea. Let's pick up Dad, some more beer, and cracklins and head over to his place. His place is secluded enough to not worry about prying eyes."

Rex parked the truck near the high-pressure water pumps on the side of Johann's shop to flush the mud from the chests. Johann and Gabrielle were out back under the massive live oak tree cleaning up some branches that had fallen in the storm.

"What's under the tarps, boys?" Gabrielle asked as they approached. "I doubt you've got a marlin or red fish under there . . . though I thought you two went deep sea fishing last night."

Rex motioned for Heinmot to grab a corner of the tarp and pull it back to the tailgate. Both mother and father gasped.

"After chatting with Old Man . . . with Mr. Patterson, we contracted a charter boat and its captain to bring us near Vermilion Bay and dug this up."

He and Heinmot spent the next thirty minutes laying out their tale in every detail.

"I think it only fair that we open this in the presence of Mr. Patterson," Rex concluded. "After all, if it hadn't been for him, we'd be empty-handed right now."

"And still tromping around in a mosquito-infested marsh," Heinmot laughed.

"Too right! Dad, are you game to ride over with us?"

"Let's do it! It'll be good to see Eamon again. But I think your

Mom won't let you two hear the end of it if you don't have one of her sandwiches to tide you over."

The pair washed their hands, wolfed down the two hero sandwiches, then headed toward the Cajun Café to pick up the obligatory boudain and beer for the old swamp tenant. On the drive, Heinmot noted the road seemed rougher than before, though he wasn't sure how that was possible. The break in the road was wider as well, and most of the underbrush appeared to be trodden as if a large piece of equipment had been dragged up and down the edges. The trio navigated the rough surface, dodging the ever-widening holes to stop at the edge of the clearing as they had on the last visit. Rex looked around suspiciously. Though he couldn't quite put his finger on it, he was certain something was different.

Johann wasted no time in strolling up to the door and rapping sharply on the rough edge of the doorframe with no result. A second knock yielded the same. No answer. He tried a third time and was all set to give up when he heard movement inside the old cabin, and the weathered door creaked and slowly opened to reveal Eamon Patterson holding a steaming mug of coffee and balancing himself with his cane. He propped it against the door and shielded his eyes from the morning sun. As his vision focused, its tone changed from one of apprehension to that of charity.

"Johann, my friend, it's good to see you!" he nearly shouted.

"Eamon, indeed, my old friend. I see Mrs. Aldridge is keeping things in order around here?"

"I *knew* you'd put her up to coming out and cleaning up my place. I wouldn't let her know, but I'm glad to have someone to talk to every now and then." He looked past Johann to see Rex and Heinmot waiting with more food and beer. "What are the three of you doing out here so early in the morning?"

"The boys have something to show you. They took a ride into the swamp last night and made a discovery they think might interest you."

The old man's eyes widened as he found a burst of energy he hadn't possessed in decades. He motioned to the trio to have a seat on the dusty porch then walked without the assistance of his cane to his rocking chair. He sat and wrapped an old quilt around him to shield against the misty morning air.

For the next thirty minutes, the explorers detailed the events of the previous night, pausing at times to clarify certain events or to answer questions the old hermit posed. They concluded by revealing the package of food and beer, which the old man swatted away, thereby making it apparent that he wanted to continue the conversation.

"Well sir, that brings us to the here and now and the three chests in the back of the truck. We've been waiting with bated breath to see what's inside. Shall we open them?"

"Son, I've been waiting about forty years to see what might be in there. Open away!"

"Which shall we open first?" Heinmot asked.

"Sonny, they say that big things come in small packages, so why don't you open them in order of size, from smallest to largest. Only the three chests?"

Rex nodded.

"See. Always in groups of three."

Heinmot held the first chest as best he could while Rex worked a small pry bar into the gap between the lid and base near the locking mechanism. Rex was amazed to find how solid the fit was despite its apparent age. He twisted the bar as he wiggled it in, and the old wood began to surrender. Shoving down as hard as he could, the lid sprang open and the stench of decades old rotting mud slammed into their noses. The pair nearly retched from the stink, stumbling back for fresh air.

Regaining their composure, they found no gold or jewels in the box; instead, something that resembled globs of mud sat at the bottom of the chest encased in rags. Heinmot began lifting the small bundles from the box with a pair of tongs, and placed them in order along the edge of the bed sheet they'd spread across the ground. Rex quickly filled a bucket with clean water and submerged the bundles to remove the mud, revealing wax-covered globs. He continued the process until the globs were clean, but had to change the bucket water three times. He then brought them up to the porch so Johann and Eamon could witness the actual opening.

Rex scraped at the wax with his pocketknife until he found the internal edge and then opened it. He heard the old man gasp as the wax was fully removed to expose old parchment paper that was completely dry. Within twenty minutes, all of the globs were opened, all with the same contents inside. There were a total of thirty-three pieces of parchment. Rex unfolded each page and stacked them in order on a small table near the old hermit.

They repeated the same process for the next, second-largest chest. Aside from the familiar smell that emanated from within, it also contained the same globs of mud, though far fewer of them. Rex noticed this box was lined with purple felt that had faded from the royal color to a lavender hue. They unpacked all three and each contained the same old parchment but with vastly different handwriting.

"Well guys," Johann said, "no gold or jewels, but these papers might contain something of value. I'm skeptical though. They seem to be letters that were never delivered . . . at least that's what appears to be in the first stack."

"It's the third chest that has my attention," Rex said. "It nearly broke our backs, it's so heavy."

Johann helped the two boys position the chest so the two latches could be leveraged. This chest was far heavier than the first two combined, and the hardware on the latches was indicative of those used to protect something of value. Heinmot attacked the first one with a vengeance, releasing the latch fairly easily. The second buckle, however, defeated every trick that he tried. It appeared to be welded to the chest. Rex did not want to destroy the old chest, but with every minute that passed, he drew closer to taking a hammer to it.

In a last-ditch effort, he hammered the crowbar into the latch, and, with some hearty prying, the old metal finally gave way. The latch popped off so suddenly it flung Rex forward, onto the chest. His belt caught on the edge of the lid and lifted open when he hit the ground.

Rex got quickly to his feet, but not before he heard the gasps of his companions. He leaned over the lid to peer inside, expecting a bright pile of gold. Instead, more of the same: nothing but globs of muddy parchment like the first two cases. *Why the* hell, Rex thought, *would a band of pirates go through all the trouble to bury a bunch of letters? It simply didn't make any sense.*

Instead of taking each goo-covered blob from the chest and washing it individually, he elected to refill the bucket with clean water and pour it over the mud. The mud washed away to reveal wax nearly the same color as the mud, but there were no individual packets. This wax fully encased the opening of the chest.

"I think we bombed out completely," he said to Heinmot. But maybe there's something under this wax.

"I got this," Heinmot said, unsheathing his knife to trace the wax against the inside opening until he had cut through on all four sides. He worked the blade under the closest edge and lifted out an inch-thick slab of wax. "Pahana!" he cried, "We've done it!"

Rex let out a sharp whistle when he saw what his friend had uncovered. There, sitting in the chest surrounded by wax on all sides, looking as new as the day they were stored inside, was a mound of shiny gold coins. By his guess, there were thousands of them—perhaps tens of thousands, and all of them appeared to be the same denomination.

Slapping Heinmot on the back, Rex cried, "We've have done it! Dad, Mr. Patterson! We've found Lafitte's treasure!"

The old trapper got down on his knees and ran his fingers through the coins.

Johann let out a sharp whistle. "Boys . . . I can't believe it. Wait until your mother sees this! Call Arieanna and Sebastien. We have to let your parents know too, Heinmot!"

Rex scooped up a handful of coins and began to examine them closely. He could barely contain his excitement. His heart literally skipped a beat when he saw how familiar they were: a bust of Napoleon on one side and a circle of olive branches on the other, both with raised dots on the perimeter. The same inscriptions were there just as he saw on the other two coins and they were all forty francs in value. The dates on the coins were the same too—'AN 13. .A.'. The last and most important identifier was there as well: the prominent "JL".

He looked up to see tears running down the old man's wrinkled cheeks. Rex fought for words to say, but the old man simply shook Rex's hand, slowly and firmly. He turned to Heinmot and Johann the same.

Rex helped Old Man Patterson back to his rocking chair, where he took a sip of cold coffee. Rex handed him a beer. After a sip or two, he finally spoke.

"Gentlemen, I've been searching for that gold nearly all my life. I've lost one of my sons in the search, I've seen friends go bankrupt and mad in the quest . . . I've nearly gone mad myself. I had all but given up on the legend. I can't begin to express my appreciation for all you've done for me through the years Johann. And now this."

Johann started to speak, but the old man went on.

"There was a time when people treated me and my kin like some kind of walking plaque—avoiding us, disparaging us, going out of their way to mistreat us. You changed all of that Johann. I am forever grateful.

"Rex, when you and Heinmot first came here, I didn't think you had a chance. I never trusted the feller that gave me the information about those chests, but I figured that was all I could tell you. This is a lifelong dream come true."

Patterson bent into coughing fit. After a few moments, it quelled. He looked up at Rex again.

"Shall we count 'em up? I *have* to know how many coins are in that chest."

Rex and Heinmot proceeded to count the coins, placing them in stacks of ten, starting near Patterson's feet and crisscrossing the porch until they completed their task nearly three hours later. Rex took the time to count out the last five one by one.

"24,995, 24,996, 24,997, 24,998, 24,999! Twenty-four thousand, nine hundred, and ninety-nine coins?"

Everyone marveled at the number for a moment.

"Wait," Heinmot said. "Why not an even twenty-five thousand?"

"Is one stuck in the wax in the chest? Seems it should be an even million francs."

"Twenty-five thousand isn't divisible by three is it?" asked Patterson. "I'd bet the farm I'm right."

"Indeed, you are Eamon," Johann said, nodding. "24,999 divided by three is 8,333. Three 3s. It's almost too perfect!"

"Seeing something like this breathes new life into this old heart," the old man said. "But you know there's more out there . . ."

"Of course!" Heinmot said. "This isn't all of them. There are 225,001 coins remaining!"

"And these coins aren't part of the original stash, either," Rex added.

"Not part of the original stash? How can you be so sure?" Johann asked.

"Because, my dear Johann," the old man quipped, "there's no way a bass fish could swim from Vermilion Bay to the burned-out bridge, and there's not a continuous portion of fresh water."

"Remember, dad, my bass was the first and was caught at the burned out bridge and the second was a redfish caught near High Island? To me, this means the original stash is somewhere near fresh *and* salt water. Maybe brackish water somewhere?"

"The original stash has to be somewhere between the burned-out bridge and High Island."

"OK, I'm convinced. But what to do with this batch?" Johann asked.

"I think there's only one thing to do with it. Heinmot?" Rex said.

"Absolutely. Mr. Patterson, these coins are for you. I'm sure Mr. Rhineheart can sell them and put the money into an account for you."

The old man started to protest, but Rex interrupted.

"Nonsense. Had it not been for your information we wouldn't have found them in the first place. The only thing that I'd like to keep are the letters so that I can study and catalog them. Perhaps, there are some clues hidden within."

"Of course! Please keep the letters. I don't know what else to say," the old man quietly said. "The whole Rhineheart clan has been so good to me through the years." He quickly added in a near shout, "BUT, we'll split the money three ways—I insist!"

"I think I speak on behalf of everyone when I say—thank you and that you're more than welcome. Hopefully, in some small way, this makes up for your losses through the years spent searching for it," Rex said.

"Do you have something to put the coins in?" Heinmot asked. It'll need to hold a few pounds," he added with a laugh.

They spent the next hour storing the coins in an iron lockbox the old man had in a storage shed in the back of the house. Then Rex and Heinmot gathered the empty chests, the letters, the tools and their part of the coins. After placing all of it in the back of the truck, and they said their farewells.

As the Ford bounced down the road towards the Rhineheart homestead, Rex had a feeling of foreboding he just couldn't shake. Something told him they'd just visited Eamon Patterson for the last time. But at the same time, he knew that he and Heinmot had just made it big. Not sure how big, but he was certain that Johann would find a buyer for the coins.

CHAPTER 11 – THE CURIOSITY SHOP

FOR THE NEXT FEW MONTHS, REX AND HEINMOT SPENT ALL OF THEIR FREE TIME studying the old parchment letters in the hope that something would lead them to the remainder of the treasure. Johann found a buyer in the UK for Eamon's coins, or, rather, the buyer found Johann after reading an article detailing the treasure find in a prominent newspaper. The buyer didn't flinch at the initial offer of $1,300 per coin and the unlikely trio made a little over 10 million dollars each on the sale. Johann had to admit his surprise and delight at the figures, but the buyer's overall demanding demeanor was an absolute turn-off. He vowed never to do business with him in the future. They could always find another buyer, even if for a little less money.

The adventurers were in awe and had been making general plans about what they would do with their share of the money. Of course, they would be upgrading their lifestyles to a certain degree and both parents would benefit from the windfall. The partnership would be officially formalized, and they agreed a foundation was likely the way to proceed. Deep down, Rex knew they had just found their new way of life, and there could be worse ways to spend one's days than treasure hunting.

Rex hoped something in the letters would point them to another clue, but no magic bullets appeared. They determined the letters were written by three different people: 'JL,' who Rex assumed to be

Jean Lafitte, Antoine Meriwether, who was the first mate of a ship named the *Bienville*, and the cook of the *Bienville*, Francois "Cookie" Fontenot.

Each author had his own style of writing, and wrote about their separate lives, though there was some overlap. Typically, 'JL' talked about the last port of call or the future voyages of the *Bienville,* but they couldn't ascertain for whom his letters were intended. There was never a subject and the only names mentioned appeared to be part of the crew. Lafitte's letters were the most mysterious, but Rex did discover that the pirate loved curios of all types. From music boxes to figurines to collections of sea charts, he collected all sorts of things. He was a no-nonsense captain who ruled his ship with an iron fist. He tolerated zero disobedience but was extremely fair in all of his decisions, and was a true swashbuckler at heart.

Meriwether, or 'Tone as he was known onboard the ship, wrote of his feelings about a woman named Karena and how much he missed and loved her. He also described some of the places the ship visited in great detail. He seemed to add a portion of the ship's log in each of the letters; from this, Heinmot and Rex loosely pieced together a few of the voyages, but there were many gaps. It was impossible to know much about the ship's history with any accuracy.

Cookie's letters were the most surprising, for they were all addressed to his mother. Neither of the pair could tell if she was actually alive at the time he penned them; based on the way they were written, it could have gone either way. Rex could tell that Cookie had quite a repertoire when it came to cooking, and that he could make tasty dishes from most anything. The captain gave him more latitude than many of the other sailors simply because he kept the bulk of them so satisfactorily and well fed.

But, alas, save for placing them in chronological order and learning some traits about the three men, there wasn't much else contained within them. No secret codes, no directions, no map; in fact, simply *nothing* of useful value.

Heinmot decided that he would take a break from the adventure and go spend some time in Galveston. He needled Rex into going, but Rex decided to stay a while longer and help Johann with some projects around the house. Gabrielle had departed a few days earlier to spend Mardi Gras with Arieanna, leaving Rex and Johann alone in the house.

The eldest pair of the males in the Rhineheart family spent the better part of a week cleaning the property line, removing remnants of the old oak tree that had fallen so many years ago, and doing general repairs to the house and shop.

The last task the duo performed was upgrading part of Johann's shortwave radio. There were several vacuum tubes that had to be replaced along with the main power supply. Once that was done, Rex installed an additional forty feet of antenna stand. The built-in jack system Johann had developed was pure genius; it took him about a half day to complete a task that should have taken most of the week. Johann had a number of people he conversed with around the world. He would receive weather reports from Australia, food recipes from India, stock market tips from Japan, and just chat with friends in Britain. The favorite part of his day, though, was between midnight and one in the morning, which was between eight and nine in the morning in Tanzania.

Sebastien had taken a job as a zoologist in a nature preserve in Tanzania, and though Johann would never admit it to any of his children, he missed each of them when they were away from the homestead. The Katawani Preserve would have been a handful for a seasoned zoologist; it was nearly *impossible* for a greenhorn like Sebastien. Though his younger brother always had to prove himself to everyone and everything, Rex thought he was far in over his head at this point. Johann maintaining a near daily presence with him pleased Rex to a large degree, for although he would never admit it, he deeply loved his brother and would never want him to fail.

A typical conversation would start with Sebastien asking Johann about British trucks and other mechanical tips on the various maladies he'd encountered on the African preserve. Johann always had good advice for him, and Rex was certain that he was following the advice to the letter. The larger problem seemed to be whether or not

Sebastien's employees could interpret and execute the advice. Rex knew he was struggling with the administrative part of the business, much less having to deal with the animals. Sebastien extended an invitation to his brother to visit the preserve. Johann thought that would be a great idea and would do the both of them a world of good. Rex agreed that he should head over at some point in the near future and knew that he would share some of his good fortune with Sebastien and his passions.

Sensing the irritation in his oldest son over breakfast the next morning, Johann loosely asked Rex what his plans were moving forward. It had been an arduous week. Johann could tell that not knowing where to turn next was a huge source of Rex's frustration.

"You know, Dad, I don't have a way forward yet. I've gone through the letters over and over and haven't found anything. I'm more than a little frustrated, though I know that I shouldn't be—hell, we just struck it rich, but you know how I hate an unsolved mystery. I guess Heinmot sensed it and just headed out to give me some space. I need to give him a ring, but the wind's been knocked out of my sails."

"You know, you shouldn't fall into the same trap that Eamon and all of the people that he talked about have over the years. The remainder of treasure that may or may not be out there might never be found. You mustn't blame yourself for that. It's just one of those things."

"I know, but I can't help but think it's just around the corner, and all I have to do is reach out and grab it."

"You just described a recipe for heartache and disappointment. Have a look at Eamon and the way he reacted to the gold. I think Heinmot had the right idea. You should take a break. I'm not suggesting that you run off to Africa, but maybe something a little closer might be good for you."

"What did you have in mind?"

"Why don't you head over to New Orleans and have a good time with Arieanna? I'm sure some Cajun food and Mardi Gras would relieve some stress."

"True . . . but I'd also have to survive Arieanna's shopping sprees . . ."

For a February afternoon, the drive to New Orleans was remarkably clear. It was too cold to remove the targa top, but he did swap the Corvette's painted roof for the clear one, and loaded up some Eric Clapton tunes.

Although Mardi Gras and visiting his sister should have put him in a good mood, Rex still felt frustrated and sullen when Arieanna answered her hotel door with eyeliner in one hand and a compact mirror in the other. *Girls,* Rex thought, *in a perpetual state of applying.* At twenty-six, she'd done well for herself, following the lead of their father in the sciences. She was always the math whiz in school, so physics was a perfect fit for her. She had helped Rex more than a few times with complicated equations in class, despite her being four years his junior.

"Why, Rexy, you're looking fit!"

"Why, Arieanna, you're still putting on makeup!"

"Now, Rex, why the sour mood? We're going to have a great time today—I have a festival, shopping, and dinner all scheduled for the four of us."

"The *four* of us?" Rex quizzically posed. He hoped she hadn't set him up on some sort of date as she had so many times in the past.

"Yes, the four of us. I have a surprise for you, dear brother."

"Another blind date?"

"No, silly. It's better than that!"

Rex was about to dive deeper into the topic when Gabrielle and Sebastien poked their heads around the corner.

"Mom! Sebastien!" he nearly shouted. "What are you doing here?"

Gabrielle laughed, pulling him close to hug and kiss him on the cheek. "Rex, you should know I wouldn't miss a chance to see my oldest son, and your dad thought it would be a good surprise."

"Well, don't just stand there gawking," Sebastien said. "Give your little brother a hug."

Rex quickly hugged his mother and his brother—thrilled to see both of them—then turned to Arieanna. "For once I agree with you. This *is* a good surprise!"

"About time!" Arieanna teased. "I didn't think we'd ever see a smile on that sourpuss of yours again."

"Yeah, but Mom always hugged the pouter first," ribbed Sebastien. "He could do no wrong in her eyes."

"Ha! That's because you always messed up worse than me."

"No matter," Gabrielle laughed. "It's good to have all of my children together."

"Unfortunately, it'll be shorter than I'd like—I have to meet with Dad a little later to discuss some of our findings with the animals," Sebastien said.

"I think breakfast at *Cafe Du Monde* is in order. Rex can't pass up beignets and chocolate milk."

Breakfast was amazing. The foursome relived the good times they had shared as a family. Indeed, the Crescent City had been a wayward home and when Galveston was added into the count, there was a proper mixture of old and new world to suit the tastes of all things Rhineheart. Although Rex could tell at times the lack of German culture in some of the family outings left Johann a bit forlorn, he enjoyed the flair of the French nonetheless. After a long breakfast, Sebastien headed west towards home and his research, leaving Rex to the agony of shopping with his mother and sister.

Uncharacteristically, he did not keep his word, and as the day wore on, Rex's mood became even dourer. He began to wonder just how many of these French Quarter shops they could slip in and out of in a single day. While she had bought a few things, he knew Arieanna enjoyed the *act* of shopping more so than actually buying anything.

They meandered down Royal Street toward Jackson Square, where Rex hoped they would stop for a break and he could find something to slake his thirst. He raised an eyebrow when the trio strolled past Pirate Alley, which made a direct path to the square. Chattering about some trinket or other, the pair was nearly oblivious to their surroundings. He stood fast at the intersection of Royal and Pere Meriwether Alley and cleared his throat. They pivoted on their heels and started up the alley. They were just steps away from Chartres Street and a cold mug of beer when Arieanna noticed a sign hanging above them.

The sign was shaped like a fleur-de-lis, and contained a black background along with the obligatory yellow, green, and purple hues most commonly associated with the infamous New Orleans holiday. The marquee for the *Magasin de Mystère* hung at an odd angle; its weight had long overcome the ability of the anchors to support it.

Upon Arieanna's insistence, Gabrielle's curiosity, and Rex's capitulation, the trio entered the shop in order of ascending age. The ancient boutique held a distinct aura with the smell of old wood, books, and pipe tobacco not unlike Johann's. Spotting some harlequin dolls and masks, the two women left Rex to fend for himself near a shelf stuffed full of dusty knickknacks.

Though he was probably there the whole time, the shopkeeper appeared to Rex's right like an apparition from the fog. He held out a hand, inviting him to peruse the contents of the store. Quite certain there would be nothing of interest to see, Rex indulged him by pretending to look over a few books. As he was flipping absentmindedly through the pages of an old book on home remedies, a small music box caught his eye on a shelf close to where the old man was standing.

The shopkeep's gray eyes sparkled as Rex carefully removed the curio from its resting place.

Intricate scrollwork ran along the square, golden base, upon which an egg was affixed. A fleur-de-lis was carved on either side of the base, and, what appeared to be diamonds circumnavigated the body. The tiny door at the center of the egg was adorned with a much larger symbol of the iris, and the glossy, garnet-red bauble contrasted magnificently with the gold trim. A small golden crown capstoned the ornament. It was beautiful, but of no particular interest to Rex until a detail on the bottom of the base caught his eye. He looked closer.

His heart skipped a beat. It was hard to tell, but it appeared to be engraved with the initials 'JL.'

He refocused his eyes and brought the egg within a hair's width of his face. Yes, the letters inscribed there were certainly a J and an L, but the year carved next to it, 1841, couldn't be right. Lafitte left the mortal world in the winter of 1823. Perhaps it should read 1821, he thought.

After a final going over from top to bottom, Rex carefully returned the music box to the shelf under the wistful gaze of the old shopkeeper and turned with Arieanna and Gabrielle for the door.

"Leaving without your prize, sha?"

"I beg your pardon?"

"We both know that you must have that bauble," the old man said with a knowing smile. "It possesses some historical significance to you, yes?"

"Oh, it's a nice piece, but I'm certain it's out of my price range." In actuality, Rex was certain he *could* afford the music box, but didn't want to show his hand.

"Mon ami," the man said, laughing as if he could read Rex's mind, "we both know that leaving without it would leave you wanting it all the more."

Definitely confused by the man's ability to practically see into his soul, Rex simply repeated, "Oh, it's a nice piece, but I'm certain it's out of my price range."

Laughing, the proprietor further demonstrated his mysterious powers. "Now, we both know it currently holds your full interest and to depart without it would leave you wanting in more ways than one. That egg has sat in the same space, untouched, since I placed it there some thirty-seven years ago. Its destiny will be fulfilled when you walk out with it, and we both know you will."

Returning the grin, but not wishing to show his hand, Rex simply said, "Well, that will all depend on how much you are asking for it."

With a flat stare that apparently read the contents of his mind and wallet, the old man said, "I'll take a hundred and seventeen dollars for it and not a penny more."

"Not a penny more? Usually it's not a penny less?"

Laughter danced in the old man's eyes as he securely wrapped the egg in old newspaper and placed it in a small wooden box.

Rex counted out six twenty-dollar bills, all the money he had and set it on the counter. "Well, I guess you may as well make it an even one-hundred and twenty since that's exactly what I have."

"Nonsense," came the reply as counted out the change. "One, two, and three dollars makes one hundred twenty. Now you have the music box *and* just enough cash left for that frosty brew you've been pining for."

"Well sir," Rex said, shaking his hand, "I have no idea how you're so tuned into my thoughts, but I've been tasting a cold beer now for the last two hours."

He turned and exited the shop, thoughts floating in his head of how its shopkeeper possessed such powers. He had heard tales of people with psychic abilities who lived deep in the swamps, but, until today, he never expected to meet one of them. With a final glance back at the tilted sign, he rounded the corner to find Gabrielle and Arieanna waiting impatiently for him near the trolley.

CHAPTER 12 – THE CIPHER

AFTER A BRIEF STOP IN JACKSON'S SQUARE TO FINALLY PARTAKE IN A COLD BEER, THE remainder of the day was uneventful. However, it still found the two female members of the clan purchasing additional trinkets and the latest fashions to the point where Rex could not carry anything more.

Rex wrestled the bags up the steps to Arieanna's apartment, setting them, with a heavy sigh, on the floor of the small living room. Looking around the cramped room, he realized that despite the age-old differences between the male and female genders, he and Arieanna were not so different, particularly in their penchant for collecting odds and ends. Small harlequin figurines and masquerade masks were positioned in various places around the space. Old movie posters were affixed to the walls at varying angles to simulate an old French Quarter movie-house parlor. He had to admit the room held a certain atmosphere that was both inviting and somewhat mysterious.

Wading through the bags to make his way over to the glass dining table, he turned on the small chandelier to closely examine the trinket he'd purchased. Again, he saw the initials engraved with a precise flair and wondered if the 'JL' on the music box was indeed his quarry. The music box had the obligatory hole in the bottom where the square rod could be found to attach the key, which he saw the old man had packed along with the box.

The tag on the key had some text scribbled on it from an unsteady hand, which he assumed to be the old man's handwriting:

Acquired March 30, 1964 from Marie Comeaux, Larose, La.
Music box full of mud, may not work.

Arieanna appeared in the room again wearing a short blue-and-green dress that gathered and fanned out just beneath her knees. She called out for Gabrielle for her opinion. She looked at Rex as if to ask for his, as well. Walking out of the kitchen and wiping the flour from her hands onto her apron, their mother smiled warmly. "Oh, Arieanna, it looks so *nice* on you. What do you think, Rex?"

Rex gave his normal smirk of approval. "It looks the same as when she tried it on in the dress shop."

"Men are all the same," quipped Gabrielle. "Spin so that I can see how it fans out and—"

"No!" Rex cried out, but his warning was a half second too late. Arieanna spun quickly in a tight circle. Centrifugal force caused the dress to blossom out in a wide circle, catching the music box with the full force of the turn, slamming the music box against the wall.

Bouncing from the wall, it careened in a diagonal arc, seemingly picking up speed on the way to crashing against the ceramic tile floor. Everyone watched helplessly as dozens of pieces of crimson-colored glass mixed with bits of golden metal rocketed away from the point of impact. One of the tiles developed a long crack across it as the musical apparatus did not shatter, but acted as a small chipping hammer on the face of the floor. As the glass atomized at the point of impact, something dark slid away along with the cylinder and winding mechanism.

Though it took mere seconds from the instant of impact with the dress to the point where the box was destroyed, seconds seemed to drag into minutes. Rex, now thoroughly aggravated with Arieanna, merely sat there with a deep frown on his face.

"Rex," Arieanna said, "I'm *so* sorry—I never meant to break it. If I had known . . ."

Rex merely held up a hand.

"Arieanna, one thing is certain, with you it is never a dull moment. I can only imagine what your boyfriends must have to endure."

"Rex, I'll pay you for the trinket," Gabrielle interjected. "How much was it?"

"It's no big deal, Mom, the cost doesn't matter. I would've enjoyed examining it for another minute, though. I think it might have been another clue."

"Arieanna, don't just sit there. Come in here and help me clean this mess!" Gabrielle scolded.

Arieanna grabbed a broom and started sweeping as Gabrielle found a bag and a dustpan to gather the pieces of the now-ruined music box. On the last swish of the broom, she reached as far under the edge of the refrigerator as possible, and along with the mud-encrusted music mechanism, a small, square object equally caked in mud slid out from beneath.

"Let me see that," Rex snapped before she tossed the remains into the trash.

"What is it?" Gabrielle asked.

"Not sure. Give me a few paper towels and let's see if we can figure it out."

Rex carefully studied the glob of dirt to find it measured approximately two inches by three inches, and was about one inch thick. He cracked the dried dirt and, in short order, managed to remove the outer wrapping to find a wax-encased inner section. He tried in vain to scrape the wax away with a knife, but grew concerned that he would cut the object contained within.

"I wish Heinmot was here—he's a master with this kind of stuff. He would know how to remove the wax without destroying it at the same time."

"Allow me, dear brother; it's the least that I can do."

He started to protest, but then decided to see what she was going to do. In a blink of an eye, she returned to the room with a blow dryer in tow.

"Ah, I see the physicist coming out in you. Good idea—that *might* actually work," he teased.

She started the blow dryer on low and, within a few minutes there were two apparent changes—the wax slowly began to melt and a stench of sulfur started to fill the room.

"What is that smell?" Gabrielle gasped. "It smells like rotten eggs."

"Arieanna! Stop! Open some windows!" Rex shouted. "Everyone out onto the terrace!"

He threw open the sliding door and ushered them out onto the small portico.

"Everyone breathe deeply—in and out. I'll explain in a minute." For several minutes, the trio stood repeating the motions that a diver must undergo before donning his or her equipment for a deep dive.

"We were releasing hydrogen sulfide in there," he said. "The heat of the dryer melting the wax likely opened pockets of trapped hydrogen sulfide created by bacteria. Although this thing appears to be solid, there was enough mud and gunk on the outside that it is plausible. I experienced whiffs of this almost daily at the refinery, so I suppose I'm sensitive to that odor. We need to continue removing the wax out here, and use a fan to push the smell further away from us."

They regrouped outside with proper ventilation to remove the next layer in proverbial onion-like fashion, layer upon layer. Rex was tempted to hurry the process along, but decided to wait and allow the progression to proceed at the appropriate pace. He had to admit to himself that his heart was beating much faster than he expected; in fact, he was more thrilled at the prospect of the contents of this find than he had been of the chests that he and Heinmot unearthed.

After a few more passes with the dryer, the final part opened like a budding flower—opening from the center to the perimeter to reveal a beefy skeleton key and another, small wax-encased piece of paper. The head of the key had a hexagon shape with three diamond-openings inside—one diamond-shaped opening rested above the other two with a small fleur-de-lis symbol on the top.

So, there it was again: a group of three.

The bottom of the key was the normal overall square shape, but when the head was held in the left hand and the square pointing down, the shape was unique. He noted it resembled two "E" letters, but back to back and only attached at the top of the "E." There was a long notch cut through the common part where the backs of the letters joined with a small horizontal cut between them. When viewed from left to right, it formed a backward facing "E," and crucifix shape, and then a forward facing "E." The key was quite unique. He'd never seen anything like it.

Arieanna and Gabrielle each let out a gasp of amazement as he set the key on the table for them to observe. He then turned his attention to the wax-encapsulated object that remained inside the outer shell. After carefully removing it, he used the dryer to melt the wax covering, revealing one final piece of paper. With the skill of a surgeon, he carefully unfolded it to reveal text formed with a rich handwriting that resembled calligraphy:

Step smartly and rifle stealthily through not the last but instead the first,
For ye to discover the last of the first who fell from the jack of yellow,
Thrice around and then off to the left else ye'll visit Paris the Cursed,
Look high, but remain reverent so that ye finally see the resting fellow,
It seems safest at noon, but seek ye instead when the moon will burst,
Dast be vigilant for water on rise, and then ye'll find the circles of yellow.

It was signed with the initials 'JL' and dated August 20, 1841.

Gabrielle and Arieanna stood there completely speechless.

Rex let out a deep sigh and sat back in the chair, closing his eyes to take it all in. He felt the pent-up frustration slowly leave his body from head to toe and allowed himself a moment to revel in the discovery. While he was not a believer of fate, he paused to question how this could have simply fallen into his lap. In fact, he felt as though he had been guided—nay, *manipulated*—by some unseen, unknown force to discover the old curiosity shop.

He collected his thoughts and his posture. "I need to call Heinmot. He is *definitely* going to love this! It seems my sails have fresh wind, and we have a new mystery to solve! I think he's in Galveston at the Hotel Galvez."

Rex wasted no time in packing his few things, saying his good-byes, and heading toward Texas. He considered exiting the highway to visit a few minutes with Johann, but decided he should press on toward his destination. The Corvette made good time, and rolled up onto the Bolivar Ferry at half-past eleven. He knocked on Heinmot's door about ninety minutes later.

The door opened to reveal a slightly disheveled Heinmot. "Pahana! What're you doing here!?"

"Mon ami, it's a long story, but for the price of a cold one, I'll share it with you."

"Well, come on in, the mini-bar is fully stocked with the usual suspects. I can tell you've been up to something."

Rex laid out his adventure from the beginning, and closed it by showing him the key and the inscription on the parchment.

"Well my friend, it appears that we have a riddle to decode, but I think it'll have to wait for morning—I'm bushed and you appear to be as well."

"Yeah, Arieanna nearly walked me to death today with her shopping tour-de-force. That couch is looking pretty comfy right now—I'll see you in the morning."

That morning, they inspected the parchment together over coffee and Rex's obligatory Mountain Dew. Slowly, Heinmot read the text aloud:

"Step smartly and rifle stealthily through not the last but instead the first,
For ye to discover the last of the first who fell from the jack of yellow,
Thrice around and then off to the left else ye'll visit Paris the Cursed,
Look high, but remain reverent so that ye finally see the resting fellow,
It seems safest at noon, but seek ye instead when the moon will burst,
Dast be vigilant for water on rise, and then ye'll find the circles of yellow".

"Well, what do you think? It would seem prudent to break it apart and into sections, thereby solving it in a structured way."

Heinmot chuckled, scratching his thin beard with his thumb and index finger. "Well, it's never that easy, my dear Dr. Watson. You know that pirates—if that's who wrote this—rarely did anything in a structured way, so I think we'll have to improvise. Let's start with 'Paris the Cursed.' That sounds like a person to me, not the city, though I hear some tell that grand old Paris is indeed 'cursed'. Agree?"

"Indeed. We should head over to the library and see if they have a computer. Otherwise we'll be looking through books for the rest of our lives."

"You know who would be great at this?"

Rex tilted an eyebrow, but when he didn't offer anything.

"Why Sebastien, of course. He used to spend days researching tidbits of this and that for his papers."

"Sebastien! Yes, indeed, he would be, but I suppose he probably headed back to New Orleans and he's sleeping late, along with Arieanna and Mom. I'm not gonna wake him. Looks like it's you and me, Dr. Iiniwa."

Ten minutes later, the pair arrived at the Galveston County library and started the arduous process of decoding the riddle. They started with 'Paris the Cursed' and found nothing relating to a place named as such or any person named Paris who would have lived in the mid-1800s. Rex put the reference materials to the side for that subject, and focused on 'the jack of yellow'. In short order, Google informed them the term was not a person, but instead an illness. Jack of yellow was a slang term for yellow jack or malaria.

"So, who lived in the mid-1800s, knew Jean Lafitte, and died of malaria?"

"Are we playing *Jeopardy,* Heinmot? If so, could you ask an easier question?"

Heinmot continued to flip through the pages of the books and Rex followed suit. After perusing no fewer than five books each, neither had a further direction or clue from which to go. Heinmot suddenly said, "Let me see the parchment again."

Rex pulled the Ziploc bag containing the old paper from the protection of his padded portfolio and handed it over. Heinmot studied the text, going over it several times and then glanced up with an 'I might know something' look on his face, but said nothing.

Creating a small disturbance with his outburst, Rex practically shouted, "Well!?"

In response to the many 'shushes,' Heinmot quietly said, "When you read the text through a few times, don't you get the feeling that this is describing a cemetery?"

"Pray tell, how do you come to that conclusion?"

"Well, see here it says, 'For ye to discover the last of the first who fell from the jack of yellow.' We know what 'jack of yellow' is, so where would you find someone who died from malaria in the mid-1800s?"

"OK, that follows. He or she would likely either be in a cemetery or an urn on someone's parlor room mantle."

"Right, so what would 'Step smartly and rifle stealthily through not the last but instead the first' suggest? A cemetery, wouldn't you say?"

Perking up in spirit, Rex replied, "Yes, it would, and we don't have to worry about many of them."

"Really? There must be thousands of them between here and New Orleans and—"

Rex cut him off by saying, "It's only New Orleans that we need to worry about. At least, I believe that's true since the music box was in a curio shop there and it was recovered from a swamp near the same area."

"I'm not so sure. Why wouldn't it be somewhere else? I could buy that it's in New Orleans, but this seems to be coming together a little too easily."

Frowning, Rex said, "You're right, of course, but let's continue to see if we can narrow it down to the least common denominator. We don't need to find just *any* cemetery; we need to find one that could flood with the tide. Remember this part 'Dast be vigilant for water on rise'? I'm guessing this refers to tidal rise and fall . . . so the cemetery has to be close enough to a body of water that the tide could flood it."

"OK, I'll buy that. So we have to find a cemetery that houses someone who died from malaria *and* it can flood with the tide *or* a storm. I think we just narrowed down the possibilities from millions to tens of thousands." The two turned back to the script again. "Here's another point of clarity, 'Step smartly and rifle stealthily through not the last but instead the first.' The first what? First gate? First town? This could be most anything. But what if it's the first cemetery in New Orleans or perhaps the first in a series of them."

Smiling, Rex put his hands behind his head and leaned back in his chair and sat quietly until he was prompted out of his dream state by Heinmot kicking him under the table. "OK, what gives? I've seen that look before. What do you know that I don't?"

"Simple, Holmes. It's Dr. Watson to the rescue once again. The cemetery in question is indeed the first one in New Orleans, but it's also the first in a series of them.

"How could you—"

"You forget that I've spent years with Mom and Dad going to old locations and poring through their notes on the history of Louisiana. Plus, Mom and Arieanna dragged me through most of New Orleans yesterday. Somewhere along the zillions of footpaths, I happened to read a sign pointing the way to St. Louis Cemetery *No. 1*. At the end of one of the other alleys, there was another sign indicating the way to St. Louis Cemeteries No. 2 *and* 3. I think we have it!"

"Well done! Now that we know the cemetery, we should be able to piece the remainder together. So, what about the lovely 'Paris the Cursed?' Who, or what, do you suppose that is?"

"I've been thinking about that one, and have already taken the liberty to thoroughly check Google. As it turns out, St. Louis No. 1 has a prominent resident. Marie Laveau was a voodoo queen in New Orleans in the 1800s, and was married at least twice. Jacques Paris was her first husband and at different points throughout her life she used his name when it suited her. I believe she is 'Paris the Cursed,' and the cursed part is a play on words. She, indeed, could do the 'cursing' of unfortunate souls when requested by anyone equally as devious and for a price."

"Who is 'the last of the first'? That one has been bugging me too! Last and first of what? I—"

Rex was interrupted by the librarian announcing the closure of the library in fifteen minutes.

"Geez, it's already after five o'clock. No wonder I'm starving. Let's clean this up and head out for some dinner. By the way, we need to buy some computers so that we don't have to keep going to the library for our research."

Rex agreed, and well within the allotted time they had all of the books returned to the proper locations and shut down their computers. On the way out, they both thanked the librarian for the assistance, and drove out of the parking lot toward Seawall Boulevard for dinner.

On the way, they both thought about who the person could be in the cemetery they needed to find and what they could do to narrow their choices.

"You know, Pahana, there's something else that's bothering me. The dates don't match up."

"You mean the 1841 date? I agree, and based upon what we know thus far, Jean Lafitte died sometime around 1823 . . ."

"Which means the music box, and likely all of the coins we've found to date, aren't his." Heinmot continued.

"I'm not sure that I agree with that. Everything to date points to Jean Lafitte as the likely candidate—so who is this new 'JL', and how does he play into this?"

"I don't know, but how can a guy who died some eighteen years prior rise from the grave to bury his treasure? The only explanation would be that someone else did it, by either using his name or just by burying more treasure that Lafitte never had a chance to, in the hope they would return to dig it back up again.

"That makes some sense, and I agree that *some* of the coins are probably Lafitte's. I've also been wondering about the letters we found back in the swamp. We've gone through most of them, but not all. I can't help but wonder if there is more information there which we can use to unravel this mystery."

"I'm with you on that. I'll see if there's room available at the Galvez, and we can work on those letters later tonight to see if we can find anything."

"You have them with you?"

"Right here in the console; I never go anywhere without them. Although I should probably find a safer place for them."

"I'm game if you are. It does seem strange to me though, that pirates would both have the time to write so many letters and that they would actually take the time to do so."

"Indeed! Well, here we are!"

Back at the hotel, they set up in the Coral Sea meeting room, which seated about fifteen people comfortably. The overhead projection lights could be turned downward, illuminating the conference table to near surgical brightness. Spreading the letters across the table, they quickly divided them by date and author. Rex started on Meriwether's letters and Heinmot ground through those written by 'JL'. After about two hours of reading, Rex broke the silence in the room that previously only contained the sounds of shuffling parchment.

"I have something here that explains a few things. It may be good or bad. I'm not sure what to think . . ." he trailed off.

"Don't keep me in suspense, what do you have there?"

"I know who 'JL' is and it's *not* Jean Lafitte."

"Oh? Who else could it be then?"

"According to the first mate of the *Bienville*, 'JL' is one Jacque LaFleur who is, believe it or not, one of Jean Lafitte's nephews. As it turns out, LaFleur is the son of one of Lafitte's three sisters. Meriwether goes on to say that LaFleur took over as captain of the *Bienville* when Lafitte died."

"Great! Like it wasn't complicated enough with the timelines and now we have to keep up with two different 'JLs.'"

"I know what you mean, but it should be easier than we think to keep them separated. We simply have to remember that anything past 1823 would almost certainly be Jacque LaFleur, since Lafitte died sometime in that year. It's the time prior to 1823 that'll keep us on our toes. Now, that doesn't mean that the gold was LaFleur's—it's likely all Lafitte's, if that matters at all."

"I'll agree with that," Heinmot said. "But this also means that we have two sets of pirates to—"

"Two sets of pirates, of course! Don't you see!? The last of the first! The riddle's talking about the last pirate to join the first group of them! So all we need to do is figure out who the last pirate was to join Lafitte's gang, and who died of malaria, and that's the grave we need to go to."

"I can tell you who that is right now. LaFleur writes about a guy who joined the gang at the end of one of Lafitte's final voyages, who barely made that journey before falling sick from 'yellow jack,' and had to be brought back to New Orleans for treatment. He didn't survive, and Lafitte was beside himself about the whole thing because this guy apparently promised to design a cabana along with a great villa on a large estate somewhere along the coast of Cuba or Mexico."

"The coast of Cuba! Isn't that where Lafitte stopped to bury one million francs to make the lot he acquired from Napoleon divisible by three?"

"Both your dad and Mr. Patterson described that scene vividly."

"Any chance the gent's name is posted within the body of the letter, or am I asking for a miracle?"

"Wish granted! LaFleur writes that after ten days of fever, this man named 'Lafon' sat up in bed one night, said 'Vive la France!' and then fell into a coma from which he never recovered. He died two days later. His name was Barthelemy Lafon."

"Are you sure?"

"Pahana, it has to be. I didn't struggle though Mrs. Broussard's 'Classic French Architecture' sophomore class to forget about this guy. He was slightly famous during his time, but the real reason he's remembered is because he led a double life—half architect and philanthropist, and half smuggler and pirate."

"So let me get this straight—you're saying that we have to break into St. Louis Cemetery No. 1; figure out where Barthelemy Lafon is buried; find a door or lock near his resting place that fits this key; pray that said door or lock will open after more than a century and a half; dig up or carry out whatever is behind said door or lock . . . *all* the while watching for rising water and without a doubt the police, in the middle of the night; and last, but certainly not least, all without getting caught?"

Smiling as widely as he could, Heinmot said, "Umm . . . yea, I think that about covers it."

"I see. And here I thought that you were going to describe something difficult." Returning the smile and matching the sparkle he could see in the eyes of his friend, Rex said, "Well, when do we leave?"

CHAPTER 13 – THE CEMETERY

FOLLOWING BREAKFAST THE NEXT MORNING, REX MADE TWO PHONE CALLS: ONE TO Johann to see if he could borrow his truck—again—the second to Arieanna's apartment to speak with Sebastien to find out how long he would be in town. After confirming the details of both, he and Heinmot piled into the 'Vette for another ride east. There were times that he missed driving the Trans-Am, but the Corvette was light years ahead of the old F-body in terms of technology, and he still had the 'Bird stored neatly in the corner of Johann's shop.

The trip was quiet and Heinmot slept most of the way, save for the time it took to cross the Bolivar ferry. It was nearly noon when they rolled up at the Rhineheart homestead to find Johann puttering around in the garden with a new tiller he had just bought. He was working on the rows for the obligatory crop of corn and okra when he saw the Corvette pull up into the drive. He stopped the tiller and walked over to greet the duo.

"Howdy boys, was the trip over a smooth one? Car handling as expected?" Johann had a certain admiration for the generation of Corvette that Rex also adored.

"It was like glass, Dad! Especially since I put these new tires on it; they ride much smoother."

"Well, I need to share some disheartening news with the two of you. Eamon had to be moved to a constant care unit. For reasons still unknown to the doctors, his health declined rapidly after we shared your discovery with him. I have him in the best care unit in the region; if anyone can help him, they can."

"I didn't want to admit it at the time, but I noticed him practically changing before our eyes as we dug through those chests. He seemed to lose the fire in his eyes after we counted out all of the coins."

"I have to agree," Heinmot added. "He didn't seem to be the same at the end of the day. Almost as if someone had delivered really bad news instead of him seeing his lifelong quest come to fruition."

"We sold all of his coins and opened an account for him at the bank. It was the first eight-figure deposit they ever had. Of course, the bank manager acted as though he were a long-lost friend of Eamon's, and laid it on pretty thick. Eamon made me joint executor on the account, and I smiled when I broke the bank manager's heart by telling him this was a temporary account. We would be moving the majority of the money to a New York bank that was accustomed to handling sums of money this large and the account at his bank would be a utility account. He pulled out all of the information about FDIC and the like, but I simply waved him off. There was no way I was going to leave all of that money in such a small bank with no other branches."

"Wow! Eight figures? It's nice to know what we all may stand to gain should we find the remainder of the treasure."

"The agent for the coin collector said he'd never seen coins in such excellent shape or quantity. Initially, we thought the engravings might have discounted the value somewhat, but the collector said due to the potential notoriety of the person whose initials they belong to, and his apparent connection to Bonaparte, the value actually increased. He had to call in a few collectors to jointly bid on the lot of them, but within three days the deal was closed with one collector rapidly outpacing the others. They offered thirteen hundred for each coin, but Eamon had them drop it to twelve hundred a coin—he wanted to honor Lafitte all the way by remaining consistent with the 'divisible by three' rule. I pulled Eamon to the side and informed him that he would be losing about two and a half million dollars by doing that, but he wouldn't hear of it. There was no question; the dealer jumped at the chance to save that much and, to be honest, I think the initial offer was conservative already. Anyway, there's one piece of business I have to conclude with the two of you, however, and it's my first action as joint executor. Follow me into the house."

Heinmot and Rex looked at each other quizzically, then shrugged their shoulders and followed Johann inside. If there was one thing they had learned about him, it was to never argue when he was in this serious a mood.

They entered the log cabin and walked straight into the study only to wait for him to make up his pipe. Johann then flipped open the cover of a black business-check binder, and began scribing onto a check with his nearly stencil-like handwriting.

While he wrote, the pair of adventurers stole glances at each other, wrinkling their brows as if to silently question the scene before them. Johann removed a second check and then paused to write some additional figures on the record log of the binder. He then replaced the pen into its golden holder, closed the binder, and opened his middle desk drawer. He pulled an envelope from the drawer and slid the binder into its place.

Rex looked at Heinmot and then back at Johann and started to speak, but the patriarch held up one hand and removed the pipe from his mouth with the other.

"I swore an oath to Eamon that I would do this in a certain order, so I have to complete this ritual before we talk."

He opened the letter and pulled out a sheet of paper surprisingly formal in appearance. Rex could see the colored fibers impregnated into the grain of the paper. From his position, he could also see that a shaky hand had written the brief text on the paper. He and Heinmot shifted nervously in their seats and sat back to listen to Johann read.

"Dear Rex and Heinmot,

I can't begin to explain to you boys what finding this treasure means to me. I've spent most of my life looking for these circles of gold, when I should've been out living and spending time with my boys. I know they would've been equally pleased at seeing those boxes opened after some many decades of being sealed. I genuinely felt like a kid in a candy store as the chests were opened one after the other and then again when you counted out the coins at my feet.

These days, I feel my age, and I know I don't have much time remaining on this earth, so there are a few things I need to take care before I cross over into the great beyond. I have now completed all that I need to with the exception of one last piece of business. I have named Johann my joint executor in a foundation that he helped me set up. After I am dead and gone, this foundation will continue to make annual donations to schools and libraries that have an interest in maintaining Cajun heritage and its way of life. Johann tells me there is a certain amount that I can give each year without touching the principal, and so this gift that you have given me will be perpetual for those schools and organizations.

Now, to the business at hand. You should have just watched Johann write two checks. One is for you, Rex, and the other for you, Heinmot. There'll be no arguments, and you better abide by the wishes of a dying old man—else I'll come back and haunt the pair of you. I want you to take this money and stop searching for the remainder of the treasure. You'll waste your life away, and you both have your whole lives before you. Take some advice from one who knows—time is the only thing we can't replace, so please don't waste yours. I remain eternally grateful to you both.

Your friend,

Eamon G. Patterson"

The group sat speechless for a moment before Johann spoke. "Well, if you think that left you with nothing to say, then this should still your voices for the next month or so." Johann stood and handed one check to Heinmot and the other to Rex.

"Dad, what is this? You can't be serious?"

"Mr. Rhineheart," Heinmot stammered, "This can't be right. Can it? Math has never been my forte, but I just roughly calculated in my head that all told the coins would be worth just shy of three million dollars."

"Heinmot, in your excitement, I think you missed a zero. The coins sold for $29,999,800 dollars. Had Eamon accepted their first offer, it would have been nearly thirty-three and half million, which I believe was still low. Eamon simply divided the total in half and then halved it again to give you your portions. It left him with nearly fifteen million dollars and if I've done the math correctly, the two of you should have $7,499,700 dollars each. Naturally, I'm sure that you'll both want to continue to fund the schools Eamon named in his will."

Each in turn looked closely at the check to find the name of the foundation, JG Patterson, and the totals, which matched the numbers Johann gave to the penny. For a full minute, each of them sat in disbelief until Rex finally spoke.

"Dad, I'm sure I speak on behalf of Heinmot when I say . . . I don't know what to say . . . of course, we'll fund the schools, but I don't really want to keep this check." Heinmot nodded in affirmation and Rex continued, "Mr. Patterson should keep this—"

Johann cut him off. "Boys, I can assure you that nothing would hurt Eamon more. He sincerely wants you to keep this money and to use it however you like. He said that it was really yours to begin with, since you found it and he was merely returning a part of it."

"Johann . . . you're like a second father to me, but I feel the same as Rex. It's going to take a while before it sinks in that we just became millionaires. To be sure, we made some money on the muffler system on the PWC deal, but nothing like this, unless, of course, Rex held out on me," Heinmot said, winking at Rex.

"I recommend the two of you take these checks to Eamon's bank and have them wire the money to your own bank accounts. It's better to be safe than sorry. That's a lot of money to have on a piece of paper."

"I agree! Heinmot and I'll go do that now, and then head over to see Mr. Patterson and thank him in person."

The smoke from his Butz-Choquin encircled his head as Johann solemnly said, "Rex, don't expect much when you see him. The last time I was there, he was slipping in and out of a coma. I'm afraid he doesn't have much time left, but I know how you both feel—go and see him and you'll be able to say goodbye if nothing else."

Driving over to the bank, neither said anything, remaining deep in their own thoughts. Though they should have a sense of glee—and to some degree they did—there was also a sense of melancholy.

Stepping out of the car, Rex said, "You know, mon ami, I should be happier than this, but inside it feels like I've just lost a best friend."

"I was about to say the same thing. But let's shake this off! We're millionaires, and if we don't accomplish another thing from this point forward, not many can say they've done what we have. We need to celebrate a little when we have a chance and you should come up and see Mom and Dad. I know they would be thrilled to see you again."

The inseparable friends shook hands, then walked into the bank and made the necessary arrangements. The bank manager had a sour look on his face as he wired the money to their respective accounts. Both adventurers ignored the bank manager's mood and exited the bank with a livelier gait than the one they had upon entering. Rex double-timed it over to the care center to see the old trapper. Both of them had seen older relatives in hospitals when they were near the end, but nothing really prepared them for the scene that was to unfold in the next few minutes.

The nurse filled them in on his current condition; it seemed that, indeed, the old man was slowly but surely slipping away. They walked into the room and straight up to the bed to find Eamon

Patterson wired for sound, along with untold tubes entering and exiting his body. Heinmot gave a questioning glance at the doctor adjusting one of the intravenous drips. A slight shake of his head told both of them what they needed to know.

"Thanks for all of your guidance and the exceptionally generous gift you have bestowed on me and my family," Heinmot said softly to the old man. "I'll certainly make good use of the money and not squander it away. My parents would be so proud to meet you, so you must get well soon, sir."

Rex started to speak, but at that moment the old man opened his eyes and attempted to speak even though the feeding tube and breathing equipment wouldn't allow him to.

Heinmot made a gesture to let him know it was okay, that he didn't need to speak, he only had to listen before Rex continued.

"Mr. Patterson, my family has known you and yours for many years now. I can honestly say that I wish I would've spent more time with you so that I might have learned more about the swamp and everything in it, as well as your way of life. From the bottom of my heart, I want to say thank you for all you've done. I also wanted to let you know that we have to keep looking for the remainder of the treasure, but that we have really good clues, so I don't expect that it'll be a waste of time or take a lifetime to find the remainder."

Eamon Patterson motioned for the two of them to move closer and weakly held out his hands for them to hold. Rex and Heinmot moved to opposite sides of the bed to slightly squeeze their benefactor's hand. Inside of Rex's hands, the old man's felt like a child's—tiny and weak. It was nearly the same in Heinmot's case.

The old man squeezed both of their hands and then made the universal motion for 'thank you'. He continued to communicate by giving the sign for 'love to you' to which Rex and Heinmot reciprocated. Tears welled up and rolled down the sides of the old man's face as he smiled at both of them one last time, nodded once, and slowly closed his eyes.

The EKG monitor began to fluctuate and then alarms started to activate. The medical team rushed into the room, pushed both of them into the hallway, and drew the curtains. Rex and Heinmot could hear a tremendous amount of activity in the room with the cardiologist calling out for various tools and hypodermics. The pandemonium continued for another few minutes before all went silent.

Heinmot could tell from the expressions on the retreating staff's faces the prognosis wasn't good. The cardiologist was the last to leave the room. "I'm sorry," he said, "he's gone. We tried everything, but he simply didn't respond."

"We understand, Doctor. Thank you for trying. He's had a really big adventure these past few weeks. He went out a happy man."

"Again, my condolences. Feel free to say goodbye to him. The group from the medical examiner's office won't be here for a short while. Just let the nurse know when you're ready to leave."

The pair thanked the doctor again and went in and said their goodbyes to the old trapper. Heinmot had to admit he really did look peaceful. If he didn't know better, he would swear the old man was smiling more now than when he was when they counted out the coins at his feet.

"You know Rex, I'm glad that we were able to see him before he passed away. He seemed to give his approval despite telling your dad to dissuade us from looking further for the treasure."

"Heinmot, it's the times like this that I'm glad to have my family around. I think we'll stay an extra day to find out what arrangements are going to be made for him, and attend the service. He deserves no less than that."

"Agreed. Besides, I need to be sure that we have all of the equipment for this next little escapade we have planned. I may have to pick up a few things to complete the ensemble."

They spent the afternoon preparing for that night's excursion into the cemetery. Heinmot checked and rechecked their gear. Rex had to admit, Heinmot was one of the most thorough persons he had ever met; *nothing* was left to chance when he was involved. Rex had called ahead and had Sebastien go to the graveyard's tour office and gather as much information as he could about Barthelemy Lafon's final resting place. Within a few hours, he had all they needed to take the most direct path to the mausoleum, but Rex was under no impression that such a direct path would be possible when the time came.

For his part, Sebastien was apprehensive about this 'adventure.' Rex understood his misgivings, but it was not as if they were going to rob the Louvre; in fact, Rex wasn't sure they were robbing anything at all. They possessed the key which entitled them to whatever it opened, provided they could find it. Should they report it? Possibly. Would they? Not a chance! It would be tied up forever in a bureaucratic mire, and why reward lame politicians with the hard work they had performed?

No, he and his team would reap the product of their efforts.

His team? Now, there was a thought. Provided there was a level of success, perhaps he should consider forming a treasure-hunting team with Heinmot and his family. Indeed, they could easily set up a business to handle all of the details, maybe a salvage company specializing in recovery operations that just so happened to find million-dollar treasure on occasion.

Well, Rex thought to himself, at a minimum it was something to ponder for the future. He already had a great teammate in Heinmot who could handle just about any logistics and computing needs. His dad was an excellent planner and engineer in his own right, and Sebastian could sniff out just about any tiny piece of information they could ever need.

The part they were missing was security. Though the episode with Fats on Weeks Island was benevolent, it could have easily been the other way around. The tempting nature of their work was bound to attract unwanted attention, no doubt about it. He'd have to shop around for a security man if this idea were to go any further. It would have to be someone well skilled in self-defense and weapons but who could also train others to defend themselves and those around them. Indeed, a special type of person.

Rex made no reservations about remaining legal, but he also had no misgivings if he needed to cross slightly over those lines and back again to find the right person. Many of the most spectacular feats ever accomplished were right on the gray area of legal versus not. He decided on the spot that proper consideration over the prospect of forming a team needed due consideration as well as the required equipment and location when time allowed.

His daydream was broken by Heinmot instructing him to hand him the last bag so he could complete the packing of the truck. As he lashed the oiled tarp over the supplies, Rex tossed their bags into the truck and climbed in. Johann saw both of them off and bade them to be careful. They pulled up at Arieanna's just as the sun was setting. Piling into the small dining room, they visited over dinner and Sebastien informed all that there had been some trouble at the nature preserve in Africa, which drew some pointed questions from Gabrielle.

"Not to worry, Mom. Ayoub has things well in hand, and the Tanzanian Army is involved in this as well. We have more than ample protection with these guys handling security."

"Still, I'm not sure I ever liked the idea of you running off to that place, and now you tell me that poachers are as lush in the preserve as the animals?"

"Mom, Sebastien is old enough to make his own decisions. He's managing the place, and I have to surmise based upon what he's told us, that everything is under control. I know it's hard for you, but lighten up a little on him."

"Oh, don't even start with me, *Mr. Let Me Crawl into the Cemetery in the Midst of the Night to Dig up Buried Treasure!* I'm starting to think the entire group of you like testing my nerves and making me worry. Your only saving grace is that your father called me to let me know the risk was minimal. Otherwise, I'd be all over you even more than I am now."

Arieanna jumped into the conversation. "But Mom, they *do* know what they're doing. Look at what they've accomplished so far. Though I hate to admit it, I'm going to have to agree with Rex."

"Fair enough, but that won't stop me from worrying. Besides, I checked the forecast. There's a full moon out tonight." This last bit was said with a slight smile that diffused the tension in the room.

The clock chimed eleven, and Rex gave Heinmot a knowing look. After obligatory hugs with Gabrielle, they donned the equipment and headed out and down the stairs for the walk to the cemetery.

The street was eerily quiet, but then again the world's largest annual party had just ended, so most of the citizens should have their fill of celebration for a while. As they neared the corner of Royal and St. Louis Streets, Heinmot motioned toward the street lamps, or rather the lack thereof. Only every third block or so had a functional light, no doubt a consequence of too much alcohol and too many people. If his count was right, the light near Basin and St. Louis Street was also out and so their entrance might go undetected. Still, there were roaming guards and just across the street there was a New Orleans police station as an additional point of contention. He supposed they would cross that bridge when they came to it.

Sebastien had gathered quite a bit of information in the short time he had been given, including a map of the cemetery; and Heinmot had studied and committed all of it to memory, noting the path they had deduced, despite its notoriety was the most direct path to the tomb. Once they entered near the southeastern part of the site, they planned to move in a northern direction for at least ninety yards until the lower center part was reached, then move off to the left in a systematic fashion, denoting their location periodically. While studying the map in Arieanna's apartment, Heinmot noticed a crypt stood slightly apart from the others. When he asked Sebastien about it, he informed them it was the final resting place of 'Paris the Cursed.' *Bingo!*

Though part of the riddle seemed pointless—'Thrice around and then off to the left else ye'll visit Paris the Cursed'—Heinmot explained that back in those days, there was but one entrance instead of the typical four that existed today to the cemetery. He surmised this part of the riddle was to give would-be seekers a general direction in which to gather their bearings, since there would be no illumination, except for perhaps the moon. This also explained the need for the phrase—'It seems safest at noon, but seek ye instead when the moon will burst'. Without moonlight, one would be blind—unless you had a candle or coal oil lantern, but that would draw much unwanted attention.

As they continued north, Rex noted the age of the buildings in the area were certainly the correct period for the era they were hoping to explore. Much of the brick was crumbling or outright collapsing. Construction scaffolds erected along the sidewalks served to protect passersby also served to conceal Rex and Heinmot as they stole their way toward the cemetery. As if to further assist their need for stealth, a slow drizzle began to fall, followed by thunder and then lightning off in the distance on Lake Pontchartrain. In the lead, Heinmot stepped through a gap in the scaffolding. Rex scanned ahead and could just make out the outline of the entrance gate. He nodded, and Heinmot continued on toward the entrance.

As they drew nearer, the police station loomed out of the mist, where handcuffed suspects were being pulled out of the rear of patrol cars, motorcycle units were deploying and returning, and a general buzz of action rose into the otherwise near-silent dark—definitely not what they needed to maintain a low profile. Both knew they would receive much more than a glance in their military garb.

Quietly, they turned west, away from the station to the intersection of North Rampart and Conti, then switched back to the north until they found Basin Street. One last turn to the east had them walking along the southern wall of the cemetery. Within five minutes they were inside the boundary. Heinmot counted out the steps as they moved past the molded gravestones and crumbling mausoleums. Silvery moss swayed in rhythm as it hung from massive live oak and cypress trees, while the wind gently whistled through the overhead branches. The occasional croaking of an amphibian broke the deathly silence, which seemed befitting considering the locale. He motioned for Rex to stop when they reached the first mark, which was a tall monument which appeared to be made of black granite. He knelt to read his tritium-enhanced compass, and started moving in a west-north-west direction until they found themselves between four evenly spaced tombs, at which point they stopped again. After one last reading, they walked up to a mausoleum that stood much taller than the others in the vicinity. Based upon the design and style of the exterior, Rex knew this had to be the one.

Heinmot attached a red lens to the end of his flashlight and switched it on, while covering the bulb-end with his free hand. He slowly spread his fingers to allow some of the light to escape in order to judge how much would be visible. The rain had turned to a heavy drizzle, so he deemed it safe and completely removed his hand. He scanned the face of the edifice, finding the name plate in the oval of the beam. There, in weathered lettering, mold partially masking the sharp edges of the inscribed characters, they could read but a single word: *Lafon.*

Both took time to enjoy the moment before deciding what to do next. Rex pointed at the door to the crypt and motioned for Heinmot to try it, though he expected it to still be locked tight. Heinmot braced himself and fixed a grip on the knob that could have broken the hand of a lesser man. Taking a deep breath, he twisted with all his might, nearly falling face-forward when the knob twisted off in his hand. Rex, down on one knee, hung his head to prevent from laughing out loud. Heinmot regained his composure and went back to work on the door, pausing to study the locking mechanism before taking any further action. It appeared to be the original lock, not having been touched in, perhaps, a century.

Bracing himself this time, he put his shoulder against the door and pressed his weight against it. It didn't budge. The door seemed welded in place. Heinmot doubled his force and, after a few seconds, the door hinges finally started to release a screeching sound that would have awakened most of the citizens of the facility. Snatching a can of penetrating oil out of his pack, Rex quickly sprayed the hinges and the metal frame, and they waited silently for the lubricant to do its work.

After several minutes had passed, Rex pulled a small pry bar out of the pack and inserted it into the hole where the knob was once affixed. A muffled clang could be heard from inside the crypt. Both froze to wait for the sound to stop echoing. Once all was quiet, Rex indicated that he would use the pry bar to gain leverage on the door and Heinmot should use his shoulder against the door once more. He pointed at the bar to show that he could become trapped between it and the door if Rex lost his footing. A quick nod acknowledged his concern, and Rex did a countdown using his free hand. When he clicked off 'zero' the pair pushed and pried in unison against the resistance of the ancient door. The door was no match for the two muscular bodies working as a team, and the door slowly but silently opened wide enough for the pair to enter. Once inside, Heinmot removed the filter from his flashlight and switched on a battery-powered lantern, providing just enough light for them to see the full interior.

The room hadn't been opened in decades. Dried floral arrangements sat in the corners, pretzel stick stems crumbling to dust at the slightest touch. Nothing in the room appeared to be from the twentieth century. A formed arch climbed the wall opposite the door, as if to hold a piece of stained glass. The floor appeared to be one solid sheet of stone, but with a ledge that ran along the wall all the way around. Under the arch, there was a depression in the floor, perhaps due to the ground sinking beneath the mausoleum. Other than a few sconces built into the walls for holding candles, of which some were melted down to stubs, the remainder was depressingly bare. Not joyful in the slightest, Rex thought, but then again, he reminded himself to acknowledge where they were.

Heinmot shined his light into the vaulted ceiling where three nests teemed with paper wasps. Fortunately, it was relatively cold at this particular time of year, and it was night; thus they would remain dormant unless provoked, something neither of them intended to do. The roof of the mausoleum was domed with leaded glass panels inserted between the beams to allow some natural lighting into the tomb. Heinmot quickly moved his light way from the panels to prevent the dome from being illuminated and becoming a beacon advertising that someone was inside. As the clouds shifted, spare rays of moonlight broke through and cast their dull glow into the room.

The entire building appeared to have been hewn from southern limestone; the building material of caves. The fit was extremely precise between the stones. Rex was certain that would have pleased the occupant of the building, who made his life designing such tolerances—at least the part of his life best known by the public.

As if reading his mind, Heinmot shifted the lantern and his own flashlight to examine Lafon's final resting place. In the center of the room stood a rectangular structure that rose about five feet from the floor of the crypt. Measuring about four feet wide and seven feet long, it was constructed of the same stone as the mausoleum. The base had a rounded bolster that circumnavigated the entire pedestal. Save for some ornamental trimming engraved into the sides, it was quite spartan, considering the profession of its resident.

On the convex top of the western end of the lid, 'Lafon' was engraved again, but this example was crisp, and had no mold on it. Rex gave Heinmot a look of exasperation; other than the fact this was the tomb of a famous privateer, there was nothing to set it apart from the several hundred other crypts of St. Louis Cemetery.

Heinmot was the first to speak. "Now what? This seems to be a dead end, no pun intended."

"You've got me, man. I mean . . . I see *nothing* here that I wouldn't find in the other seven hundred-odd rooms like this one. Nothing at all out of the ordinary."

"Let's have a look at that key."

"Sure, but it's equally unremarkable."

Rex fished the key out of his pocket and handed it to Heinmot who examined it meticulously and then handed it back.

"See. Nothing that stands out. Just a key."

"Yes, but not just any key—it's a key attached to a riddle. We're missing . . . *something*."

"Well, either we're missing something, or too many things have changed from then until now. I mean how could anyone from that era expect something as ingenious as this to still exist for us to find?"

Heinmot rubbed his chin. "Maybe they didn't have to. Think about it. What would be the one thing, despite all other things that would still be here hundreds of years later? If the building were somehow destroyed what would remain?"

Rex raised an eyebrow and pivoted on one foot, then shined his light on the pedestal standing in the middle of the room.

"Right! Our dear friend Mr. Lafon would still be here in some shape or fashion. So whatever we're looking for must rest with him."

"Wait a sec . . . there is something in the riddle we haven't deciphered as yet. What was it? 'Look high, but remain reverent so that ye finally see the resting fellow'? I think that's right. Remain reverent . . . Do you know if Lafon was Protestant or Catholic?"

"We're not in the Protestant part of the cemetery and, in those days, nearly everyone was Catholic, anyway. Why?"

"I'm thinking that 'remaining reverent' means to pray and nearly every religion kneels to pray. So let's pray."

Confused, but willing to try anything at this point, Heinmot followed Rex's lead and knelt at the end of the pedestal opposite Rex.

"Well, what do you see?"

"I see a lot of gray stone. What do *you* see?"

"Heinmot, remember the phrase 'look high, but remain reverent'? What do you see when you look up? Anything out of the ordinary?"

"I see the edge of the pedestal where the lid meets the base—about a four-inch overhang, but nothing other than stone."

"Nothing here either. Let's try the other two sides and see if we find anything."

The two moved to the long sides of the pedestal and knelt again and looked up, but neither saw anything that helped them in their search. Rex stood and walked around the perimeter of the pedestal and felt every crack and crevice. Heinmot followed suit, running hands along the wall and floor.

After an hour of searching every nook and cranny, Rex finally gave up with a sigh. "I don't know what to think," he said. "Any ideas?"

"If someone, presumably a member of the family, came here to pray, and they were Catholic, wouldn't they do it around the base of the vault?" His eyes widened. "Wait. No! They *wouldn't.* There would've been a kneeler and a place for holy water and candles. In fact, they would've used a place like . . . this," he said as he turned and pointed at the indentation in the floor below the arch.

The pair closely examined the space. Not only was the floor indented; there was a gap in the ledge that ran around the room.

"There would be a candle stand on each side of the gap here," Rex said, "and a holy water well beneath a . . . a crucifix! That's what's missing and that's what was on the wall! It wasn't a stained glass window, there was a crucifix hanging there years ago. I'd bet my life on it. See here, there's a small depression where a holy water well could have been hanging. It would have to be filled at the church because only priests would've carried the water around in a bottle back in those days. So that means a person would be kneeling about here. I'll demonstrate."

Rex knelt on the floor. "Shine your light up there about where the crucifix would've been."

Heinmot stood behind him and shined his light back and forth to no avail. "Wait a minute . . ." Rex said. "'It seems safest at noon, but seek ye instead when the moon will burst', now why would this need to be done at night time? What if light is necessary, but the room needs to be dark? I have an idea—you climb on top of the vault with your flashlight. Hold it above your head and angle it toward the wall like a moonbeam coming through one of the glass panels above us. I'll turn off all of the other lights.

After climbing onto the lid of the vault, Heinmot switched on his light and slowly moved it back and forth and up and down on the wall inside the stone archway. Again. Nothing. Heinmot was about to give up when Rex's voice boomed between the walls. "Wait! Go back and move it more slowly until I tell you to stop.

"There! Stop! Do that again, but move the beam back and forth slowly. Now stop! What is that? There's something reflecting from the stones in the wall. They're slightly glowing in . . . a . . . three-diamond pattern!"

Rex moved over to the wall and put his chin against it and looked at the spot where the light shined.

"Would you look at that? You did it, Heinmot! This is what we're looking for." He pulled the key out of his pocket. "Look at the design on the top of the key. It matches the arrangement of these stones. They're angled in such a way that the light shows up only for person kneeling."

"But that answers only part of the riddle," Heinmot said, jumping down from the vault. "What about the rest? What does the key fit?"

"There must be something on this wall. It stands to reason that if one could only see the three stones while kneeling, then we should continue to be reverent and search low on the wall."

"Take a break and let me be reverent for a while."

Pulling a headlamp from his bag, Heinmot went to work. Within minutes, he struck gold.

"Here you go, it's not on the wall, but on the end-cap of the ledge. I found something here that has an oblong notch, and I'll bet this is the keyhole. Do you want the honors?"

"No, my friend, it's all yours."

He bent down to insert the key, but paused to glance at the face of the stone on the opposite site, noticing an identical hole. He turned back to Rex and said, "I think we've got a problem here. There are two keyholes, one on each side. Booby trap?"

"Although I wouldn't expect a trap 160-plus years old to still work, I don't think we should take the chance."

"Especially since it's my hide that could be boobied," Heinmot joked.

"Especially . . . Left or right? It's a fifty-fifty gamble, but I'd like to improve on those odds. Do you think it's safe to say that 'JL' would be the one returning to collect whatever would be stashed here?"

"Yeah, that's a safe bet. I doubt he'd trust one of the others to retrieve his stash."

"You read the majority of his letters, right? So, was he left- or right-handed?"

"He was definitely a southpaw. The letters all slanted to the left. Left-handed."

"Then open the right side."

"Right side? But he was left-handed."

"Too awkward to open with your left hand from here. The geometry isn't right."

"Geometry *was* always your subject. I prefer trigonometry. Here goes."

"Regardless, I could be wrong. You should probably open it while standing to the side instead of facing it."

"Your confidence and sense of deduction is awe inspiring," he joked as he inserted the key and turned.

The key rotated in the lock with surprising ease, considering its age, with a sharp click and a dull thunk followed by the stone on the top of the ledge shifting slightly. Rex reached down and lifted the edge of the stone, while placing his body as far to the side as possible. When nothing happened, he lifted it a bit more and Heinmot shined his light into the opening to inspect the crevice. Rex continued to lift, but the weight of the stone required both hands. He gestured for Heinmot to slide the pry bar under the edge so that he could manage a better grip. He had second thoughts about placing his fingers into an unknown hole, so he grabbed the other pry bar, and together they worked the ends into the space. Then, with the lid hanging over the edge of the coffin, they pushed down on their bars and flipped the stone onto the floor with a massive boom. They waited with pounding hearts and ragged breath for what seemed like hours, expecting at any moment to hear approaching footsteps. When none came, both released a sigh and laughed, as quietly as they could, with relief.

Rex shined his light down into the opening and let out a soft whistle. Heinmot shook his head and thanked his guardian angel for small favors. Inside the opening, running parallel to the ledge was a rusty blade with a spring mechanism attached to it. Had he been bent down looking into the keyhole and attempting to open the opposite side, the blade would have rammed into his head.

Rex motioned for Heinmot to step back, and lifted the stone adjacent to the first one. He then jammed the pry bar into the catch holding the spring and, as a testament to its 1800's craftsmanship, the blade shot out with a snap. Upon closer examination, Rex could see the exterior panels that sealed the ends of the ledge were notched so they could easily fall out, but they were not able to fall in. This all but guaranteed the other side contained a similar blade and mechanism.

Checking for further traps, Heinmot poked around inside the opening in the area where the blade was attached with the pry bar and hit something solid. Not wanting to induce further risk, he and Rex poked around until they found an edge, and then scraped out the remaining edges, uncovering a small stone. Despite its small size, it wouldn't budge. Working to gain more leverage, Heinmot jammed the point of his bar into the space near one of the corners. He leaned against the bar, and the stone moved ever so slightly. Rex used the end cap to the ledge as a point of leverage with his bar, and gained about the same amount of movement.

They worked as a team and alternated between pushing and releasing; the slab began to wiggle back and forth until it finally gave way and flipped up. Heinmot reached down and grabbed the stone. It was heavily coated in thick pitch, which had served as a sealant for over a century. The small opening contained a chest that measured about one foot long, ten inches deep, and eight inches across. It was removed without further incident, leaving Rex to study the interior of the makeshift stone box. All of the edges of the remaining stones had the same pitch applied at the seams, creating an airtight, but, more importantly, watertight storage device.

Behind him, Heinmot studied the chest and exclaimed, "Bingo! We've done it again!" He then extended his hand toward Rex who grasped it and shook it.

"Indeed we have!" Stealing a glance at his watch, Rex stated flatly, "It's nearly zero four hundred. We need to wrap this up and make tracks out of here; it'll be dawn soon."

"Agreed, but there's one last thing—"

"The other side?"

As Heinmot nodded, Rex said, "Yep, that was on my mind too. We should open it, if for nothing else but to disable the other trap. Ready?"

Together, they jammed the pry bars between the wall and the

stone cover and pried enough to break the mortar seal. Remaining cautious not to create any unnecessary noise, they carefully slid the stone off to the side of the ledge. As anticipated, a twin to the first blade was sitting at the ready for some unsuspecting soul to encounter. Heinmot took great pleasure in disabling the spring catch, which performed just as efficiently as the previous one. He looked over and Rex and said, "I wonder . . ." and began to probe the earth beneath the former location of the blade.

His pry bar echoed the same dull thudding sound it had before. Another box.

Rex grinned from ear to ear and walked over to assist with the removal of the stone. They found and retrieved an identical chest beneath another pitch-sealed slab, which was retrieved and placed with its mate. They quickly detached the blades from their holders and pushed them straight down into the earth inside the ledge. Each, in turn, stepped on the top of a blade to force it beneath the surface of the soil, then quickly cobbled the stones back together. The two adventurers loaded the chests into backpacks and Heinmot told Rex they would not return the same way they had entered—the western gate would be the exit of choice. He had a surprise for him. After thanking Mr. Lafon, then closing the door to the crypt, they quickly made their way toward the exit, pausing only once to allow a pair of intoxicated lovers to stumble by their location.

While they waited for the couple to move along, Heinmot attached the red filter to his flashlight. One last group of crypts stood between their location and the exit, so Heinmot turned on his light and tapped on the Morse code button a few times to force the light to flash on and off. About a block away, they saw headlights on a car turn on and off again. Within seconds, Rex heard an engine start up. The headlights came on again, and it advanced toward their location. Heinmot nudged Rex. "Looks like our ride is here."

Chapter 14 – The Flintlock Pistol

After escaping from the confines of the Lafon Mausoleum, the pair of adventurers headed for the Rhineheart homestead at high speeds to examine their find. Rex pulled the truck directly into the large shop and closed the door behind them, so they could work without the fear of prying eyes. The massive run of mercury-vapor lights spanning the ceiling of the shop softly buzzed as the dark-blue glow of the phosphor-coated bulbs slowly shifted toward the white end of the spectrum, illuminating the room. Johann, as always, was happy to see the pair of his 'sons,' and the chests with their potential reward was a perk beyond description.

"Boys," he said warmly, "this is getting to be a habit—you disappearing into the night, digging and finding a buried chest . . ." he glanced over at Heinmot, "or two."

Flashing a titanium-white smile, Rex said, "We've been thinking about this since we found the chests back on Weeks Island, *and* we have a hypothesis. We believe that Lafitte, who was probably constantly on the verge of being caught by the government or the military, stopped in a few places up and down the coast to bury parts of his treasure to prevent anyone from seizing all of it in one fell swoop. In case they couldn't remember where all of it was buried, they left clues inside of letters only they would recognize.

Because this has been a piecemeal affair thus far, we don't believe we've found the main treasure, and we don't think this is part of it either."

He continued, "There are *two* 'JLs', it turns out: one we know a lot about—Jean Lafitte—and one we don't know much about—Jacque LaFleur. It makes me wonder if both men buried treasure, or if this is something part of the crew was doing. At any rate, what say we open these babies?"

"I have all of the tools here—who wants to do the honors? Else, I'll jimmy them if you two don't stop gabbing," Heinmot jested.

Perhaps this time we don't need to force them open. The opening to the lock appears to be about the same size as this," Rex said as he pulled the old key from his pocket.

True to his word, the strange key slid right into the lock, the notches aligned, it hit the bottom of the slot, and the tumblers clicked loudly, as though they had moved for the first time. Before he lifted the lid, he paused and passed the key to Heinmot for his chest.

Hands shaking with anticipation, he grabbed the corners of the modest lid and lifted. It creaked as it opened, but only just enough to be audible above the soft hiss of air that escaped from the chest. The cover flipped back to reveal faded purple silk that lined the interior of the lid and covered the contents of the chest. It was in the late stages of deterioration and, as he touched the cloth, it transformed to dust, a small cloud of particulates floating about in the bright light. Between the bits and pieces of cloth, gold could be seen reflecting in the beams of the overheads with twinges of royal blue, emerald green, and claret red.

"This might help," Johann said, handing Rex a small air nozzle.

Rex lightly pressed the nozzle trigger on and off in quick succession. The remnants of the cloth vanished into the surrounding air, leaving only a trail of shimmers as a reminder of what once was. He could hardly contain himself as the dust settled to reveal a small cache of forty-franc coins with sapphires, emeralds, and rubies sandwiched between. He slapped Heinmot on the back and shook hands with Johann.

"Guys, I'm speechless. So far we're batting a thousand! I want to keep doing this sort of thing from now on. There must be more treasure buried that needs to be found."

Heinmot let out a slow whistle and said, "This just keeps getting better and better. Before we count the booty, as they say, shall we see what we have in the other one?"

"By all means, let's see what's behind door number two." Johann joked.

Heinmot repeated the process on his chest to find it lined with desiccated silk cloth that evaporated under the slightest touch just like its twin. After puffing a bit of compressed air over the matter at hand, the contents were revealed, but they were not what any of them had expected. Inside the small space was yet another wax-covered object of some kind. But there was something else they hadn't yet encountered.

Slipping on a pair of latex gloves, Heinmot reached lifted out a piece of grease-covered metal and wood. Glancing over at Rex with a smile, he proceeded to wipe the grease away. After a few minutes of work, he sat back with a satisfied look on his face. "Well, fellows, now there's something you don't see every day—just your everyday run-of-the-mill flintlock pistol in absolutely pristine condition. In fact, I don't think it's ever been fired. The corrosive nature of black powder would've long since eaten this away to a rusty hunk of useless metal."

Johann lifted the pistol from the workbench with one hand, and slipped on his bifocals with the other. Puffing hard on his pipe, he spent the next ten minutes studying the old weapon as Rex and Heinmot separated the valuables into small piles. One would never guess the pistol was as old as it surely had to be. The metal and the wood had lines that were crisp and clean, with no signs of wear or pitting. The wood was dark and in its natural state, though perhaps a shade darker from the grease that it encased it for decades. A burled pattern was apparent throughout the grip and the forearm, and the finish on the wood was exquisite, with insets for the side metals and grip base. The barrel was precisely inlaid into the channel as if the cuts were made with a laser. Side and butt plates were engraved with scrollwork that rivaled modern, precisely machined designs.

A small buccaneer could be seen in the center of the gray side plate, posed in swordplay; the flash pan was directly above the tip of his sword. The frizzen and hammer displayed the same intricate engravings with one noted exception being the hammer's extra curves, which enhanced its overall appearance. The base of the buttstock had a lion's face affixed in a growl, with the whiskers leading up toward the sides of the grip. On each side near the bottom of the grip, the metal formed a triangle with thin strips tapering to a point inset into the handle. The trigger and its guard completed the stylish look with the end of the trigger curling backward into a small circle. Johann was in awe of the quality of the craftsmanship, and reflected on the fact that this pistol had to have been built for someone of power or importance. A layman would not have owned this pistol in the 1800s.

Rex, reaching out to hand him a fresh cup of coffee, broke his concentration, and he set the pistol down onto a towel on the bench for all to see. The three took a moment to drink and reflect, then Johann said, "Boys, though we can't downplay the importance of the remainder of your discovery, this one probably belongs in a museum. I've seen a few flintlocks in my time, but with the exception of the embedded grease in the crevices, which can be removed with further cleaning, it appears that it just rolled out of the gunsmith's shop. This is a brilliant example of an early- to mid-1800's pistol. I'd wager that if it was loaded, it would fire without a problem."

"While you were admiring the flintlock, Rex and I counted the coins and jewels. True to form, it's all divisible by three. It appears 'JL' was truly obsessed with the number three. Two hundred and thirty-seven coins, and thirty-three each of rubies, sapphires, and emeralds for a total of three-hundred and thirty-six."

"Why not three chests then?" Johann asked.

"Well, Dad, we believe it's because these chests belong to Jacque LaFleur, who had no superstitions about the number three. Heinmot and I have worked hard to keep those two separated, as it becomes very confusing otherwise. But suffice it to say that if one of the letters has a date past 1823, it has to be LaFleur and not Lafitte. These dates are 1841."

"Some of the jewels," Heinmot said, "are quite large. Where do you guys think they even found this stuff?"

"You mean from whom did they steal it?" Rex asked with a grin. "Some of what they did probably had some knowledge driving it, but I'm tending to believe there was a fair amount of luck associated with it too."

"Say, what about our old friend here?" Heinmot said and motioned toward the wax-covered square.

"Right! I nearly forgot."

Rex walked over to the tool cabinet, pulled a heat gun from inside, and connected it. He switched it on low and began to soften the layers of aged wax, pulling the layers off as fast as they peeled. After a few minutes of work, the wax was removed to reveal another familiar object—a folded piece of parchment.

"In the words of some famous person whose name currently escapes me, 'Here we go again.' Does this look like anything you've seen before?"

"Only in every way that it could, considering what we've found thus far. Let's see where this leads us," Heinmot quipped. "Dad, will you do the honors?"

Johann reached out and took the paper from Rex and read through it silently and then again aloud:

April 7, 1841

"In this chest, ye'll clearly find my favorite to date,
Yet consign ye must to instead discover its mate.
Strange it must seem to divide from one's possessions,
If one flaunts, it could be seen as having an obsession.

Aye, some wonder, question or accuse my daft actions,

But the game is afoot and the booty's hid from a faction.
My loot's not safe in a vault or bank, for there's a diddle,
There's safety in codes, earth, and sea added to a riddle.

So go smartly to the place where the river meets land,
But the side opposite where Spain showed their hand.
Tis but a speck of a trail leading from the water to earth,
Over to the first settlement that my kinsmen gave birth.

Find a forest whose trees start roots near the water's edge,
Within an arch of gray stone is where the pistol I did wedge.
Lowest on the corner on the side that subtly favors France,
Check inside the grip for a clue to provide your next chance.

Now, 'tis true I've led ye on a grandiose chase thus far,
Give ye up not, for a motherload awaits favoring a Tsar.
Twon't be a smidge too easy finding that long favored twin,
But alas, this in the hands of another surely signs the end."

Signed 'JL'

"You've got to be kidding! I'll give old 'JL' one thing, he certainly enjoys a good riddle," Heinmot said, unable to contain his sarcasm at yet another puzzle to solve.

"That's true," Rex said, acknowledging Heinmot's frustration. "But has anyone noticed something? We seem to be working backward."

"Backward?"

"I see where Rex is going. You mean we're working backward in *time*," Johann clarified.

"Yes. Time. What was the date of the other parchment we found in the music box? August 20, 1841 and this one is dated April 7, 1841. For what it's worth, I agree with Heinmot, 'JL' does appear to enjoy the breadcrumb treatment."

"It also seems like he was traveling from west to east during this time, but then again, it all depends on where he left the music box," Heinmot said.

"Rex, I think it's something else, though. After you two found the treasure on Weeks Island, I started researching pirates and their mannerisms—the real pirates mind you and not the fiction of lore. I had some help from an old colleague who told me that one of the things they all did was bury treasure in different spots, so they always had some money nearby in case they had to run. They would leave themselves clues as to where the other caches were, so they could find them at later times. So although this seems like a letter written for a would-be treasure hunter, this is likely so that any other pirate or one of the crew could not read it and go straight to the other treasure."

"That's what we were thinking," Rex said.

"The other thing that I can confirm is Heinmot's suspicion that 'JL' could not be Jean Lafitte—at least in this context of time. Lafitte is believed to have died somewhere off the coast of Cuba in the winter of 1823. Nearly all piracy had been obliterated by the late 1820s, leaving our friend 'JL' here a sailor without a port. That is, if 'JL' is indeed his initials and it's not just one of the surviving crew attempting to impersonate Lafitte."

"Dad, the 'JL' who lived in the 1840s is Jacque LaFleur—Lafitte's nephew. Just based upon some of the changes in the tone of the messages and the way they're written, I'm confident that LaFleur is the one currently throwing the breadcrumbs."

"Got it. That explains a number of things. I do wish that Eamon could've seen this. He would've loved it.

"I think he's seeing it, Dad. He's looking down right now cheering us on—though he would probably be chastising us in person for ignoring his wishes!"

Heinmot released a slow breath. "OK, so we've uprooted another cache of valuables and I'm thrilled that we did, but I'm equally antsy about this new mystery, and am growing more so. What are the odds we can find any of these landmarks based on these clues? They certainly would've changed by now, or could be erased by modernization. For all we know, this loot is buried under a McDonald's by now!"

"You may not believe this, guys, but I think we're in better shape than you think. I know a little something about this "arch of stone."

"How could you possibly know anything about this, Dad?"

"Simple. I served on the Board of Trustees for Ward Seven for about fifteen years."

"And what does that have to do with it?"

"We spent about six months scanning every bit of history associated with Ward Seven. Some of what I scanned, I read, and I know exactly to what arch that 'JL' is referring."

"Well, let's go!" Heinmot practically shouted.

"We can't. I'm sorry to say it no longer exists."

Heinmot's spirit couldn't have been more rapidly deflated than a balloon popped by a razor-sharp pin. Rex didn't mask his melancholy either. "Well, where does that leave us? Have we hit a dead end?"

"Hardly. I said it no longer existed, not that all hope is lost!" Johann proceeded to tell that tale of the stone archway that was erected to welcome visitors into Louisiana territory before it or Texas was admitted into the Union as a state. "Most everyone of that era used horses and wagons as primary transportation. There were no maps—at least no good ones back then—and no mile markers. So, to indicate the spot where unsettled territory ended and Louisiana more or less began, the governor of the region had a stone arch built. This was sometime around 1810, a few years before Louisiana was admitted as a state. It was designed in the shape of an "X" when viewed from above to provide a much more stable footing than a simple arch would have. It stood there at the western border for about forty years—until 1850 or so—without any maintenance or repairs. It was then moved in five complete sections to mark the entrance of Millspaw's Bluff, where it remained for nearly a hundred years until it was decided the stone arch no longer fit the needs of the park—which has been renamed to Niblett's Bluff. Arguments ensued for the next few years about what to do with the arch, since the park was rural and neither the parish nor the state wanted to pay to remove it. Sometime in 1949, a clever young civil engineer named Richard Kibodeaux went to the park management and offered to take the arch off their hands for the tidy sum of one dollar—and it was a take it or leave it proposition. They bemoaned the whole thing, but weary of fighting about the disposition of the arch, they agreed. Kibodeaux had the base of the arch moved once again in four complete sections, leaving the arch itself to ruin, to the construction site of the new bridge spanning the Calcasieu River in Lake Charles. The base section of each foot of the arch was used as the four cornerstones of the eastern ramp and the remaining parts of the arch were distributed within the concrete that was used in the main roadbed."

"But if they moved it twice and if this is the same arch where LaFleur stashed the twin pistol, then why didn't someone already find it?" Rex asked.

"Remember they moved it in four complete sections. So, other than the main arch piece, the remainder was intact during both moves. This was well documented in the history of the park with the clerks of the park taking some nice photographs and detailed notes on the subject. It seems the moving of a stone archway was big news back then."

"So where does that leave us?" Heinmot queried.

"I think can answer that one—sneaking up to the base of the bridge and guessing which corner is made from the stones that hold the pistol," Rex joked.

"Right. Sounds simple." Heinmot said with a sigh.

"Oh, I think it'll be even easier than that," Johann said, patting Heinmot on the shoulder. "I'm fairly certain the original dates are engraved in the lower corner of the stone, so if you can find that one stone, you're on the right track."

"Well, alrighty then! When do we leave?" Rex said.

"Are you an adrenaline junkie or what? We've barely sorted this haul and you're ready to go for another? How about some sleep?"

Rex laughed. "Of course. You're right. I could sleep too. Dad, will you take care of this and add it to the account for the foundation?"

"What foundation?" Heinmot asked, with a quizzical expression on his brow.

"Right," Rex said, "sorry! I forgot to tell you that we are now partners in the newly established *Thundering Heart* foundation. There are some papers Dad has for you to sign. I think you'll agree we needed a structured approach to the finances, and Dad consulted a lawyer who recommended it. I've consolidated all the money that I have received and deposited it into the account." As his smile broadened, he continued, "Of course, I'm not saying that you have to do the same."

Shrugging his shoulders, Heinmot said, "Works for me—one for all and all for one. We already have more money than I could spend in two lifetimes. I'll transfer mine into the foundation as well. I assume the bank holding the funds is well diversified?"

Johann piped up and said, "Indeed! One of the oldest in the UK: Hong Kong and Shanghai Banking Corporation (HSBC). It's been around since some time after your infamous pirate's heyday."

"Along with the creation of the foundation, there are some improvements we need to make to our routines, and I think we're going to need to add some security to the team. If we ever catch our breath, I want to detail my thoughts with you on that part."

"I'm with you on that one, Pahana. That episode in the swamp with Fats could have turned out a different way if that had been anyone else. I'm all for beefing up our security so long as we're properly trained."

"Guys, how about we lock this stuff into the vault and head into the house where I'll whip up some sandwiches."

As he closed the door on the massive walk-in vault and spun the locking wheel, Rex said, "I'm in! I don't think we've eaten in nearly a day!"

After lunch, Johann stoked his pipe. "Rex, how do you propose to remove the cornerstone and replace it without damaging it? I mean, it's not like you can't put it back."

"I've been thinking about that. I think the easiest thing to do is simply work on the mortar until it loosens and then pry out the stone. Based upon the construction, it shouldn't be load bearing—at least I hope not! We'll have to scout it out first and when we return we'll have some fresh mortar as part of the supplies. Heinmot has done a fair amount of brick and mortar work with his dad; between the two of us, we should be able knock it out in a few minutes. What do you think Heinmot?"

"That sounds about right. The average stone usually has less than four linear feet of mortar on its edge, so that won't take long. Gravity will do the work for the removal, but there may be some straining for the replacement. Let's pray it doesn't weigh more than two hundred fifty pounds or so."

"Sounds like a decent plan," Johann said, and then added, "You both should grab some rack time and check it out in the morning, and return to do the deed later tomorrow night. I'll call in a favor and see if I can get a construction zone set up to cover the real reason for the supposed work."

Rex looked over with a look of disappointment.

"What?" Johann asked. "Surely you two had a better plan than to just go and pull the stone out of the wall, right?"

Rex and Heinmot just stared at him.

"I see. The Lake Charles Police have a small annex station not far from the foot of the bridge. They'll probably want to know why two random dudes are digging around their bridge."

It was Heinmot that responded and said, "Indeed, we had to tiptoe around a district police station in New Orleans, and I'd rather not repeat it."

"OK, you two worry-warts win. I'm hitting the shower and then the bed. See you both in the morning."

"Bet you twenty bucks," Heinmot said, as they neared the bridge, "that it's the southeastern corner that we need."

"I think it's the northeastern corner. I guess that means we needn't waste time on the western side. We'll try yours first and then mine."

Rex exited and made a U-turn at the first overpass to drive the mile or so back to the west to double back under the bridge. He found a parking place near the edge of the beach where he let the truck roll to a stop and then set the brake.

"After you, Dr. Iiniwa!" Rex exclaimed, and made a grandiose motion to cross the narrow feeder road.

"With pleasure!"

The pair crossed the road in two hops and immediately began to examine the face of the first cornerstone. Heinmot's sharp eyes scanned the edges of the stone to no avail. Rex pulled out his Gerber survival knife and began digging around the bottom of the stone. After several minutes, he finally reached the concrete foundation and paused to remove the loosened earth. Wiping the blade clean, he returned the knife to its scabbard and flicked on his mini-flashlight to examine the freshly exposed surface. After less than sixty seconds, he switched the light off and slipped it back into his pocket then reached into his wallet and fished out a twenty-dollar bill and handed it to Heinmot.

"There it is, plain as day. 'Set 29 September, 1810 by R. Mouton'. Well, I think we know where the construction cones need to be set up."

"Easy as pie to find, probably crazy-hard to remove," Heinmot joked.

"Let's head out to grab the gear and let Dad know about the location."

The pry bar suddenly made a screeching sound that would have carried far across the glassy surface of the lake. Thankfully, a semi-truck rumbled past, providing ample cover noise. Heinmot gave him a look that would have stilled the fastest river. Sighing, Rex paused to gain a better grip on the cold steel, but then loosened his grasp on the lever to reach around and swat at the plethora of mosquitoes nipping at his legs. The night air was stagnant and muggy. Sweat dribbled from their brows stinging their eyes, but it was the pungent chemical smell from the nearby Conoco refinery that nagged at them the most. Heinmot could hear the makings of a heavy storm brewing in the distance, but grabbed hold and forced the tool deeper into the crevice. He leaned harder into it and felt the stone begin to budge. The spine-grating sound of stone sliding on sand made the pair shiver as traffic on the bridge rolled past with thundering rumbles. Rex was thankful they were hidden by the escarpment provided by the base of the bridge.

He then thrust forward and dug his feet in deeper, the block finally gave way, tumbled over, and nosedived into the soft earth. Briefly hesitating to look around for spectators, he switched on his flashlight, covering it with his palm a bit to cast a narrow beam into the small opening. Sitting just as it had when sealed into the cornerstone nearly a century and a half prior, Rex could see a small artifact carefully wrapped in cheesecloth encased in grease. He motioned to Heinmot who reached inside and removed the old pistol. He unwrapped the upper portion of the cloth and, all at once, the sheen of a dull gray barrel reflected in the bluish light.

Such fortuity did not happen often, he mused, as Heinmot concealed the barrel and placed the package into his backpack. Together, they quickly replaced the stone and applied fresh mortar around the edges. Taking only the briefest of moments to admire his work, Heinmot made one final wipe on the edge of the stone and deemed it good enough, mentally thanking Áápi for teaching him his trade. After gathering their accouterments, the duo sprinted over to the waiting truck and drove off into the now-falling drizzle.

Fighting fatigue and the rain that had mutated from the gentle showers of moments ago to a torrential downpour, Rex maneuvered the truck back onto the freeway toward Johann's shop. He gambled for a glance at Heinmot, who was carefully wiping the animal fat from the old flintlock in the dim light, and saw the pistol was in an unspoiled condition, rivaling that of its twin. After a few more minutes of intense polishing, Heinmot sat back and looked at the pistol with the eyes of a hawk. In the dull illumination afforded by the instrument panel, he couldn't discern any particular differences between the two.

"Pahana, this will have to wait for the lights in the shop and a decent magnifying glass so we can make the comparison. But, so far, I don't see *any* obvious variations."

"We're almost there," Rex said as he navigated the truck around the steep curved exit ramp towards the long drive down the state highway.

Though it was well after two in the morning, Johann was still working in his study, the smoke from his pipe causing his desk lamp to appear as if it was flickering on and off. When the engine and headlights on the truck were switched off, the adventurers saw him slide his chair back and head toward the door that led to the shop walkway. Rex and Heinmot met him on the path, with the latter nodding ecstatically to Johann. This served to perk up Johann, who seemed to be slightly distracted.

He revealed to the two adventurers that he had expected Gabrielle to arrive late the prior evening, but she called to say she was staying another week with Arieanna to help her settle in and decorate her "spartan apartment". Rex chuckled at this last part. He'd seen her apartment; spartan was *not* the word that he would use to describe it. His facial expression conveyed what Johann was already thinking, and he returned a knowing smile.

Heinmot opened the door to find the shop in the same condition they left it in some hours before. The bench was set up with his pistol's twin still under the bright white fluorescents and magnifiers. He wasted no time setting it down next to its mate and the trio began examining the pair for discrepancies. After a full five minutes of side-by-side scrutiny, Johann broke the silence. "Boys, there's no doubt about it—these two pistols are the same, and were made by the same person at the same time." He then spent a few minutes pointing out the irregularities that appeared on each pistol in the same places and the pair agreed with his assessment.

Rex looked up at Heinmot. "Well, shall we check the grip?"

Heinmot took a moment to examine the butt of the pistol. "See the lion's face . . . it's almost exactly the same as the other one, but with *one* difference. Notice the tiny nicks on each side of the mouth? One at the upper right side and one at the lower left side?"

"Yes, I can see them. Dad?"

"I agree. What are you thinking?"

"I'm thinking the head is actually a threaded cover plate serving as the head of the screw and the mouth is the groove. Whoever tightened it made those nicks with whatever screwdriver they chose to use. Hand me that brass wedge over there, and we'll test my theory."

Rex handed him the small wedge and Heinmot gripped the pistol firmly in his offhand and worked the wedge with his left. As he increased the pressure with both hands they all suddenly heard a shrill squeak as the head began to slowly turn. Not giving any quarter, he continued to apply force until there was a gap between the head and the base, and, finally, he set the wedge down with a final twist. The lion's head came off in his hand to reveal a perfectly drilled and threaded hole. He handed the cap to Rex and moved the pistol under the light for closer examination before reaching into the hole with a pair of tweezers, emerging with a small piece of particularly delicate parchment affixed between ends.

The condition of the parchment, unfortunately, was nowhere near as immaculate as its predecessors. Small holes appeared at random on the parchment and the entire piece seemed to be on the verge of becoming dust. This parchment didn't contain the smooth edges the other parchments had. In fact, this one appeared to be ripped from a book, because three sides were slightly tattered as frequently seen with deckle edging while the fourth was quite ragged.

As they stood there and looked at the old paper, it was Johann who sighed then spoke. "Guys, it appears this goose is cooked. Without the protection of wax like the others had, time and the environment have been efficient with their work. We can try to examine it, but we should probably let Gabrielle work her magic to see if anything can be recovered. She is quite adept at recovering old documents."

"We've got nothing to lose, so I say that we try to take a look at it. Let's sandwich it between some plastic wrap just in case," Rex said as he walked over to one of the shop cabinets and retrieved a roll of cling wrap.

Using a second set of tweezers, Heinmot and Johann worked to spread the small paper onto the waiting sheet of plastic, then held it until Rex could apply a second piece, thereby sandwiching the parchment between them. After carefully smoothing the plastic, they paused to take a few digital photos of the paper on both sides. Then Johann placed the whole arrangement into a large brown envelope for protection.

Using Johann's newly upgraded computer, they reviewed the digital images on the monitor. While it was apparent that at least two paragraphs of text once existed on the parchment, only a handful of words were visible to the trio. Johann worked with the contrast and brightness to try and bring out more of the words, but it was of little use; they could discern only seven words: *pyre*, *departure*, *storm*, *sickness*, *mouth*, *horseshoe*, and *buried*. The remainder of the note would remain a mystery, at least for now.

Three sets of bleary eyes looked up at nearly the same time. "Gents," Heinmot said, "I'm not sure about you two, but I'm beat. I'm calling it a night."

"I'm with you, mon ami. Dad, I'll see you in the morning; we can decide what to do from there."

"Agreed. All hope is not lost, guys. Gabrielle is a miracle worker at this type of stuff, and I'm sure that she'll pull something out of this. See you both in the morning."

After showering, Rex examined his muscular frame in the mirror as he shaved, grinning at the extra-heavy stubble on his face. He stretched out onto his waterbed and felt the heat from the trapped liquid go to work on his sore muscles. Mentally questioning his current state of fatigue, his irritated mind reminded him that things had been going well; the pair had successfully accomplished more in six months than many men had in two lifetimes.

Still, his frustration ran deep, and he began to realize it was not because there was more treasure yet to be found, but it was the matching of wits with pirates who had lived and died a century before him. The mystery and excitement of unsolved riddles and puzzles were the prime driver for Rex to continue, and though Heinmot was not a vain as he in this area, he knew his friend loved the challenge.

As sleep finally enveloped him, he gave thanks for his good fortune, family, and for the friendship—nay—brotherhood he shared with Heinmot. To be sure, he'd go to the ends of the earth for him and he was certain his adopted brother would do the same.

CHAPTER 15 – THE TRAINING

THE DAWN WAS BRIGHT LIKE MOST OTHER DAYS THAT TIME OF THE YEAR: MOSTLY COOL at the start and roasting before the end. Rex and his crew were working a shutdown at one of the twin oil refineries separated by an old state highway. Rex was a pipefitter's helper and clever at his trade, more often than not possessing more knowledge than the journeyman who was supposed to be his mentor. They had just completed a particularly difficult lift with one of the larger cranes. He and his pipefitter had mounted an eighteen-inch control valve station for a twelve hundred-pound superheated steam line, and had subsequently stopped for a break.

As Rex was walking back to bring some water to the pipe crew, the sudden, roaring sound of a freight train caused him to turn and look back over his shoulder. Blinded by the sun, Rex hesitated a moment before the shape plummeting from the sky registered in his mind: a massive Boeing 747 with black smoke pouring from its starboard engines.

Less than five hundred yards away, the nose of the airliner punctured the wall of a floating-roof storage tank as if it were made of paper. Speed and weight merged the fuselage with the crude oil inside, and twisted the steel of the tank until they were indiscernible save for the plane's rudder with the prominent red triangle painted on it and the blue "V" inside the triangular logo signifying Victory Airlines. In the blink of an eye, the 2.6 million gallons of crude oil stored within the tank ignited, and flight 264 headed for Buenos Aires—along with its 451 souls—disappeared in a fireball the size of the great pyramid.

The explosion rocked through the tank farm, leveling the remaining tanks, and causing a chain reaction of detonations that, Rex would later learn, measured 6.2 on the Richter scale.

He turned back around and ran toward the crew, shouting for them to grab onto anything they could and hold on. The initial shockwave took less than five seconds to reach the crew in the break shack, killing the five inside. The blast was so hot and fast that it blew clothes off the rest of the crew and covered them in debris. Thinking the immediate danger had passed, the men stood and began running in the opposite direction of the blast. Unbeknownst to them, the initial detonations coupled with the shockwave had ruptured the oil storage tanks within their own defunct refinery.

They stopped when the first of the explosions began, and froze in horror. A colossal wall of flame enveloped the men, instantly turning them to dust. As Rex sprinted ahead of the wall, he heard the men following him screaming in pain before they fell silent.

"Help! Rex! Help!" one of his crew cried out.

Sliding to a stop and turning to his coworker, he grabbed the man with one steady motion and slung him over his shoulder, the firewall loomed above him as he turned and continued to run. In his peripheral vision, he could see fireballs erupting. The concussions from the myriad explosions racked his mind and stilled his hearing. Sprinting deftly in and around the maze of pipes, he suddenly found himself at a dead end. The only escape was to go back and try a lateral direction. But it was too late, the fires had completely encased his escape route, so he did the only thing he could: he climbed. His legs were screaming, but he ignored them and continued to climb. Crossing back through the control stations, he found an opening with stairs leading down and took it. He could see his freedom just ahead when another explosion knocked him to the ground, the weight of his colleague pinning him to the ground like a butterfly in a glass display.

He rolled over to see the fear in his co-worker's eyes, then flames were closing in on them, and the moan of steel girders signaled a deck above was collapsing. One of the steel plates embedded in the earth next to his arm, and yet another detonation signaled his doom.

Through the smoke and flames, he could see the main control room in the distance. It was designed to survive such incidents. If he could just get them there . . . mustering all his strength, he scrambled to his feet, hoisted his journeyman onto his back, and dodged the falling shrapnel and flames as he ran full-out for the control room. A final blast slammed the weary pair through the door, and Rex fell into nothingness.

The imaginary flash of lightning and the sensation of falling jarred Rex from his nightmare. *Would that dream ever go away,* he wondered, as he slowly released his death grip on the edge of the bed. It had been more than nine years since that fateful day. Every time he re-lived it, the details grew more vivid, it seemed, than the actual experience.

The dream was particularly unnerving that morning, for he had decided it was time to realize his lifelong dream of becoming a hot air balloon pilot. After purchasing the required equipment—envelope, basket, burners, and countless accessories—he found an independent airfield that was secluded with limited clientele. Exactly the privacy he was looking for. He knew it would take at least twenty-five hours to earn a license, so he dedicated the entire week to the task. Though it was certainly a cool hobby, Rex figured that, at some point, he and Heinmot could use the balloon to search for the treasure. After all, a plane couldn't be landed just anywhere, and hiking through snake-thick swamps wasn't exactly a dream come true.

Gulping down another piping-hot cup of coffee, Francis Rosario

Gianelli, balloon pilot extraordinaire, reviewed his schedule for the day. He remembered the entire week had been blocked out except for one appointment: Rex Rhineheart.

Yesterday, when he first saw the name in his planner, the name was merely familiar, but as he sipped his coffee, a memory slowly emerged of squatting in the dense bush with the sweat trickling down his back in rivulets while pondering how he had come to be in Africa. At twenty-six and far from his New York home, he was not all pleased with where he was in life. Growing up with two female names wasn't easy, and his hooked and slightly flattened nose was a testament to the many protests he'd staged to that effect. To be sure, in the early days he lost more fights than he won, and changing his first name to Franco had helped reduce the altercations, but he wasn't one to hide from conflict; in fact, he embraced it. He never felt more alive than when he was dancing in a circle on his tiptoes with his massive fists landing blows with the force of a sledgehammer—of course, that was before he learned a more efficient way.

Though his Italian heritage and growing up in the Bronx all but ensured that he would be a street fighter of some sort, his moniker had *guaranteed* it. The number of fights he won or lost had become a blur, as had the countless cuts and bruises tended to by the equally unknown women in his past. Never keeping a steady girl, he played the field from left to right and all points in between. At times, he couldn't remember the name of the last one he'd had before he moved on to the next.

Having never met his father, he'd been more or less adopted by an older Japanese man with a penchant for Italian food, who helped to focus his energy on more constructive ideals. Ishikawa Miyazaki, a sensei in the most direct form of the word, taught him the intricacies of aikido, karate, and kendo over a period of ten years. The two developed a unique bond that could only be described as father and son. When the day finally came that student defeated the master, Miyazaki couldn't have been more proud if Franco had been his biological son. For his part, at sixteen, Franco was likewise satisfied to know he had pushed the limits far beyond their breaking point. Thus ended the antagonistic attitude of many would-be teasers regarding his name; he simply gave one warning and then snapped the nearest appendage with a lightning-fast strike of Aikido when the assailant failed to heed his warning.

When word spread of his talents, he soon found himself in high demand by those with deep and willing pockets. Few questions were asked about his background. There were no drug screens. And the interview process lasted just long enough for him to best the lead henchman under the boss. The shadow world welcomed him with open arms, and seduced him like a lover. The transformation from innocent young adult to experienced thug-for-hire was completed in less than three months. His relationship with Miyazaki crumbled even faster. Franco always meant to go back to try to make it up to him, but, somehow, the time never seemed right.

Upon hearing the news of the old man's death, Franco went into a rage. He began by evacuating his current employer's workers from his many sweat shops, hostels, drug warehouses, and money laundering operations before burning them to the ground. When Freddy the Weasel offered a $250,000 bounty for his head, he proceeded to erase Freddy and his entire gang of thugs from the face of the earth.

He followed suit with his first employer, leaving those in between in his mercy. Hot tears streamed down his face as he came to the realization that no matter how much trash he took out, or how many wrongs he righted, his friend, mentor, and surrogate father was gone forever, and he'd never had the opportunity to say goodbye.

He vowed at that moment he would become a force for good. Evil would be squashed wherever he discovered it. Never again would he use his skills to help the strong at the expense of the weak. Though five years after making that oath, like the proverbial sinner he backslid into his old ways and found himself supporting evil again, but in a slightly different way. He was squatting in the bush and sweating profusely in the midst of Tanzania working with poachers. *How did he come to be with these idiots, a group of rabble far less worthy than the animals they were unmercifully capturing or killing? It would serve them all right to run into the Tanzanian Army right after they took down a bull elephant, an offense punishable by death.*

On this second hunt, he found himself more disgusted and distanced from these men than ever before. He felt a flash of rage when they shot a female elephant, sawed off her tusks, and left her baby to scavengers and predators. He contemplated killing the lot of them and leaving them to the wills of the wild. He vowed to break free soon, and steeled himself into accepting the fact he had to return to the good forever more.

Two of the poachers, Boseda and Rashidi, took great pleasure in the hunt; the fact of it being illegal provided an extra shot of adrenaline to the whole business. The other two, Klevon and Saleem, were cleaners who skinned the animals and removed anything of value from the carcasses: ivory from the elephants, the head and paws from the male lions. When they captured a specimen suitable for sale, they caged them for transport.

Franco's job in all of this was to protect them from the Tanzanian Army. He had accepted the fifty thousand-dollar advance without a drip of emotion, but now that he was on the hunt, something about slaughtering these animals twisted in his guts like a knife. He would feel no more remorse for turning the tables on these buffoons than he had for the pack of criminals back in the Bronx. The longer the hunt took, the higher the chance that he would end up flushing them all and making his way back to America.

Suddenly, Klevon and Saleem pointed out a small group of men, under the cover of brush, holding rifles aimed in their general direction. Within moments, the poachers began to fire upon the partially camouflaged men. The group returned fire, but Franco noticed the bullets were not hitting their marks nor, was the gunfire creating the expected echo, but were instead making a muffled sound. Boseda and Rashidi began firing as Klevon and Saleem advanced on the group to obtain a better target angle. As the small group became pinned down in a near crossfire, Franco realized they would all be killed if he didn't act. A familiar feeling exploded inside him; he pulled his Walther P99 AS and shot Boseda and Rashidi in the back of the head. He then worked his way around to the rear of the group of attackers and called out to the leader, who was a tall, muscular man reaching for another bolt action rifle.

"Don't shoot!" Franco yelled. "I'm here to help."

"Who are you?" the leader queried, "and why should we trust you?"

"Because I'm the one that took out half of the bad guys shooting at you."

"Well, in that case," Sebastien Rhineheart said, while setting his tranquilizer rifle down and tossing him a .300 Winchester Magnum, "welcome to the party."

It was that night he had decided he really was through with a life of crime. He had seen enough and been in enough killings to last a lifetime. He knew wasting the poachers was the right thing to do, but it was enough. For him to kill again would mean good had to outweigh evil, because it was only good that he would practice going forward. He possessed a myriad of skills so he would search to be a security specialist of some sort, perhaps combined with training for occasional flying classes. He preferred the former, but it was the latter where he felt most at peace—especially in a hot air balloon.

Though it had been several months, it seemed like years. And while he'd had enough money to make it back to the US, he wasn't completely sure his current situation was an improvement. But he was happy despite the lack of steady income. The sound of a vehicle door slamming announced his student's arrival.

Yesterday, the training had begun with the usual classroom instruction. Today, they would be flying. The fully-inflated envelope of the balloon sported the typical rainbow color scheme that contrasted sharply against the green of the surrounding woods. The balloon sporadically tugging at its tethers was reminiscent of a small child attempting to pull away from its mother in a toy store.

Trainer and trainee boarded. From the basket suspended beneath the great orb, Rex pulled on the lanyard to increase the propane gas jet to full burn, and the balloon began its initial ascent into the damp morning air. As it rose, Rex watched the fog unfurl its misty tendrils and penetrate the spaces in the verdant flora below.

After several ascents and descents, Rex's first flight was uneventful save for the slightly rough landing.

"Sorry about that," Rex said with a frown, "I should have floated it a little more before shutting off the burner."

Franco shrugged with a smile.

"Yep, but hence you learned something in the process. It'll be easier and become second nature with more experience."

"I appreciate your confidence and guidance."

"Not sure about you, but I'm starving," Franco said, his stomach echoing the sentiment. "How about some lunch?"

After the heading to a local diner, the pair had ordered, then sat quietly, awkwardly looking around the deserted space, but then both attempted to speak at the same time and then simultaneously stopped.

Rex finally broke the silence. "You first. I wanted to talk about hot air balloons, but I'm sure you'll find that boring."

"OK, I wanted to tell you a story about your brother Sebastien and Africa."

"Sebastien? You know Sebas—"

Rex's phone buzzed on the table. Johann.

"Dad?"

"Rex? It's Dad. You better get over here. We've had a break-in. Heinmot's been shot."

"What? When? I'll be right there."

Looking over at Franco, Rex said grimly, "I have to go. I'll drop you back at the airfield."

Franco, sensing a potential chance to explain further, asked, "Mind if I tag along?"

CHAPTER 16 – THE ROBBERY

REX PULLED UP AT THE SHOP TO FIND JOHANN STANDING OUTSIDE WITH A GRIM LOOK ON his face.

"He'll be fine," Johann told them as he approached the vehicle and softened his features a little. "It was two shots, but neither of them were life threatening, and in fact, one of them was a glancing shot."

"What happened?"

"Someone broke in and took one of the chests. Heinmot walked in and caught him in the middle of the job. Despite being shot himself, Heinmot managed to get the gun from the thief and shoot him. We found a trail of blood leading out of the shop. Apollo and Gemini are after him in the woods now. Gabrielle is on the way to the hospital with Heinmot, and I was about to join the dogs in the hunt. Want to join me?"

"How about you wait at the shop and wait for Mom to call. I'll take care of the thief." Raising an inquisitive eyebrow at Franco, Rex made a beeline for the house to grab a rifle and some ammunition.

"Count me in," Franco called after him. "I'll take an AR-15 if you have one."

Rex grabbed two AR-15s and, after loading the magazines, they proceeded to catch up with the dogs, which were raising hell deep in the woods behind the shop. Thrashing through the thick underbrush, they heard someone crossing, Rex surmised, Foreman Creek.

He spun around and indicated to Franco that they could cut the thief off by outflanking him to the left. No doubt, the thief didn't know the area nearly as well as he did. Scrambling up a bank of a dry rice water canal, they turned left for 100 yards, then proceeded straight for another hundred, then turned back to the right and found themselves in a prime location to intercept the thief as he emerged from the brush.

As they lined up the shots, off to the right, Rex heard a vehicle start and rev its engine. For a moment he assumed they were too late; the thief was making his final getaway! Then Franco elbowed him and pointed to an olive-skinned man in a shredded suit holding his side with one hand and cradling the chest in another emerging from the woods. Apollo, the black-and-tan male Doberman Pinscher, leapt out of the brush and clamped down on the thief's right calf, twisting his head from side to side.

Though Rex couldn't believe what he was seeing, the man managed to kick the dog in the face hard enough to inflict more pain than the dog was willing to endure. As the dog yelped, pausing to lick its wounds, Gemini, the cinnamon female, began her assault. The red spray of blood and a man screaming filled the air. Turning, the man swung the chest into the dog's head, forcing her to release his arm, she fell and remained still as he ran for the getaway vehicle plowing through the underbrush. Franco fired two shots at the truck just as the man attempted to leap into the bed with the trunk. The truck fishtailed and knocked the man away from the bed, but somehow the trunk managed to make it into the bed. Rex fired two shots through the back glass, shattering it to pieces, and Franco landed three more shots into the tailgate of the truck as it disappeared from sight.

The pair trained their weapons on the thief and cautiously approached. From his vantage point, Rex could see the man lying motionless, with his face to the ground. Rex motioned to Franco to cover him and rolled the man over with his foot. Rex placed a foot on his chest and pressed harder incrementally until he had the man's full attention.

"You've got one chance and three questions," Rex said. "Who are you, where is that truck going, and who sent you?"

Gasping for air, the thief managed to utter, "I'm Smiley Grogan. I don't know where the truck is going, and I work for Stratford."

Flipping off the safety on his AR-15 and pointing the barrel between the thief's eyes, Franco said, "Not good enough. You have exactly three seconds to answer the man's question. Where is that truck going?"

"OK. OK. Relax. He's headed back to the Andrews warehouse in Lake Charles near the docks and then to the airport for a flight back to the UK."

Franco safetied the weapon. "Thank you." Then he flipped the rifle around and smashed the butt of the rifle into the side of the thug's head, rendering him unconscious.

"Call the cops while I check on the dogs," Rex said, tossing Franco his phone.

Apollo met him halfway down the makeshift trail, still nursing his wounds and whining for Rex to follow him. Rex found Gemini laying the grass bleeding profusely from the head wound, but still breathing. Removing his shirt, he bound it around her head as Johann pulled up on one of the ATVs.

"Put her on the back. I'll get her over to Doc Hudson's. Did you find out anything?"

"I did. We're on it. Did you say the name of the guy who bought Mr. Patterson's coins was Stratford?"

"Yeah. Richard Stratford from the UK."

"That's what I thought. I guess he didn't like the fact that we weren't going to sell any more coins, so he took matters into his own hands. He orchestrated this little escapade."

"Oh?"

"Yeah, Franco *persuaded* the first thief to give us that bit of information."

"First thief?"

"Yeah, there was another in a getaway truck. He escaped—for now."

"Rex, the stolen chest had the letters and papers in it. The thief would've taken both of them had it not been for Heinmot."

"I can't worry about that now. I need to grab your truck and a pistol with some ammo."

"Where do you think you're going without me?" Franco said flatly. Seeing a quizzical look from father and son, he added, "I'll explain later. Besides, 'Smiley' isn't going anywhere and I gave enough information to the dispatcher to find him. The police can catch up to us later for the details."

It was late afternoon by the time they had armed themselves with the appropriate weapons, ammo, and supplies. Rex figured the second thief had a flight out of New Orleans or Houston.

They exited past the Calcasieu river bridge and headed toward the port. Rex remembered there was a set of deserted warehouses off to the side. This, he wagered to Franco on the drive, was the target and base of the thief.

Parking a few blocks away, he and Franco worked their way to the west side of the complex and entered through a hole in the fence. They passed several buildings with no signs of life until Rex motioned for Franco to stop. Motioning and drawing his SIG P226, Franco replicated the move. Rex pointed at the camera on the corner of the building and eased backwards into a side alley.

"This has to be it. This place has been deserted for years but that camera's a dead giveaway."

Franco nodded in agreement. "There's a break in the siding over here out of its view. Let's see if we can get inside."

Inside, the pair squatted motionless with their eyes closed for a full two minutes to acquire their night vision as they listened to an excited voice in the center of the warehouse. The British accent was unmistakable and was, in no uncertain terms, telling the person on the other end of the phone that the payment wasn't enough and that they were considering just keeping the chest. The person on the other end clearly said something to change the thief's mind because his demeanor suddenly changed. He hung up the phone and returned to packing his gear oblivious to Rex and Franco slipping up behind him.

As he jammed the pistol into the thief's ribcage, Rex felt the man cringe in fear. Spotting an old chair in the corner, he motioned at Franco, who walked over and grabbed the chair and a piece of rope. He forced the man into the chair and lashed him down so tightly the thief struggled to breathe.

"Your buddy's probably already dead back at my place," Rex said, slamming the butt of his pistol into the back of the would-be-thug's head, creating a spurt of blood. "You have exactly ten seconds to answer my questions, or experience more pain than you can in two lifetimes."

Groaning in pain, the thief had no constitution for torture. Though he feared his boss, this was the here and now, and he knew he had to capitulate or face torture, perhaps even death. The stale air of the warehouse combined with the ferric smell of his own blood permeated his senses, and he relaxed his body in surrender.

"What do you want to know?"

"The same three questions I asked your partner—who are you, where is that chest going, and who sent you?"

Sensing a pause in an effort to conjure up a story, Franco brought the butt of his weapon down on the man's collarbone, shattering it instantly. He pushed the barrel of his pistol into the back of the man's head until it drew fresh blood. "He's not kidding, friend, so I suggest you get on with it."

"OK! OK! No more. Not that it matters, but the name's Wild, Nigel Wild. If you tortured Grogan, then you already know the chest is headed to the UK and that we work for Stratford."

Rex backhanded Wild across the face and threatened another, then shouted, "Give me more information or so help me you'll wish you were never freaking born!"

"Is that the best you've got? Sorry boy, you'll have to do—" the thief began but was unable to finish his sentence before Franco high-kicked Wild, knocking out his front teeth out and sending him flying backwards at the same time. The chair smashed into multiple pieces and Rex walked over to pick up one of the chair legs.

Tossing the chair leg to Franco, who was jerking Wild's shoes off, he spent the next five minutes bashing the bottoms of his feet until the soles were torn and bloody. Not giving any quarter, Franco kicked Wild onto his side and, using the now-splintered chair leg, smashed Wild's ribs with surgical precision. Rex started to speak, but saw a primal look in Franco's eyes and nodded.

Rex rolled Wild onto his back and straddled him using the chair leg to pin his throat to the concrete. Franco's rage temporarily sated, Rex moved close to the thoroughly beaten thief and said, "If you *ever* want to breathe again, you damned well better talk. Now, *where* is that chest going and *where* can I find Richard Stratford?"

Coughing and spitting blood, Wild felt one of his ribs puncture his left lung and knew he either had to talk or die. He chose the former.

"Stratford lives somewhere in central London," Wild said through a bout of coughing and blood. "I, I'm not sure exactly where, but once a call came from the Bishopsgate area of London. That's all I know, I swear."

"You better hope that's all you know," Rex said, rising to a stand. "If I ever see you again, I'll kill you and that's a promise."

"He's not joking," Franco said. "And even if he were: if *I* ever see you again, I'll kill you myself."

Rex grabbed the chest and the two made their exit as stealthily as they appeared, leaving Wild to lick his wounds and ponder his future.

CHAPTER 17 – THE COMPOUND

AFTER THE ADVENTURES OF THE DAY BEFORE, REX CHOSE TO UNWIND AT THE GYM with a moderate weight-lifting session and a five-mile run around the track. Johann had updated him on Heinmot's condition so he taken the time to blow off some steam. He then made his way to the hospital to check on Heinmot, who smiled weakly when he awoke to Rex watching over him.

He had a flesh wound in the thigh that went clean through, with no impact on any of his vitals. He would be sore and would walk with a limp for about a month or so, but would fully recover.

"Well, lazybones, have you had enough rest?" Rex kidded, to mask his concern.

Heinmot laughed. "Seems like old times—just in reverse." Sparing no details, Rex filled Heinmot in on the actions after his altercation as well as Franco's role in the aftermath. "Richard Stratford will have to be handled sooner or later, but we're ill-equipped to do so right now."

"Agreed."

"But it was all too easy for him to find us and practically stroll right through the front door of the shop. Had you not been there, we would've never known what happened to the chest—probably both of them. And us being there is putting my folks in danger. My mom's pretty pissed."

"I've been thinking about that too . . ."

For the next hour, the two brothers-in-arms mulled over potential locations for the shop, until it dawned on Rex: "How about Eamon Patterson's old place—with major improvements, of course?"

"Pahana!" Heinmot exclaimed. "That's perfect."

The pair spent the rest of the day going through the details. Both agreed it would be costly, but they had plenty of money, and it would be well worth it, even with the expense of seriously ramping up security.

Rex knew that Johann lived for this kind of stuff, and Heinmot was appreciative of his second father's talents. In fact, he could already see him in action doling out orders and inspecting the work. Rex was certain he was the man for the job. But something was missing.

"Heinmot, I was just thinking . . .we're missing part of the equation. I mean, we have you as the computer wizard and mechanical engineer, me as the marine biologist/pilot/backup engineer, Fats & crew handling sea borne operations, and Dad as the financial/equipment manager, but we're missing a security/weapons guy."

"True. But we can hold our own . . ."

"Still."

"You have anyone in mind?"

"As a matter of fact—I do."

Rex left the hospital and headed toward the old airfield. He found Franco puttering around with one of his older balloons. He waved, and Franco returned his gesture.

"You have a minute?"

Wiping grease from his hands with a rag that may have been even greasier, Franco climbed out of the balloon. "Sure."

"I have a business proposition for you, but first I wanted to say thanks for your help with that nasty piece of business we had yesterday, I really appreciate it."

"Anytime. But you could've handled it by yourself."

"Maybe so, but my colleague and I are in need of a security man. I spoke to Sebastien this morning and he speaks highly of you. What are your future plans?"

"Funny you should ask . . ."

Franco proceeded to tell Rex the short version of his life as well as the poacher encounter in Africa when he helped Sebastien. He finished his sordid tale and leaned back against the hood of the SUV. "I imagine someone with my past isn't what you're looking for."

"Look, I'm no saint, either. Though I can't claim to have killed anyone and have no desire to do so unless I'm forced to. I'm willing to give you a second chance, but you must not deviate from the path, my friend. We have a good thing going; each member of the team is an integral block in the foundation. Your part would be to train us in martial arts and weapons as well as be the armory manager . . . that sort of thing. I can offer you a percentage of whatever we bring in as well as equipment, housing, and a salary. While I can't say things will always go as planned or that we'll be rich, I can promise my loyalty as long as you stay clean on- and off-mission. What say you?"

"Mission? Are you doing some kind of paramilitary work? How close will we have to shave our skins?"

Rex laughed, slapping Franco on the shoulder.

"No, no. Nothing like that. We've been involved in tracking down a few . . . artifacts. Our shop just got robbed, as you know, and Heinmot and I have been in some sticky situations we were lucky didn't get stickier. You proved to my brother to be a good man. I'd like to have you looking out for us."

Without a word, Franco extended his right hand and placed his left hand on Rex's right shoulder.

"Welcome to the Thundering Heart Foundation, Franco," Rex said, as they shook hands, "I'm sure we'll benefit from your talents. Make out a list of what you need to get started, and I'll have it delivered to our new compound—at least as soon as we have it built—which I'd like your input on, especially the armory.

The next day, with Heinmot still on the mend, the trio met with Johann and laid out the plans. Johann generally agreed with the concepts, but offered his expertise in a number of areas. Unbeknownst to Rex and Heinmot, Eamon had willed the entire property to them, so as it turned out, they already owned it. Equally unknown to everyone in the community was that Eamon had owned over ten square miles of land, including the marsh. Rex and Heinmot signed the property over to the foundation, and Johann commenced the execution of the work packages.

Eight weeks later, Johann called them to the house and informed them the compound was ready. After toasting to their success, Rex, Heinmot, Franco, and Johann strolled over to Johann's new and expansive garage and entered the open bay. Upon seeing the new Ford F-350 4x4s, Heinmot let out a whistle and said, "What's this? He then chuckled when he read the license plates—THDRHRT1, THDRHRT2, and THDRHRT3.

Rex tossed the pair of adventurers two keys for each truck.

"We all needed something a little more suitable to our current line of work. These should fit the bill nicely."

Laughing despite himself, Heinmot said, "I just bought one of these for Dad, and yes, they are nice trucks for most any off-road situation."

"These have something that factory models don't have, for an extra boost of power—boost being the operative word. I had twin turbos installed on both of them so we should be able to get out of nearly any jam. Oh, and there's the suspension and security upgrades as well."

"Rex, my friend, you never fail to amaze me. As always—my thanks."

Franco, who was usually quiet, let out a long whistle and took a moment to peruse his truck. Upon seeing indications the glass was bulletproof all the way around, he smiled and gave Rex a knowing look of approval, and merely said, "Thanks!"

"It's my pleasure—you both deserve it. Besides, one of you is driving."

The last bit was said with more than a little jest for it was normally Rex who did all of the maneuvering. With Johann in tow, and Heinmot at the wheel, they drove down Johann and Gabrielle's new driveway, which was complete with security fencing and cameras.

As they turned off the main tributary onto the smaller road, Rex was pleased to see that Johann had work crews replace the pock-faced road with a new concrete base and had installed a similar security system around the boundaries of the property. As if on cue, the heavily reinforced gate swung open in response to the proximity of Heinmot's approaching truck. When Rex noted the reaction on his face, he simply winked in response and nodded at Franco. Pampas and salt grass lined the roadway providing natural camouflage for the winding road from all angles except from above. As they approached the end of the roadway, Rex could see the road veer in an opposite direction from its original course. The old road base had been removed and redirected, and as the turn straightened, another equally massive gate opened and quickly closed behind them.

Cameras were mounted at equidistant points surrounding the space of the old homestead, which had been expanded to more than triple its size. The old shack had been razed and replaced with six, concrete pillar-supported buildings, one of which was an immense workshop that dwarfed Johann's by comparison. Solid concrete ramps extended in multiple directions from all of the buildings except for one. Both fortune hunters knew at a glance it was the new office building, complete with a laboratory.

On the southern end of the property, four new docks and landings had been constructed to extend from the marsh up to the workable areas of the compound. Rex could also see the waterways had been dredged to provide enough draft for a substantially sized vessel to navigate—including one the size of the *Bienville*. Parked under the extra sturdy canopy, a new bass boat and center console bay boat floated lazily in the murky water. Equally new power plants sat at the ready on the transom of each vessel. A winch system was mounted above each boat, ensuring that lifting either of them from the water would be a simple task.

As the truck rolled to a stop in the center of the compound, Rex eyed the motor pool with maintenance bays, lifts, and a covered parking area. At one end of the motor pool, triple-walled fuel tanks were housed in a fortified containment wall. If Rex knew Johann, there were likely subterranean tanks as well. The opposite end boasted a new generator large enough to power the majority of the parish.

On the western side, Johann showed off the compound's runway. It was huge. Long enough for a medium sized jet to land and circle back to the hangar. Rex looked over at Johann with a quizzical expression.

Johann shrugged. "You never know . . ."

Rex nodded in approval, looked over at Heinmot and Franco. "Well, partners, what do you think about our new base of operations?"

"To be honest," Heinmot said, "I'm amazed all of this could be built in less than ten weeks!"

"Couldn't have said it better myself," Franco said.

The foursome spent the remainder of the afternoon examining the rest of the compound. Heinmot was impressed with the workshop, which had all of the machines needed for any task he may be faced with, as well as a state-of-the-art computer center which scratched every geek itch he had. Rex loved the quick egress into the marsh, which would afford him maximum freedom to perform his marine biology work. All three were amazed at the layout of the lab and equipment, and the communications room, computer center, and motor pool area were all top-shelf. Franco, for his part, was thrilled at the layout and arrangement of the armory.

They could see the pride beaming in Johann's face when he demonstrated the hurricane protection system. Massive formed steel plates mounted a hydraulically operated ram system would lift from underground bunkers to form a wall-to-wall shell surrounding the main operational parts of the compound. Rated to withstand more than three hundred mile per hour winds, the wall system doubled as an invader repellant device. No weapon short of an atomic bomb could penetrate the reinforced steel plates, and they could be deployed in less than ten minutes with the turn of a key and the push of a button. But there was more.

With a wink, Johann walked over to what appeared to be a sprinkler control station and entered some numbers on a keypad housed behind a door. A hum and then a muffled mechanical thunk could be heard, followed by a panel sliding back in the concrete. A stairway appeared within the opening and, in succession, the process was repeated twice again with the openings appearing one hundred and twenty degrees apart in a circle that encompassed more than five hundred feet in diameter.

"The vault. A series of subterranean chambers all connected underground. There are exits at various locations around the complex. The motor pool, workshop, boat dock, hangar, lab, and the living areas. Perfect protection from just about any emergency. Follow me."

As soon as they entered, the door slid closed behind them and, on both sides of the tunnel, lights at the tops of inset cutouts came on and fully illuminated the space. Heinmot's unasked question was answered within a minute; places for handguns, rifles, shotguns, tactical equipment, emergency food stores, purified water, and other pieces of equipment too numerous to detail were everywhere. All of the spaces had precise metal tags affixed to them with a short description and a bar code. Cases of ammunition and sealed pallets of firearms lined the hallways, waiting to be stored in their respective racks.

I see the two of you have been hard at work," Heinmot said.

"Indeed, my friend," replied Rex with a smile. "The whole point is to do our work undisturbed by man *and* nature. Franco was the architect behind all this; our equipment training begins next week."

"Well, to say these tactical rooms are impressive is the understatement of the year," Heinmot said with a smile. "The gulf coast, though, isn't an area that supports underground facilities without incident. The arid climate in here should make the walls sweat, but they're dry as a bone. How's that possible?"

Johann chuckled. "No easy feat, Heinmot, but with the proper design, all that's required is moving some dry air about and a pump system. I can show you later, if you like."

"I would like to see the design of the entire facility, just so that I'm able to commit to memory the intricacies of it. Now, for the literal million dollar question—what did this place set us back?"

Rex started to answer, but Johann interrupted. "Guys, you need to know that Eamon left all of this land to the two of you as well as all of his money from the first find, including a substantial amount of interest revenue. That was the part in his will that was directed to me. I simply created an account for it at the time and, when the foundation was formed, I transferred the money and the holdings to the foundation. In essence, you've yet to tap into any of the money Eamon split with you, and there is still a small fortune left of his part, even after the bills were paid for all of this and the donations he requested I maintain. The foundation is definitely in the black, and unless something changes, it is poised to remain that way. Of course, the foundation will continue to fund those interests that he named in his will, but those costs are inconsequential."

Winking at Heinmot, Rex said, "Motion to make Johann the CFO of the Thundering Heart Foundation!"

"Motion seconded," Heinmot said.

"Motion carried and acknowledged. How about it, Dad? Will you take the job? It's not like you aren't already doing it now."

"Boys, I'd be happy to and it'll give me something to do in my 'spare' time," he said with an immense smile on his face, shaking hands with the trio. "There are a few other pieces of business before we move on. Your work could become dangerous, hence the need for a place such as this, and I think it best if you two don't share much of this with your mothers. No need to worry them excessively, since they'll worry either way. The second thing I wanted to share was that of the money Eamon left, he wanted me to donate two million of it to the state wildlife fund. I did that in his name and those of his two sons. Although it doesn't impact any of the foundations interests, I wanted you both to know about it. Last but not least, you looked over the operational areas of the compound, but not the recreational ones. I feel a good barbeque coming on, and we have just the equipment to host it."

"I think I speak for Rex when I say we have no issues with the donations. I grew up respecting animal wildlife, perhaps more than the average animal lover, so I'm delighted the money was given. In addition, you've done a fantastic job here. I couldn't have designed and executed this any better if I had a team of ten engineers."

"I echo Heinmot, Dad. Brilliant work! Now, how about that food? I'm starving!"

The evening was time well spent with family and friends. Rex made a call to Fats and invited him and the boys to visit the compound and partake of Johann's secret recipe. Fats was pleased to see the duo again, meeting Franco in the process, and not surprisingly, he and Johann chewed the fat, literally, late into the late evening. Johann took care to show him the new docks and that all of them could house the *Gittaloadodis,* as well as a much larger vessel. Fats promised to bring them a load of fresh shrimp and some fresh oysters on his next haul. They departed, leaving Rex and Heinmot sitting around the fire contemplating their next moves.

Quickly, their conversation turned to the old piece of parchment. Gabrielle hadn't been able to recover more of the parchment, though she tried many tested and proven methodologies—save for one item of note. At the upper right corner of the page, she recovered a date—December 4, 1821. But this was a dead-end, unless they could make something of the mystery with only a few clues. The date also told him they were dealing with Jean Lafitte rather than LaFleur since the year was 1821, though he wasn't sure that revelation helped at all.

"Well," Heinmot said, "I don't know about you, but I've had enough of a break for a while. I think it's time to solve the remainder of this mystery."

"I agree, mon ami."

"So what can we make of *pyre*, *departure*, *storm*, *sickness*, *mouth*, *horseshoe*, and *buried?* These words might describe something or someone. So what if we assume this is a chronological document as opposed to the riddles we've already found?"

"Chronological document? You're a veritable genius, Heinmot. That's exactly what it is! Remember the paper had a ragged edge as if it were torn from a book? Let's also assume it was torn from the captain's log. Perhaps this is even an entry detailing part of their journey. I forgot to tell you, Mom was able to find a date on the corner of the paper—December 4, 1821. Of course, you know what that means . . ." He trailed off.

"Right, as your dad said, it means Jean Lafitte, not Jacque LaFleur. Which might also mean there's a considerable cache of coins out there waiting to be found."

"Exactly. So let's assume that it's Lafitte. Where would he have been on that date?"

Heinmot sat back in thought. "Well, he left Galveston in October 1821, and if his old habits hold true, he would have gone somewhere between Galveston and New Orleans."

"Agreed. We need a map to plot it out. Let's head over to the lab."

They pinned a large map of the western gulf coast to a drafting table, and, using a magnifying light, Rex marked the spot where Lafitte had his camp in Galveston and began scanning the coast.

"What's the next word on the list?"

"Departure."

"We'll assume that meant toward the east and New Orleans. What was next?"

"Storm."

"Which he may have encountered at any point in the voyage, so not much help there. The next word?"

"Sickness."

"Sickness . . . I remember reading something in one of Antoine Meriwether's letters about the whole crew experiencing some type of fever in one of the last voyages?"

"Yeah . . . I remember that too. Didn't you say that your dad moved all of the things that we found thus far to here?"

"Yeah, now where to find it."

"Find what?" Johann stepped into the office. "What are you guys looking for?"

"The letters that we discovered in one of the chests from Weeks Island."

Unlocking and pulling out a file drawer, he said, "Right here under "W" for Weeks Island."

The trio went through the old papers until Heinmot hit the mark. "Here you go! The entire crew had a strange fever at the beginning of the voyage that lasted much longer than any fever they had experienced to date. It says here the illness struck sometime the day after sailing from Galveston. Assuming they were too sick to make much headway, and considering there was a storm in there somewhere, I'd say that put them at about High Island, Texas, when the fever and storm subsided. Agree?"

"Agreed," Rex said and marked the map accordingly. "And the next word?"

"Mouth."

"Must be a river, right? Dumping into the Gulf?"

"I'll buy that," Johann said. "The first one they would've encountered would be the Sabine River, which forms the border between Texas and Louisiana, and which, by the way, was the main waterway back in those days on the western border of Louisiana. It also stands to reason, at least somewhat, that it plays a role in the overall mystery, since the first fish that you caught with a gold coin was in a small slough off the Sabine."

"Yep, I agree with that. Can you mark it Heinmot? Now, the next word?"

"How about the final two—horseshoe and buried?"

Smiling at Heinmot, Rex said, "I'm going to assume they didn't have any horses on that ship and that none of them believed in good luck from horses—"

Interrupting, Johann held up his hand and said, "Sorry guys, there were plenty of superstitious sailors back in the day who believed nailing a horseshoe to the mast will help their vessel avoid storms."

Snickering, Heinmot said, "Well, I guess it didn't work so well for these guys. But joking aside, we should assume they were not talking about a horse's shoes for the sake of argument since the word buried was not much further along in the same sentence of the same paragraph."

"Agreed. Now what else would have to do with horseshoes?" Rex queried.

"Rex, I think the answer might be under your thumb. There seems to be a number of horseshoe-shaped lakes along the Sabine as you go north from the mouth of the river. See here?" Johann pointed to two definitive lakes and one long switchback turn that might be construed as a horseshoe.

Yes, I see those, Dad. Of course, it would take months to search all of that marsh and river." Seeing Heinmot grinning from ear to ear, he continued with, "What? What're you grinning at?"

"Simple, my dear, Dr. Rhineheart. As you once taught me, allow me to teach you. What was Lafitte's favorite number? Three, right? And we know that we're dealing with Lafitte, so no second guessing that part. So we merely count from the mouth going north and find the third horseshoe-shaped lake or river turn, and 'x' marks the spot."

"Way to go Heinmot!" Johann cheered. "That makes it easy, there's Phoenix Lake, which would be one. Then this double switchback in the river could likely be counted as two. Lastly—"

"I'll be damned!" Rex interrupted. "We've been so focused on the map, we overlooked the obvious staring us in the face. The third lake north from the mouth of the Sabine is aptly named 'Horseshoe Lake'! I'll bet my stake on that lake being the one and if you look on the map, the spot where I caught the fish is only about five miles away! For a largemouth bass, that distance would be easily covered, and it is brackish enough for a red fish to find its way there. This lake simply must tie things together."

"So where do we go from here?"

"Dad, will you turn on the compound lights?" The sun had set hours ago, but the small team was so absorbed in their mystery the loss of light had not dawned on them. Johann switched on the lights and the total area that was cleared and developed was instantly and fully illuminated.

"What's on your mind, Rex?" Johann asked.

"I have a new gadget that I am certain will aid in the search, and we can start using it first thing tomorrow. I forgot to ask, but I'm assuming that you were able to find everything I asked for?"

A simple nod from Johann and a finger pointing the way told Rex what he needed to know. Leading, Rex walked them over to a building near the edge of the airstrip and punched in a key code on the pad of the beefy door, which clicked and opened as if on air hinges. The fluorescents began to warm up, and the room brightened from their white light. Rex pointed over to a huge crate and the basket that stood near it. Heinmot looked over and saw propane cylinders at the rear of the room securely standing in a custom-made rack and connected the dots.

"Can you pilot one of these?"

"With ease, my friend! At least as long as Franco gives the green light. I didn't get to complete my training before the robbery interrupted everything. Well, now that we have a plan and way to execute it, shall we call it a night? It's past midnight."

"Time flies when you're having fun, Pahana!"

Closing the door, they walked back and climbed into Heinmot's truck, that still smelled as though it had never been used, and drove back to Johann's one last time, dropping Franco at the airfield on the way. Rex was certain that tomorrow, they would begin the final stages of the adventure. There was no way for him to know that it had only just begun.

Chapter 18 – The Dig

The roar of the propane igniting and rushing through the large burners broke the silence of the otherwise-still morning. Mosquitoes nibbling on most every warm-blooded mammal in sight were only a testament to the time of the year and Louisiana's average rainfall. Though the sun had been awake for over an hour, the air hung heavily, like the marsh mist against the ground. Fully inflated, the colors of the envelope were brilliant and majestic and contrasted sharply with the lime-green leaves of the surrounding cypress trees. The balloon was an eight gore model, which had an exaggerated tear drop shape. It was thus one of the lighter models, making it most suitable for the task at hand. Situated within the confines of the basket, a veritable feast could be found, along with various tools including the small ground-penetrating radar unit and shovels, three pairs of high power binoculars, three hand-held radios, and extra propane bottles to allow for maneuvering. Johann had agreed to be the solo ground crew, and would bring the recovery trailer, provided that Rex landed the balloon where he could get to them—else it would be a hard walk to a clearing. Feeling the tension of the ropes pulling against the basket, Heinmot nodded to Rex when he gazed over questioningly, then braced for the liftoff.

Franco turned the burners on full, and within minutes the basket lifted from the ground and was quickly far above the treetops.

Johann gave a knowing wave to the trio, and then they were out of sight. Switching positions once they ascended, Rex continued the burn for a full twenty minutes, giving them a nice amount of elevation and some much-needed time to begin the search. Fortunately, there was a moderate breeze from the south east, and it was pushing them along at just the right pace to allow for scanning the marsh below. Rex pointed down and Heinmot could see his favorite fishing hole and remnants of the Old Highway 90 Bridge. Parts of the charred pilings could still be seen reaching skyward from their watery grave, and Rex felt a twinge of nostalgia at seeing them.

As they neared the end of the old highway, at Rex's behest, Franco deployed the rudder which would aid somewhat in controlling direction. Rex had the envelope built with lateral vents, and these combined with the rudder would allow a pilot to come as close to steering as possible. A slight elevation change netted a more northerly direction, which fit into the agenda as if planned. From their vantage point, the nearly defunct shipyards in Orange, just across the border of Texas, with their rotting docks stood as monuments to a foregone era. Slightly north, the overgrown streets of the now-dismantled Riverside subdivision could be seen fanning out in an ever-growing arc of nearly one hundred and eighty degrees from Simmons Drive. When viewed from above, the four rings of streets combined with the intertwining avenues, formed a ragged spiderweb shape that once connected the forty-five hundred buildings so many had at one time called home.

It was Heinmot's turn to point, and Rex could see his target as the Sabine River Bridge spanning the river's gap with its traffic buzzing east and west. Franco nodded at Heinmot, who subsequently turned the rudder, and Rex opened one of the vents to make a course correction further to the northeast. As the balloon straightened, off in the distance, the stacks of a paper mill came into view, replete with its sulfur dioxide aroma, causing the trio to wrinkle their noses in response. The smell prompted a memory, and Rex thought of winter when the northern wind would transport the smell practically into his backyard.

Breaking the silence, Heinmot pulled out a map and said, "Not long now, we should see it within a minute or two."

Rex grabbed his binoculars, and true to his friend's word, he could see the mouth indicating the southern edge of the lake. The river split three ways at this juncture, and he smiled at Heinmot and held up three fingers.

Heinmot said, "Your elusive captain certainly had a thing about the number three. Third lake on the river where the river splits into three?" Then laughing, "Shall we wait and land at three o'clock?"

Returning the smile, Rex said, "I see a small clearing on the peninsula part of the lake. I'm going to see if I can set it down there."

Rex began working the vents in an alternating fashion, so as to maintain directional control, but also to slow the descent and prevent a hard landing. After about ten minutes, he managed a nearly perfect landing, save for the brambles that protruded into the basket, scratching all of them front to back. The trio wasted no time unloading the equipment, and as they set across the relatively dry strip of land, Heinmot queried, "Will it be the usual suspects?"

"I've been thinking about that. Since there were coins that became a meal for a couple of fish, I think we have to focus on the banks of the lake and not the main part of the strip."

"Good point; I agree, because it was after a storm each time a fish was caught, so maybe a tree or two was uprooted, thereby exposing the cache."

"There are four banks to this lake—two outers and two inners. Since our captain favors the odd, I had originally thought we should focus on the obvious, but . . ." he trailed off.

"But? What are you thinking?"

"Look at the map, notice how the horseshoe is upside down? Now, do you see how the lake forks on the right side and that the land forms a point? I think we should start working that point to see if we get any hits."

"Sounds like as good of a plan as any. Let's do it!"

In short order the equipment was shouldered, and the three

trudged through the waist-high saw grass toward the eastern bank. Within minutes, the muddy water of the Sabine could be seen lapping against the sandy shoreline. After unpacking everything, Rex fired up the radar unit and started scanning the edge of the bank, slipping several times in the process to end up waist-deep in the swift-moving water. On his third such entry, he decided it was time to move further inland, but his situation rapidly went from bad to worse. As he moved toward the inner part of the point, the elevation rose ever so slightly, then he felt and heard the sickening crunch of something beneath his feet, but could not tell what it was. Using the head of the radar unit to clear his path, he pushed the stiff saw grass to the side and realized that he was in the middle of an alligator nest and had destroyed the entire clutch.

Instantly sickened at the thought of what had just happened, and at the fact he had been simply careless, he was caught off guard when the exceptionally large and thoroughly infuriated female swept him off his feet with a flick of her tail. Once down, she rapidly maneuvered to a position of strength to use her primary weapon as a means to an end. Partially stunned, it took Rex a few seconds to recover; it was nearly too late when he did, and both Franco and Heinmot were unaware of his situation. Moving quickly, he rolled over and then on top of the alligator, which began thrashing and bucking to dislodge him from her back. Wrapping his heavily muscled legs around her mid-section, he began to squeeze, and then locked his feet, blocking her attempt. He then put her head in a full nelson, and allowed his body weight and large biceps to maintain an unbreakable grip. She retaliated by rolling over on top of him and managed to partially wind him, but tough as she was, Rex had no intention of losing the fight. His countermeasure was to squeeze her throat even harder, and then leg press against the edge of the nest to roll her over and resume his previous position. Flip and move as she might, she was not able to get him off her back, so while he had the upper hand he pulled her head back nearly ninety degrees to her back and against his chest, then held it tight. He worked his legs deeper under her and pushed, thus causing her tail and rear feet to lose contact with the ground and preventing any further death rolls. He held the position for another thirty seconds and felt her relax. Working to catch his breath, he managed to whistle for Franco and Heinmot, who he could hear crashing through the brush to find out what was happening.

Heinmot stepped into the now-widened clearing, began to chortle, and then said, "Well, I see you've met a new friend. Now, I knew you liked women, but isn't this taking it a bit too far?"

Nearly exhausted, Rex shook his head, then laughed, and growled, "Oh shut up and help me get off her back! She is one pissed-off alligator, and I'm getting too tired to run."

Together, the group pushed her head down on the ground, and while Heinmot knelt on her back, Rex gathered his feet under him. Franco and Rex forced her head and back against the ground, then Rex threw her forward as far as he could, though it was only a few inches, then both jumped back and slowly reversed course. She thrashed and turned to face the three adventurers, hissing and snarling the whole time. Just as Rex was certain that round three was going to start, she thrashed back the other way, then dove off the bank into the water, swimming rapidly away to lick her wounded pride.

"You never fail to amaze me, Pahana. Not a critter in sight and you manage to go two rounds with a ten-foot alligator."

Slapping him on the back and laughing, Rex said, "Yeah? Where were you when I reached out to tag you?"

"Well, luckily you weren't hurt, but I can't say the same for the radar unit," Franco said with a frown. "The control pad and the head unit are crushed. It'll put a damper on scanning the remainder of the area."

"Agreed. But, we can do some old fashioned reconnaissance work and see if we find anything out of the ordinary that may help. No sense coming all this way and not at least look around."

The threesome of alligator champions tromped through the dense underbrush, remaining cautious of other alligator nests and other denizens of the swampy area. In particular, they were on the alert for old trees that were uprooted or otherwise maligned. After walking the majority of the point, they had found nothing of interest, save for a partially submerged bass boat that had seen better days even prior to its demise. Scavengers had removed anything of value from the craft, leaving the remainder to the sun and elements to devour. On a hunch, Heinmot jerked a thumb toward the eastern side of the point that had become so overgrown it made Rex long for his favorite machete. Working cautiously to minimize the number and magnitude of the blackjack vine and briar gouges, they made slow progress, and at one point had nearly given up, until Heinmot stepped into a small opening that allowed them to take a breather. Sweat ran profusely down all of their faces and backs, reminding Rex the mid-day heat of August was no more forgiving than that of July. The recent storms which nestled torrential downpours within had not only served to create an extra layer of marsh, but also increased the already unbearable humidity levels to one hundred percent saturation.

In no particular hurry, Heinmot paused to wet a rag in a trickle of what might be considered a river in some parts of the world. As he wiped the grit and sweat from his face, he noticed the glint of shiny metal near the opposite edge of the bank. He had all but dismissed it as a lost tool of the trade for a would-be angler, but something about the color of the metal captivated him. Silently questioning his sanity, he stepped into the slow moving water to sink nearly waist deep in the mire beneath the surface. Goose-stepping across the water, he forded the stream in five large hops and paused to shake the water and mud from his boots. He then squatted, reached into the water, and retrieved the metal object.

Wiping the sweat from his eyes with the sleeve of his shirt, he focused on the golden blob and then squatted again to rinse it in the moving water. With the mud removed, he instantly recognized his prize and called over to Rex.

"Hey! I have something here, that I think you'll find familiar. Here, catch," he said as he tossed the coin across the stream.

"What the . . . ? You've got to be kidding! Where did you find it?"

"Here at the edge of the bank. I'm betting there are more."

Rex studied the coin in his hand and gleefully noted the familiar initials and date along with the bust of France's most famous ruler. So technology did not answer the riddle this time, determination and a willingness to endure the blackjack was all that was needed. He looked up and down the stream and saw that it was solidly overgrown with the only clearing the one they were standing in.

"Heinmot, it's the storms. This water probably moved the coins from somewhere upstream. I'm not sure how we're going to get through, the briars are solid."

Dabbing a cut through his shredded shirt, he said, "Yeah, I noticed. But, no pain, no gain. It looks a bit thinner on this side. Come on over."

Though Rex could not see so much as a glint of daylight up either bank, he trusted his partner's judgment and removed the majority of his gear, then forded the stream to Heinmot's side.

Franco chimed in, "You may as well leave some of your stuff here to serve as a marker. I'm bringing one of the metal detectors and a machete—not that a blade will help much."

Heinmot replicated Franco's gear, except for the metal detector, but kept a flashlight and another sweat rag from his backpack. The team began fighting their way through the underbrush, but it was slow progress, and after an hour they had made little headway and found no other coins. The heat and mosquitoes were starting to take their toll, but they were determined, if nothing else. After another fifty feet or so, Rex had a hit on the detector, but it was only an old paper shotgun shell casing whose paper had long since rotted away.

"Well, we know at least one other person has been here," Heinmot quipped.

"Yes, but it was decades ago. Paper shotgun shells haven't been produced since the late 1960s. This whole area does not seem to have been touched by humans in countless years. In fact, were it not for a few alligator slides that I've seen, I would say neither man nor beast has been here in countless years. Any semblance of foot traffic would keep the underbrush beaten down to some degree."

"True. Shall we press on?"

Heinmot took the lead and parted the way through the sun-hardened vines, pausing at times to free the end of the detector as it snagged on nearly everything in the path. Rex swung the machine from side to side as best he could under the circumstances, and soon their efforts paid off. Another coin was located under the edge of a rotted log, and the discovery forced a shot of adrenaline into all sets of veins. As the machete whacked and cut the brambles, the detector started pinging again, and another coin, then yet another, was found. Not waiting to rest, they trudged forward, and within twenty minutes had collected the same number of coins. As Heinmot worked the blade, a rogue vine snagged his glove, and on the next thrust it was jerked from his hand and he lost the machete in the process.

Wiping his brow with the other hand, he said, "Close, brother, we're so close, I feel it in my bones."

"Aye! I feel it too! Let me take point for a while."

Switching positions, Rex began hacking and moving forward, but then suddenly stopped in his tracks. As he strained to hear past the whine of the mosquitoes, he held up a hand when Heinmot started to speak.

"Do you hear that? It sounds like gurgling water. I mean, I know the stream is gurgling, but this is slightly rushing water. Do you hear it?"

Leaning forward after slapping a few mosquitoes, Heinmot said, "Yes, I can. It sounds like it's just up ahead and I think I see some daylight breaking through the brush."

Franco confirmed what the two had surmised and added, "Yes, see here?" as he pointed towards an opening.

Wasting no time, Rex grabbed the machete and began swinging it with both hands, but the ferociousness of the vines had finally dulled the blade, and the work was slower than ever. Bracing his calves, he made short lunges as he swung, and forward motion was again made, albeit labor intensive. The sound of the water was filling their ears and Heinmot set the detector down and began to work in unison with Rex. Daylight poked through all around the area where they stood and both knew their quarry was just ahead. The stream had widened and the water was running faster and was crystal clear beneath their feet. Rex could see the bottom had changed from clay to sandstone, which provided sure footing as opposed to the slippery bank where they currently stood. A quick nod conveyed his plan to Heinmot and both stepped into the water and were surprised when they did not sink, but were nearly waist deep. Standing side-by-side, the rushing water gave both a burst of energy and the vines began to separate and fall away at a much faster rate.

Creeping forward as they swung, they suddenly encountered the source of the vines and most of the trunks measured three or four inches in diameter. They chose to double team the largest of the bunch, but the blades seemingly bounced off the bark as if it was made of iron. Heinmot nodded at Rex, and in unison they lunged and struck with the machetes. Running water passing in and around the roots of the vine system had weakened it to the point of losing the battle and the war. As they lunged, the vines came free, and the momentum and sudden loss of traction caused them to topple face-first through the vines. Just beyond the wall of vines, a deep pool had been formed by the uprooting of a massive cypress tree, and they found themselves suddenly having to swim to stay afloat. Sputtering and coughing to clear the unexpected water from their noses and eyes, they performed a sloppy breast stroke to make it to the nearest bank.

Climbing out of the cold water and dropping the machetes, the now thoroughly drenched pair took stock of where they were. There had been three cypress trees, two smaller and the one massive—the last was a casualty of a past storm. It had fallen between the two twins and had taken all of the canopy with it, but the roof of the forest had long since replenished itself, and the blackjack vines had created a living wall surrounding the pool and its banks. A pinwheel-shaped, root-encumbered stump was all that remained, but it had endured and had formed a makeshift dam on a tributary of the old river, using the two others as a stanchion for its base. As the water flowed over the edges and sides of the stump, a natural waterfall was created, and the base of the stump had been polished clean from the vast amounts of water that had flowed over it through the years.

Rex looked over at Heinmot and said, "Are you all right? That was a bit of a surprise and I know I wasn't ready to swallow a gallon of river water."

Coughing up the last of what he had inhaled, he replied, "I'll be right as the rain in a few minutes." Smiling and leaning back on his hands, he excitedly said, "Do you see what I see?"

Rex looked over and about two and half feet below the surface of the water, the bright glimmer of gold could be seen in a triangular shape that was wider at the top than the bottom. An area behind and to the left and right of the gold was much darker than the earth on the edges of the bank and walls of the pool. He surmised they had found the proverbial pot of gold at the end of the rainbow and said, "Rest for a minute. I'm going to go in and see what's down there."

"Ha! Rest nothing! Let's all go!"

Removing their boots in unison and stripping off their shirts, they slipped in on the far side of the pool and slowly made their way over to the gold so as not to stir up the mud and ruin the visibility. Assumptions that Rex had harbored for more than twenty years were confirmed in an instant for they could see that one of the chests had broken open and spilled most of its contents into the pool. Fish could easily swim in and out, and as a testament to that fact, Heinmot pointed at a trophy bass that zoomed away when it saw the three humans. Rex guessed the coins they found in the downstream part of the water were dumped when the tree initially fell and the water rushed past before the pool was formed by countless years of erosion.

Rex switched on his flashlight, and two smaller chests could then be seen on each side of the crushed one, their contents still intact. As they surfaced for air, Rex said, "I can't tell you how long I've thought and dreamed about these chests. On second thought, I suppose that I could. I wish that Sebastien and Dad were here to see it, but I'm glad that you were here. This is truly a dream come true."

"Pahana, you and I are two of the luckiest and most fortunate people on this earth. We've done things that we know others have spent their lifetimes attempting and yet failed. I'm thrilled to be here with you, but now for the elephant in the room—how are we getting this out of here?"

"Good question and I have a good answer, well, at least I think I do. If we can manage to get these out of the water, I believe we can call Dad on the radio and have him head over with one of the boats. Unless you want to try to pack this out through the jungle behind us?"

"I think it'll be more work to cut our way through what is ahead of us to make our way to the main river, which, by the way, is more than a mile in that direction. Let's see how heavy they are first, and go from there. We can build a makeshift travois out of some of these larger vines, if need be."

In agreement, Rex walked back to his pack, which took far less time than the first incursion. Grabbing both folding shovels and one of the packs, he double-timed it back to Heinmot and Franco, and all three went back into the pool to retrieve the chests. The two smaller chests were captured with no effort, and though they had some weight to them, their size limited the burden. The larger chest was not retrievable, so they took turns ferrying the coins out of the smashed chest and onto the bank. The old box could not have been full, or perhaps some of the coins had long since been buried in the mud, because the pack held all they could find with room to spare. Franco hacked out a six- or seven-foot piece of the largest vine and lashed the two small chests to it with the rope from the pack. They agreed to take turns carrying the gold-laden pack, and after taking one last look at the three trees and the pool, set out for the balloon, gathering the remainder of the supplies as they encountered them on the back trail.

The return trip took nearly two hours as they maneuvered though the vines, mud, and mosquitoes. Fortunately, there were no chance meetings with any of the local reptilian life forms, but that was not to say the return trip was entirely uneventful. As they neared the clearing where the balloon was tethered, Franco suddenly held up his fist in the classic 'stop' indication. He then motioned for them to quietly set the chests down and slipped off his back pack. Rex moved closer and could hear subdued voices in the clearing. Scanning the area with his binoculars, Heinmot let out an angry grunt and passed the glasses to Rex. Next to the balloon, Rex could see two ne'er do wells attempting to help themselves to the contents of the basket, including the propane burners.

Not concealing his disgust in the slightest, he said, "Well, just what we need, two thieves helping themselves to the balloon hardware and, theoretically, our treasure."

Unstrapping his backpack, he unzipped a side compartment, then reached inside and smiled as he said, "Not this time brother!"

"Franco, I trust you know how to use of one these?"

Rex handed a new nine-millimeter Sig Sauer P226 butt first along with a fully loaded seventeen-round magazine to Heinmot and to Franco who smiled and said, "Right!"

They simultaneously inserted the magazines and slammed them home followed by racking the slides and lowering the hammers using the de-cocking lever. Sliding the pistol into the small of his back and untucking his shirt, Rex said, "Ready? Let's go!"

As Rex and Franco walked into the clearing in a follow-the-leader fashion, with Rex in the lead, the would-be perpetrators took note of their entrance, stiffened, and sought to strengthen their hopelessly weak position. One of the pair had climbed into the basket and crouched down while the other stood behind the basket and watched them approach. When they were about twenty yards from the balloon, Rex reached back with his right hand and drew the pistol from his waistband, but held it behind him and motioned for Franco to do the same. Heinmot waited a little further back while the pair advanced on the would-be thieves.

Rex called out and said, "Hey you! Exactly what do you think you're doing? That balloon and everything in it is ours and I'll thank you to step back and walk away."

"Now we don't want no trouble, but finders keepers is our motto, and we aim to keep this balloon."

"I don't think so and that was not a request. I won't ask again." He then ordered, "Back away and move on, or you'll have more trouble than you'll know how to handle!"

"Trouble? From who? The likes of you two? I've had—"

With lightning speed, Rex tucked his pistol into his waistband and covered the remaining distance in three hops with Franco on his heels. Rex landed a fist to the side of the head of the loudmouth that shook him to his knees. He followed with a thrusting punch to the solar plexus that completely winded him and caused him to double over. An uppercut using all of the strength in his chest, shoulder, and biceps formed a large gash on the thug's chin and put him out for the count.

While he was working on the first thief, he heard Franco working on the other rogue in the basket, pounding him to a pulp with short thrusts from his ham-like hands. As Rex grabbed his foe by the shirt and lifted him off the ground to land another solid hit for general principle, the second would-be thief suddenly flew out of the basket with his hands flailing for purchase. Franco hopped out of the basket and finished him off with a stiff uppercut.

Rex looked over at Franco and said, "Well, looks like we win round one. Again!"

Heinmot safetied his pistol, then pulled the magazine and emptied the chamber. He took a moment to look closely at the pistol and agreed to himself it felt balanced in his hands and the ergonomics were excellent. Glancing over at Rex, he said, "You really have been preparing since the incident with Fats. It certainly caught me off guard when you pulled those out of the pack, but I'm glad you had them."

The remainder of the hardware and the chests were retrieved in short order and with Franco giving some instruction, Rex had them airborne in minutes. As they cleared the treetops, the two hoodlums could be seen below in a small clearing recovering from the incident. Rex did not have to strain to see the red stain that had grown on the chest of his adversary from the gashes on his face. Johann retrieved them once they landed, and within the hour they were back in the compound, and with some effort the balloon was stored. The ride back did not allow for much conversation, because the trio rode in the trailer, securing the balloon and basket. After briefing Johann on the details of the quest and subsequent encounter, the focus turned to the two chests and the loose coins. As the golden disks were spread out on the counter in the shop, Johann looked over at Rex with misty eyes and said, "Boys, I wish that Eamon could see this. He and Kendall spent decades in these marshes searching for the gold, and you three simply stumble upon it."

"Dad, I'm not sure that I would want to describe our discovery as 'stumbled upon it,' but in reality, I think that's exactly what we did." Suddenly feeling a sense of excitement, he added, "Heinmot, let's open these chests."

The coffers were sitting side-by-side on the workbench and for a moment, Rex wondered where the pirates procured all of the chests they used to bury the treasure. Most of the boxes were well constructed and had taken someone considerable time to build them. Cheap was not a word that came to mind when describing them, and Rex thought about the set of hands that crafted them. Heinmot nodded as Rex, using his usual set of tools, began working on the first chest. The lock gave way with minimal effort, and like all the others prior, the lid was heavily sealed with a familiar tar-like goo, but it was no match for the sharp edge of his blade. As the knife's edge wiggled into the tight seam, the glue suddenly let go and he was able to open the lid with a modest effort. Just inside the inner edges of the box another repeated theme was noted—namely the sealing wax that covered everything. Having practiced the process more than once, Heinmot ran his blade around the edge and peeled off the thick layer of wax to reveal bright and shiny gold francs, all of the same description and denomination as the ones prior.

As the coins were emptied onto the waiting stainless surface, a final item of repetition was seen in the form of the wax-encased letter. Heinmot placed it to the side for later examination, and along with Rex began counting the coins. Nine hundred and ninety-nine was the count, and Johann placed all of them into another box and set it to the side. The second chest opened as easily as the first and contained slightly fewer, only seven hundred and eighty were contained within, and Johann added the coins from both chests to the two-thousand, one-hundred seven loose francs from the crushed chest for a total count of three-thousand, seven hundred ninety-six. But, in addition, the last chest had three of the protected letters, and they were much thicker than any they previously encountered.

"Heinmot, what do you make of those?" Rex said. "They're a lot larger than anything we've seen before."

"I noticed that. Let me open one of them and see what's inside."

Working carefully, so as not to slice or tear the undoubtedly fragile paper inside, Heinmot scraped and cut at the wax until he finally had the advantage and the coating was then peeled away to reveal parchment unlike any they had handled before. This paper had the look and feel of an official government document, and had watermarks and proofing stamps in various locations. Like some of the others, however, it was part of a ship's log and it detailed what was undoubtedly, the final voyages of the Gulf Coast's most famous buccaneer—Jean Lafitte. One obvious difference stood out from the other papers they had read, this document was signed, no initials were to be seen, it was indeed the full signature of the pirate captain closing out the log.

Johann felt somewhat giddy as he read the log from beginning to end, and then over again. Less like a log, but more like a last will and testament, Lafitte reflected on his voyages and adventures just prior to this one, and Johann needed no help in sensing the spite for the US government that dripped from the ink-laden parchment. Lafitte could no longer tolerate the double-crossing and fork-tongued politicians any more than he could falling into a pool of smoldering lava. He had pulled out all stakes from Galveston and burned his settlement to the ground, leaving no traces. The *Bienville* had set sail for Barataria, and would later sail for Cuba as he had some unfinished business on the island. The ship was carrying all of his acquired fortunes within a hidden compartment, and he had expressed concern about the draft of the ship within his notes. His worst fears were realized when, during a storm they encountered one day out of Galveston, the ship began to take on water faster than the crew could remove it. His first mate, who he trusted implicitly save for his most precious secret, pleaded with him to remove some cargo at the first opportunity so they might increase the draft and make necessary repairs. Then the fever hit, and he nearly lost the majority of the crew when they fell sick and could not manage even the simplest of tasks.

When they arrived at the mouth of the Sabine, he made the decision to offload a trivial amount of his hidden ballast, but with the ship sitting low in the water, it would be quite the feat to navigate the shallow passages of the river—particularly all the way to the horseshoe-shaped lake he had chosen as the spot. He was forced to settle for anchoring the ship sideways in the river quite some distance from the final destination. After fighting the climate and mosquitoes, they prepared to bury the treasure when, in his estimation, the government, in a final double-cross, used some mechanism to steal three of the largest chests and render him and his crew unconscious for hours.

After regaining their senses, and despite the impending weather, he sent Meriwether back to the ship for writing materials and the ship's logbook so that he could record these events into the log and draft a letter to his nephew, Jacque Lafleur. Under the cover of darkness and hand lanterns, he documented the latest incidents, but then worried if the crew read his log, they might consider him mad and try to take over the ship. He then tore the sheets out of the logbook and buried them with the gold.

Heinmot handed him the papers which were inside the other two wax-encapsulated packets but saved him the trouble of reading them when he said, "Looks like these are letters to people back in France. The second mate was named Jules Desmarais and he wrote letters to his brother, but it's not clearly obvious why he chose to bury them instead of burning them. He thought that old Lafitte was losing his mind because he was making plans to stop pirating and hand the whole lot over to his nephew—one Jacque LaFleur. Desmarais commented that although LaFleur was a decent enough sailor and had been captain of a ship Lafitte had given him, he questioned his abilities to run a ship like this one with such a well-seasoned crew. Of course, that was mutinous talk, and in those days, he would've been running a marathon on a short plank somewhere out to sea. For the remainder, the cook, Francois "Cookie" Fontenot decided that his collection of recipes he had created and acquired through the years were far too valuable to lose should the ship sink, so he wrote them on parchment and had the captain promise to bury them with his wares. On a foot note, he stated the captain had confided in him they would return to the spot one day and so he felt safe in burying them there."

Joining the conversation, Rex said, "Gents, those letters are pure history, and after we find out what happened to the *Bienville,* I vote we hand these over to the Maritime Museum in Galveston so they can be displayed for all to see. In fact, that goes for the other letters, too. What do you two think?"

"I agree," said Heinmot and Johann in unison. Heinmot continued and said, "What do you mean after we find the *Bienville?* Surely, it has long since left this earth?"

"Perhaps, but then again, perhaps not. I'm certain there is one last trove to be located. Lafitte alluded to it in his log by saying they lost one-third of the treasure and they were headed to Barataria and Cuba as a stop and would decide on Mexico at that point in time. All we need to do is figure out where his stop was in Barataria, and see if we can find anything there."

"Yes, about that. What do you think he meant by a final government double cross and how they were left unconscious?" Heinmot added.

"I have no idea. I think we've been overly lucky in our quests and I believe there are some mysteries surrounding all of this that will simply remain that way."

Johann had stepped away to answer the phone, and when he returned he said, "Gabrielle just called and said that dinner was ready.

She threw some fried oysters and shrimp together into some dish or another. So come, you three, let's make tracks over there and eat before she sends the cavalry out looking for us."

Sneaking a peek at his watch, Rex said, "Whoa! I had no idea that it was getting so late. I am hungry. How about you, Heinmot? Franco?"

"Absolutely. I'm starving, and fried oysters are my favorite."

Laughing Johann said, "Now how did a boy who grew up in the middle of Montana obtain such an affinity for fried seafood? That's a mystery, that is."

"I know, I'm not sure when I realized I liked it, but I do. Let me put the gold into the vault and turn off the lights over the work benches while you guys close all of the doors."

"Sounds good. I'll take care of the coins later—there was another offer from Stratford in the UK, but after the incident a while back, we'll pass on the offer and keep these under lock and key. Honestly, Stratford seems obsessed."

"Dad, at least for now, I'd like to hold onto these coins. We may never find the remainder and I'd hate to sell them and not have some of the history of our finds. And yes, you're right. According to one of his thugs, he is indeed obsessed with all things attached to Napoleon. Heinmot, what do you think?"

"Agreed. Let's hold them for now. We have more than enough funds to hold us for quite some time."

"Done!" Johann said with a smile. "I'll leave a message for Stratford and let him know the coins are no longer for sale. That should get his goat!"

Rex and Johann brought down all of the large overheads and then stepped through the side door and climbed into the other new truck. Heinmot reached out to turn off the last light over the bench with the chests and paused to take a final look at them. As he switched off the light, he had a feeling come over him that something was different about that one chest, but he couldn't put his finger on it. It had similar appearance to the first, but something was not quite right with that box. He decided that he would leave it for now, and re-examine it the next day. The shop went dark and he made his way to the waiting truck after setting the alarm on the keypad. Though it was a short ride back to Johann and Gabrielle's, he managed to nod off on the way, but his last conscious thought was about the chest.

CHAPTER 19 – THE OLD LETTERS

HEINMOT SLEPT FITFULLY DURING THE NIGHT; IT WAS INDEED THE CHEST HE KEPT tossing over and over in his mind. Maybe it was just the fact that it had fewer coins inside—no, that wasn't it. *Something* physical, something about the chest was different, but what it was eluded him, and he certainly hated a mystery he couldn't solve.

He climbed out of bed, dressed, and went for a jog to clear his mind—the ache in his leg had long healed, and no longer bothered him. A splash off to the left of the footpath reminded him of the differences in the wildlife between Montana and Louisiana. While he may have heard the scamper of a mammal into the brush at home, here it was more commonplace to startle something of the reptilian persuasion. He finished the two and half mile trek to the main road, but still had some run left in him, so he added another mile and then started back, all the while the image of the chest flashing in his mind like a beacon.

Back at the compound, he showered and dressed, and, seeing no sign of Rex, decided to have another look at the chest on his own. He spent twenty minutes examining the chest, but nothing out of the ordinary caught his eye. Only after setting the two chests side-by-side with the lids open for comparison did he almost instantly find the source of his nagging.

The interior space of the second box was about one and one-half inches shallower than its twin. There must be hidden chamber! He was just about to further inspect the case when Rex walked in with breakfast.

"I never said that I could cook like Mom or Dad. It's only a croissant with some egg and sausage on it, but it'll keep you from starving to death." He handed the dish over and continued, "What are you working on?"

"This second chest has been bugging me ever since we opened it. It kept me up all night, but I couldn't figure out why. Well, at least until now. See here. A false bottom."

"Open it up!"

After clearing the requisite tar from the bottom, a thin screwdriver served as the appropriate lever to lift the bottom. Beneath the plate there were two well-known objects in the form of yet more wax-encapsulated letters. They wasted no time in removing the wax, and saw a familiar writing style: Meriwether. Heinmot had grown to respect Meriwether as somewhat of a romantic poet who adored the beautiful Karena. He read part of his letter aloud:

"As I stand here with one foot planted steadfastly on the gangplank and the other resting on the edge of the deck rising and falling with the pitch of the rolling tide, I know in my heart I must return to this place. I look over my shoulder and see the sun begin to extinguish itself into the leading edge of the open ocean: one half of the copper orb still visible above the threshold of the hemisphere; the other silently sinking and dousing itself deliberately and uneventfully into the oily brine. A brown pelican diving into the water at full speed after its quarry reminds me the ship is ready to be underway, so I stroll fully onto the heavy oaken deck. As I do, the crew breaks out in an old English song:

Safe and sound at home again, let the waters roar, Jack.

Safe and sound at home again, let the waters roar, Jack.

The mainsail puffs and bulges as the brisk breeze provides propulsion. The ship's bell sounds nineteen and the remaining sails slowly unfurl into the wind. I can hear the rigging take a strain against the mighty masts and feel the Bienville commence her draft through the water. I follow the pelican in flight until it flutters to a roost on a branch in a cypress tree near the edge of the bank and devours the perch in its gullet. My thoughts begin to meditate; I smile and almost hear you and your soft coos. My heart skips a beat as I remember our last encounter."

"I agree. He's definitely a poetic guy, Rex said. Here, listen to part of this one."

"The westward zephyr swishes my ebony tresses against the side of my granite cheeks, and I began to reminisce wistfully. Although the fog is particularly heavy this morning and tends to wash away all things it encounters, your fragrance still lingers on the satin folds of my crimson sleeves. I pivot on my left foot and gaze fondly at the vanishing shoreline. As the next surge of mist begins to shroud the fo'c'sle of the ship, I can almost hear you whispering my name. Ever have I longed to stand beside you and hold you close. For your skin is as fair as the wind that caresses the rooftops of Mont St. Michel in the early spring; your eyes are portals that pierce a man's soul. One touch from your hand could soften the most encrusted heart. I fear we will be shrouded within an inferno should we ever kiss."

"Well, he was certainly a charmer and seemed to adore Karena," Heinmot said. "You have to respect him for that. But here's something that might help us. Meriwether tells Karena that they were headed to Barataria with what he called a 'fully laden vessel'. I think we can safely assume he is referring to treasure; especially since they weren't in the business of transporting anything else. He also states the *Bienville* is to permanently change hands from Lafitte to LaFleur. Lafitte had more than enough of the US Government; he planned to retire in Cuba or Mexico—which syncs up with the information we've gleaned from the other letters. He made the decision to give his best ship and all of its holdings to his nephew—Jacque LaFleur."

"I've been doing some calculating as well. The legend is that he left France with ten million francs, right?"

"Right."

"So if he offloaded one million francs worth in Cuba or Mexico and we have found one million, one hundred fifty-five thousand four hundred eighty thus far, then where are the remaining seven million-plus francs? That's *a lot* of gold. It would make what we've found so far look like chump change!"

"I guess that means we're looking for one hundred, ninety-six thousand, one hundred thirteen coins—which, by the way, is divisible by three."

"Which is no small number, either in quantity or weight," Johann interrupted, as he strolled into the shop. "That many francs would weigh in at nearly half a ton."

"*Half* a *ton?* Where could it possibly be?

"Since the *Bienville* has never been found, we have to assume that it sunk, was dismantled, or it still exists somewhere. I would hazard to guess the gold is still inside her."

"Wait! The ship could still be around?" Heinmot could barely contain his excitement. "How's that possible?"

"Mon ami, I was thinking the very same. Dad?"

"Guys, that's enough for my old bones today. I think it's a good day to go fishing. We've been working too hard. One more? For old time's sake?"

Both Heinmot and Rex were bewildered, but agreed the question of the day could wait.

The pair walked out to the boat shop to grab some poles and tackle, choosing those most suited for a dip in salt water. A cursory inspection revealed that two of three reels needed new line. Working in silence, both were restrung with new monofilament, then the remainder of the tackle and supplies were gathered.

Finally, Heinmot couldn't hold it in anymore.

"Why in the *world* are we going fishing?"

"Mon ami, he's got *something* up his sleeve. Your truck or mine, and should we invite Franco?"

"Mine, and yes, we should bring Franco along. Any idea of where we're going?"

As if on cue, Johann rolled up in his old Ford and climbed out.

"It's a good day to visit Kendall. Let's head over to High Island and spin a few yarns and catch a red or two. I'm certain that he'd like to hear what we've found thus far—especially with Eamon's passing. He doesn't have very many friends; it'll perk him up. Besides, you've got to see all the improvements he's made."

Rex looked quizzically at Johann who simply winked, handed him a stack of papers and a book resembling a log, and said, "Let's go."

Two hours later, Heinmot's new F-350 pulled up at the base of the Emerald Pier. Rex was pleased to see that new railings and posts surrounded the perimeter, and that preparations were being made to replace some of the decking and the supporting piers. It seemed that business was also increasing, because they had to park nearly a half-mile from the entrance to the walkway. As they walked up onto the main pier toward the bait shop, they noticed a new addition had been added onto the bait shop.

"He probably uses that as a rest-up spot," Johann said. "He's getting old. I bet we'll find him there."

The old fisherman was more than thrilled to see the group as Rex introduced Franco. Kendall shook his hands. "Any friend of the Rhinehearts is certainly a friend of mine," he said. Franco was surprised at the strength of the old man, and Johann was pleased that he had hired some counter help to relieve some of the more tedious duties.

"What brings you four my way? I haven't seen you guys since the accident. I see that shoulder has mended up pretty well, Rex."

"None the worse for the wear."

"Just wait until you're my age!" the old man said with a laugh. "Hell, you'll be happy that something hurts just to remind you that you're alive."

"I see you've made some improvements since the last time. Nice to see business is booming, too!"

"Aye, the full railing was replaced, and some of the decking and piers, but I've also added a small room for me to sit, drink coffee, watch a little TV from time to time, that sort of thing. Mandy over there takes great care of the store, and doesn't mind messing with the different baits. I think some of the business is here to see her! So you here to fish or visit?"

"Ah! A little of both," Johann said. "But first, how about some coffee and we sit and talk for a while."

After a few more moments of idle chit-chat and a cup of Kendall's unusually strong coffee, Johann pulled out the stack of letters and the logbook.

"Kendall, with Eamon's passing he left a void of knowledge of the swamp and Lafitte that can't be filled. I'll spend some time later bringing you up to speed on the adventures of the boys, but I wanted to speak to you about some of Eamon's notes."

"He did keep an impeccable record of all his treks and findings throughout the years."

"No joke. This reads more like a diary than a log book. Eamon certainly had a passion for finding that gold. The boys have found about ten percent of Lafitte's loot. The remainder could only be carried in a ship, assuming, of course, that it's all in a single batch. While going through the diary, I found some interesting things, mostly theories, but there's one thing that stood out as a potential—the ringing of a ship's bell during a heavy storm."

"Yes, yes. There was a story . . . more of a legend really, that an old ship was lost during a hurricane off the coast back in the 1800s. It was said that every time a storm hit the coast that the sound of the ship's bell could be heard ringing. Eamon's parents told him the story over and over when he was a boy, and he came to believe it was true, though no one else did. I never believed it either, at least until late one summer many years ago when I was at his cabin during one of the storms. During the brunt of the tempest, I swear we could hear the ringing of a bell that had an echo to it. Of course, though he searched, he never found it, so who knows."

"Did you ever look for it with him? There's not much mentioned in the log."

"Why do you ask?"

"Well, we—mostly Rex and Heinmot—have concluded the only logical place for the remainder of the treasure to be is aboard the *Bienville*. Finding that ship is our last, best hope."

"Gang, I've no secrets to share. I wish I did. Eamon spent far more time searching than me. The only thing that I can say is that the bell had an echo, almost like it was inside a room. Other than that, I got nothin'."

"Mr. Tremaine, you may've helped more than you know," Rex said.

"What are you thinking?" Heinmot asked.

"Well, I think the *Bienville* is somewhere along the coast, and I don't think it's very far from Eamon's old homestead. Else, how could its bell be heard ringing in a storm?"

"But Rex, where would it be along the coast where no one can find it? Sunken? The ocean would dampen the sound of the bell and that's *if* it's even the *Bienville*'s bell that's ringing."

"Yes, it would. If it *were* sunken, but I don't think it is. I think it's inside a salt dome that, at least at one point in time, was open to the sea." Upon seeing the disbelief on their faces, he continued, "Trust me, Louisiana is full of salt domes, many of which are big enough to house a ship. My guess is it would've looked like a large cave to a ship. Perhaps in the midst of a storm, they hid in one and it may have collapsed on them before they could escape."

"Okay, that's not *impossible*, but how do you explain its ringing only during a storm?"

"Simple, Dr. Iiniwa. Occasionally, when a storm of substantial magnitude approaches a coastline, the tide falls below normal levels. I believe it's during this time, when the ship becomes free within the dome to move about with the forces of the tide and rings the bell. Although, to be heard . . . there must be an opening in the ground or shore that becomes exposed when the water recedes." Rex went into deep thought for a moment. "Therefore, we're looking for a hole of the sort that has water in it, but changes with the tide. It could be in the gulf or a nearby river. I'm not convinced they ever made it out of the Sabine if the storm was as bad as it was described."

"All this is fascinating," Heinmot said, "but that's like *another* search for a needle in a haystack. Some sort of hole with water in it? That's not much to go on."

"Not so fast," Kendall said. "I might have something for you. More than thirty years ago, Eamon and I used to fish near an outcropping of rocks on the edge of the Sabine toward the Gulf side. On one occasion, we got stuck out there in a storm, and we could hear the bell. As the tide came and went, we also started to hear a sound like the chugging of a train, but with some splashes mixed between: a tidal pool for sure. We didn't give it a whole lot of thought at the time, but I wonder if it might be the salt dome you're looking for. I've got an old map that Eamon and I used to track our fishing spots. I'll bet we marked the exact spot. Let me grab it from my desk."

The sound of shuffling papers and drawers opening and closing could be heard in the den, followed by an "Aha!" before the old man made his way back to the living room. He switched on a lamp and called them over to the table to investigate the tattered map.

"See here on the map? This is the location where we spent so many hours fishing. Eamon loved this spot because he always out-fished me there. I swear there were times that I thought he had someone hooking the fish on his line just to outdo me! At any rate, my lad, *that's* where we heard the ringing. If it'll help, the map is yours."

"Once again, Mr. Tremaine, I have to extend my thanks to you for your help. We'll investigate this spot as soon as we return."

The sounds of Louisiana's unnamed natural bird filled the morning air, as did the slap of hand to skin attempting to dispatch them. The humidity and smell of salt hung in the air like the proverbial lead balloon, but Franco and Fats Melancon and crew were happy to be up at the crack of dawn.

All were now fully employed by the Thundering Heart Foundation. Heinmot had contacted Fats a month ago and made him and his team an offer they couldn't refuse. The *Gittaloadodis* had been moved to the new compound, as well as all of their possessions. Fats had convinced the boys this was a good move for all of them since an oil spill off the coast had all but killed the shrimping for this and perhaps, many more seasons to come.

The old trawler had undergone a complete refit, sporting new paint and new hardware from top to bottom. A new Bauer compressor had been installed, as well as a Caterpillar generator. The diesels were refreshed and now sported twin turbochargers—a trademark of any engine that Rex would modify. Two new stainless fuel tanks nearly doubled its range. Fats radiated pride as much as a new father would have in the waiting room of a hospital.

His time as a US Navy Diving Officer served him well as he gave expert advice to Rex and Heinmot as to what would be the best equipment to install for underwater operations. As a marine biologist, Rex also had some knowledge about diving, and worked closely with Fats. Heinmot, for his part, engineered all of the mounting systems that would be required to support all of the equipment as well as the reels for the hoses and tethers. Franco, of course, covered security, providing some underwater tools of the trade.

Within a few weeks of the fishing trip, the pair had located Kendall and Eamon's fishing spot and backtracked in a systematic pattern until the tidal pool was located. Rex sampled the water in the pool no larger than a public fountain and found it was more than ninety percent saline. He and Heinmot agreed this was the best chance for the entrance to the salt dome that Rex had verified with a little research, had, at one time, been open to the gulf.

So here they were: Fats tending the compressor and onboard operations; his crew, brothers Matt and Mitch, minding the hoses and tethers; Franco ready to lend a hand wherever needed; Heinmot managing the lot of them; and as expected, Rex would be neck-deep in the briny liquid.

The opening of the pool had a craggy perimeter comprised of

salt, limestone, and mineral deposits. Heinmot cautioned the two brothers to keep a close watch on the hoses that could easily get snagged or cut. Rex suited up and after a few tests of the breathing apparatus, gave a double thumbs-up to Heinmot. Handing his partner a new LED diving light, he slapped him on the shoulder. "I should be going in too, but someone has to watch over you. Good hunting. Watch your head in there!"

"You're right," Rex said, pulling the regulator out and giving it a quick squeeze. "It would be more fun with both of us down there, but I need someone minding the store. Just remember: if I give two sharp tugs on this rope, don't hesitate to pull me back up. If you can't pull me back, jump in here and follow the rope down to me."

Standing in the morning sun, with sweat already running down the crews' faces, Rex took time to relish the moment. He was in the best shape of his life, with not a single gray hair in sight. Heinmot was lithe and strong enough to lift a small car. Fats, Franco, and the twins completed the ensemble. They had good fortune and great families. Neither had the right to ask for more, yet, hopefully, just below their feet was the *Bienville* with its millions in francs. He smiled at Heinmot who returned the gesture, then gave a quick salute to the crew and Franco before he jumped into the pool, disappearing in a frothy spray of sea and salt.

EPILOGUE

RICHARD STRATFORD BLENDED IN WITH HIS FELLOW BRITONS LIKE ANY NON-DESCRIPT businessman. He was quite satisfied to remain anonymous, for such a condition begat safety. His caution bordered on paranoia, but he had successfully escaped several attempts on his life by never being where he was expected. The myriad of variations of his travel routine required he keep a logbook to ensure no duplications for many weeks. Today, he chose to leave his beloved Knightsbridge manor and head south toward Vauxhall by tube train. A second tube brought him into Elephant & Castle. One last exchange found him exiting at Waterloo. Hailing a taxi was his first thought, but the calm, sunny morning—a rarity in London—convinced him to cross the Thames on foot via Blackfriars Bridge.

His guise as a mild-mannered Englishman was only skin-deep. Mystery and, to some degree, evil, resided just beneath the surface. Stratford controlled millions of British pounds on an hourly basis; he greatly enjoyed using that knowledge to further his endeavors. His motto surely had to be 'the pen was mightier than the sword,' but he used force, when need be, with equally indelible precision. Of course, he never did his own dirty work—that part was easily hired from a distance, and was usually cheaper than the monthly rent for a London flat. Through the years Stratford's wealth continued to amass to a level that, to prevent undue attention, was divested outside the UK. The accounts on the slopes of the Alps, on the beaches of the Caymans, and deep within the heart of Cyprus grew ever larger and larger.

Yet, for everything that made him synonymous with the British culture, there was one attribute that made him unique. He loved *all* things French. He obsessed over anything Napoleonic and though he would have dwarfed his idol in physical stature, there was some familiarity in his facial features and receding hairline. The obsession reached a pinnacle when, to the ire and disgust of the attendants, he climbed into the bed housed within the King's Bedchamber in Windsor Castle and rested on it with his arms crossed. Only a hefty contribution to the maintenance fund kept him out of the news and the Queen's prison.

After he was escorted from the castle, he commissioned a replica bed for his own manor. From that point on, he collected anything attached to the late emperor. Some items were acquired through less than legitimate means; many former owners had to be convinced to sell their prizes. How much convincing pivoted on the level of pain they were willing to endure, though some held out until the pain exceeded their capacity to survive. No matter—he had what he desired and fretted not over the means required to obtain it.

His latest conquest was a stack of letters from Bonaparte meant for Josephine's eyes only; the emperor had signed each sheet and initialed every corner. The price was ten thousand pounds, a broken wrist, and a promise that more limbs faced the same fate if the owner breathed a word of the transaction. Stratford would go to any length to garner former possessions, so several weeks ago, when he sat at his desk, opened the *Guardian,* and skimmed past the headline, he instantly saw his next coup: *Louisiana Man Unearths Part of Lost Bonaparte Treasure.* A quick call to the London branch of the paper gave him the desired information. His next call was to the US where he made an offer for the treasure, sight unseen. The fellow on the other end was cordial enough, but very elusive and certainly non-committal.

The offer would be considered. Considered? Who did these people think they were? No one stood in the way of something Richard Stratford wanted, particularly anything of Napoleonic connection!

He sipped his Earl Grey then noticed the light flashing on his answering machine and reached out and pressed the beckoning button. The voice on the machine was the American chap calling about the coins. He slapped his hands together and rubbed them back and forth with excitement, but when the call stated the coins were no longer for sale, the ire began to build inside him to the point of critical mass. No one refused him his quarry when he set his sights on something. If he could wrangle a Faberge egg from a former Russian general, a face-off with some young American adventurer would be a cake walk.

In retrospect, he should have known better than to send those two buffoons to grab the coins. Now, with the Americans on guard, it was high time he called in the professional. He reached for the phone and rang a familiar number. When the gritty Latino voice on the other end answered, he said only two words, "Rex Rhineheart," and the line went dead. He carefully placed the phone back on the hook. As he leaned back in his chair and sipped his tea, a sinister smile began to curl from the edges of his mouth.

TO BE CONTINUED . . .

REX RHINEHEART WILL RETURN

IN

TIDES OF FORTUNE

ACKNOWLEDGEMENTS

As one can imagine, the writing of a book is no small task, and at times it seemed to be an insurmountable one. There are so many people that I would like to thank for their efforts and contributions during my work on *Storms of Fortune,* and alas I cannot fit them all here, but here are a few:

Michal—your artwork is outstanding, thank you for bringing the *Bienville* to life in a way that amazes even me. I look forward to continuing our relationship.

AMK —thank you for your sharp eyes and even sharper feedback. I look forward to further collaboration on *Tides of Fortune!*

HS—thank you for your candor and talents. The photography was perfect in every way.

EQS—your expertise has been a tremendous help to me and I appreciate all of your guidance and knowledge. I hope you are game for *Tides of Fortune.*

ABOUT THE AUTHOR

G.D. Duhon was born in 1964 in southwest Louisiana before heading out to explore the world. He has traveled extensively in North America, Western Europe, and Asia. He attended Boston University and has a Master's of Science degree in Computer Information Systems. He currently works as a Regional Director of Information Technology for an international company, but his passion is writing fiction—especially adventure stories. *Storms of Fortune* is his first foray into the literary realm. His hobbies include traveling (of course!), riding ATVs, hunting, hiking, playing video games, reading, tinkering on automobiles, and spending time with family and friends. He currently lives in Houston with his family, and plans to continue writing for years to come.

Rex Rhineheart can be followed on Facebook at
https://www.facebook.com/RexRhineheart.

www.ingramcontent.com/pod-product-compliance
Lightning Source LLC
Chambersburg PA
CBHW070921180626
46817CB00003B/1153

9780997218404